SOMETHING
BORROWED

Books by
Alexandra Marshall

Fiction
Gus in Bronze
Tender Offer
The Brass Bed
Something Borrowed

Nonfiction
Still Waters

SOMETHING
BORROWED

ALEXANDRA
MARSHALL

HOUGHTON MIFFLIN COMPANY
Boston · New York · 1997

For information about permission to reproduce selections from
this book, write to Permissions, Houghton Mifflin Company,
215 Park Avenue South, New York, New York 10003.

For information about this and other Houghton Mifflin trade and
reference books and multimedia products, visit The Bookstore
at Houghton Mifflin on the World Wide Web at
http://www.hmco.com/trade/.

Library of Congress Cataloging-in-Publication Data
Marshall, Alexandra.
Wedding pictures / Alexandra Marshall.
p.   cm.
ISBN 0-395-81665-3
I. Title.
PS3563.A719W4 1997
813'.54 — dc21   96-29516   CIP

Printed in the United States of America

QUM 10 9 8 7 6 5 4 3 2 1

"The Ache of Marriage" by Denise Levertov, from *Poems, 1960–1967.*
Copyright © 1966 by Denise Levertov. Reprinted by permission of
New Directions Publishing Corp.

The first chapter of *Something Borrowed* previously appeared,
in slightly different form, in *Agni Review.*

To my father
William B. Marshall
in memoriam

and for
my brother, Will

ACKNOWLEDGMENTS

Elaine Markson, my literary agent, first helped me lift the idea for this book into the air, so that the wind could catch it.

At Houghton Mifflin, I'm grateful for Janet Silver, whose wisdom inspired my revisions of *Something Borrowed* and whose encouragement was my own reward; for Larry Cooper, whose meticulous attention improved every page; and for Wendy Strothman's generous support of writing, of writers, of me.

At home, my husband James Carroll has sustained me for twenty years and in all ways. He and our children, Lizzy and Pat, cause me to be very fortunate, and thankful.

The ache of marriage:

thigh and tongue, beloved,
are heavy with it,
it throbs in the teeth

We look for communion
and are turned away, beloved,
each and each

It is leviathan and we
in its belly
looking for joy, some joy
not to be known outside it

two by two in the ark of
the ache of it.

— DENISE LEVERTOV

SOMETHING
BORROWED

1

WHEN HER FORMER HUSBAND PLACED HIS HAND AGAINST the small of her back, Gale remembered how unusually warm Gary's hands always were. She and Gary were seated back to back at separate tables for this dinner the night before their son's wedding, and as Gary's familiar pulse zipped up her spine directly to the brain, Gale recognized the effect: a magnetic field more forceful than the passage of time.

Six large round tables spun with the energy of strangers destined to become intimate — in the next thirty-six hours, best friends — without any further need to encounter each other again. The power generated was already enough to give the beige walls color. And now the best man stood, tapping a water goblet with a spoon.

"With Charlie and Beth," he began, demonstrating them like an exhibit, "what you see isn't what you get." Voices popping like air bubbles on still water collected into a silence he made dense by a deeper pause. Suddenly he said, "You get more."

Gale heard herself gasp with pleasure — yes, true — as Gary clapped his hands and proclaimed "Yes!" like an adolescent sports fan, then called out "True!" as if this were a duet.

It was their son Charlie who, in marrying the girl next door, fulfilled an even older childhood ambition by bringing his divorced parents together again. Charlie and Beth presided from a table in the center of the room, their laughter combining naturally like the notes of a pleasing chord. The best man, David Haynes, was Charlie's Wesleyan roommate for all four college years, and though clearly he could divulge secrets, he only raised a glass to them and sat.

Gary had missed that college graduation by the unfortunate timing of his third honeymoon, and now his wife of those subsequent five years sat at another table, chaperoned by Gary's own Cousin Ed. Gary could hear her asking Ed what was so funny about saying you get more than what you get.

Gale heard it too, but she'd prepared herself to feel sorry for Sandra, so she did. She wouldn't want to be Sandra, an outsider flown from an uncomplicated life in Tucson east to unfamiliar Boston. Unlike Sandra — unlike Gary, for that matter — Gale's husband, Bob, had helped her raise Charlie. Bob had also known Charlie and Beth as an adult couple, whereas when Gary last saw Beth she was only nine years old. It was Gary's own fault, of course, but Gale surprised herself by feeling, instead of contempt, pity. This would explain why she could still feel his hand on her back: she felt as sorry for Gary as she did for his wife. What a rationalization.

As if Gale were a patient in her own psychotherapy practice, she asked herself the most important question: what is it you are afraid of? Why, after a dozen contented years married to Bob, would she be vulnerable to Gary? With her back to him she hadn't been able to gauge his purpose or even whether his touch was deliberate or inadvertent. But it was exactly this uncertainty that frightened her, since by the end of their marriage Gary had succeeded in making her feel like a small household appliance that gets replaced rather than fixed.

Gale looked to Bob and saw his party expression, the entirely polite face he used when the talk was small talk. Leaning at an obtuse angle away from the woman next to him, Bob wore a smile that Gale knew was inauthentic. Gale draped her gaze like a silk scarf over her own shoulder and was startled to meet Gary's intent face looking right back into hers. What was there to be afraid of? That she'd wished he'd touch her bare skin with that warm hand.

Now their daughter interrupted to ask for, and get, everybody's attention. Margo stood at her seat between Charlie and his best man to point a remote control at a screen Gale hadn't seen before. Margo had set out the place cards according to Gale's seating plan, but in order to better accommodate her presentation she'd rotated the head table and, while she was at it, two more tables, seating their parents back to back as another gift to Charlie.

The same way Charlie was Gale's son, Margo was her father's daughter. An architect like him, only more successful, Margo was accustomed to giving presentations, so she'd arranged with the restaurant for a slide projector and a screen onto which to shine images of Charlie from almost the first day of his life up to this night. It was comical, in slide after slide, to watch Charlie not change: his perfect-oval face the same, his hair staying that blond, his eyes as green. He was such proof of *plus ça change* it was hard, without her running commentary, to tell for sure which year was which. Nevertheless, a coherent future unfolded as Charlie went on from Wesleyan to study business at Northeastern, interning with Fidelity Investments and, as implied in the company name, planning to remain there the rest of his life. Margo's guide to Charlie was a promotional spot on commitment, which she termed the upside of conservatism.

On the downside, Charlie was showcased with his collections of boy things — from baseball cards to beer bottle caps — and in a mock-investigative sequence there was an exposé of the piggy banks he hid under his bed, not only as a child but, in an obviously altered photo, even right now. As Margo attested with relief, this was where Beth came in, by rescuing Charlie from himself.

There were early pictures of Charlie and Beth as a couple, in their strollers, on tricycles, and there was evidence of collaboration in the building of a tree house: Beth in a carpenter's apron, Charlie with what was interpreted as a bag of nails, until his correction, "No, that was my lunch."

Though the salad had been served before Margo began, almost everyone postponed eating it, making the room quiet enough to hear, in addition to her every word, the projector's electric hum and the clicker. Snapshot poses showed off Beth's family, six brunette Golds forming a totem pole, their matching grins fierce. This must be what it takes to remain an intact family, thought Gale. Certainly it was her smiling Charlie's long-term goal to join this winning lineup.

Here were group shots of the two families on outings, always with one grown-up photographer missing, until the year Gary gave Gale the camera with the time-release shutter so they could be complete for what turned out to be their last year as a nuclear family. There they were in the house the two families rented together in Falmouth Heights, at first intending to split the time but sharing it for those several Augusts, feasting all together on blueberries and beefsteak tomatoes and fresh-picked corn, looking over Nantucket Sound with Martha's Vineyard in the foreground.

In order to see the slides, several guests at every table had turned their chairs around to face the screen, so in effect Gary now sat directly behind Gale, as if she were a lens he could see through. From this point of view, his experience of their two children was that Gale and he had nicely duplicated themselves: two performance artists, two behind-the-sceners. More intense was Gary's realization of Margo and Charlie with none of his own faults and all their mother's strengths. Gary straddled Gale's chair so he could lean forward to tell her exactly this. To him it had come as a kind of revelation.

His voice in Gale's ear sounded much louder than it probably was, though not simply because of what he'd said. She made the same realization, but in reverse, and hadn't had the nerve to admit it to him. Just as Charlie resembled Gale, Margo's appeal was like Gary's, her own large charm equal to his. In possession of a durable self-confidence, Margo was Gale's claim to upward mobility. Before the guests arrived, with her fingers she'd stretched the rose petals open wider because, in her amateur opinion, they were looking uptight. Like her father, Margo favored open-endedness, even for these centerpieces. She liked voluptuous, she liked over the edge. She had yet to complete a single degree program in a conventional way, and yet she'd just won a competition to spend Disney money, therefore lots of it, on a design of a movie studio for the Orlando mega-expansion. Though she was barely licensed to practice, the executives claimed not to be surprised by how young she was, since in fact so were they.

When Gale whispered to Gary that she'd had the same thought in reverse, putting a hand on his knee, she could feel Gary lean up into her open palm.

∞

Beth's three brothers put on barbershop quartet hats and sang, serenading Charlie, presenting him with a red-and-white-striped jacket to recruit him for their necessary fourth voice. Gale waited until they finished singing before discreetly withdrawing — she needed fresh air more than a bathroom — and as she passed by Bob's table her discomfort prompted her to pat her husband on the shoulder. The maitre d' anxiously hoped everything was to her liking, so she told him it surely was. He directed her, without her asking, up the almond-colored marble staircase.

Gale pushed open the door marked with a W and was relieved to be alone in this soothing interior space, to press a cool damp towel against the back of her neck as if she'd drunk too much. The effect was immediate, but Gale wished she hadn't underestimated the impact Gary might have on her. Margo's assurances notwithstanding — "No, he's not your type, Mom. Sandra's his type, the same way Bob's perfect for you" — he still looked enough like himself in his twenties. He even smelled the same: Old Spice.

Gale had never met the second wife, a mezzo-soprano with the mysterious name of Chloe Fortunado. According to Margo, Gary and Chloe were always off in some exotic part of the world, although not often together, and the marriage ended with her firing Gary, in effect, at the same time as her manager. Evidently Gary's chief virtue — maybe his only virtue — lay in his being no competition for Chloe, or so Margo said. By the time of that breakup, Gale had agreed to marry Bob.

She checked her reflection in the mirror above the sink, but as if caught admiring herself by her mother, Gale involuntarily raised her shoulders to shorten her lovely long neck as she lowered her gaze to the level of the countertop. Naturally she'd prefer not to display her discomfort in a trademark gesture, but at least it wasn't as obvious as fingernails chewed down to the quick. Self-knowledge not being nothing, she lived with it, forcing a smile on her face as she left the security of this small room with no windows.

"Watch your step," said Gary from the bottom of the marble stairs. Gale's too-smooth soles meant she was doing just that. "Fall so I can catch you" was what he really meant but didn't say.

Though she might have conjured him up, she was nevertheless startled to find him there. So she gripped the railing, taking in as much oxygen as could fit in her lungs.

"I was just remembering your gorgeous legs," he told her, "rudely."

Now she was on safe ground. "Are you flirting with me?" She tried not to smile, since she too would have called him rude, but her smile must have vanished immediately, because in Gary's eyes she saw a flicker of insecurity.

Just a flicker. "I thought you therapists make your living encouraging people not to censor themselves." So he always had a quick answer, still.

"This isn't therapy, though. It's Charlie's wedding." This time when she smiled, she wasn't vulnerable.

"Therapeutic, if you ask me. Not that you did."

His tweed suit was so New England, Gale couldn't imagine him wearing, as Margo said he did back home in Tucson, cowboy clothes. In order to avoid Gary's eyes, with that shrug of hers she looked down at his feet and saw what she'd missed: custom-tooled boots.

"Nice place, the Apple Pie," he said in recovery. What could be wrong with a restaurant calling itself the Apple Pie?

Boots like that were a vanity. "Not homey enough," she answered, as if with an edge he'd sharpened.

"Meaning?" He was insistent in his interest.

But she couldn't say. "Not plush banquettes, I guess. I don't know, not cozy." It felt normal for them to be uncomfortable with each other. Gale pointed to a metal wall fixture that shoved too much glaring light up and down the wall rather than letting it enter the room. "Like that."

"Unromantic?" Gary's recognition of this shrug of hers, like a turtle retracting its head, filled him with tenderness.

"Yes, I suppose that's it," she said in a hurry. Then she surprised herself by confiding the next-larger thing: "It makes me feel guilty — so it's about lost idealism, not romance — that this whole next generation is so — what's the word? — so matter-of-fact."

Gary studied Gale's face, amazed that the cool green of her eyes could look this warm. "I agree. It's a relief to come from our generation, isn't it? A generation in common's not nothing." Unsaid was that his present wife had her own somewhere-in-between generation, different from theirs.

Because Bob was older, at times too much older, Gale thought this was what Gary meant, and because it was true, she had to reply, "Yes, it's a relief." She could have meant a relief to be with Gary again, but needless to say it was nowhere that simple. "It's not nothing, no," she told him.

From the dining room, whatever words they'd missed concluded with approvingly raised glasses and the start-up of another tribute. "We should get back," she said, as if they had left the room together and been noticed, and he said "Yes," admitting he had not been heading to the men's room, but rather to intercept her. Gary touched her arm above the wrist and asked, "To be continued?"

The neckline of Gale's dress, an olive green perfectly matched to her eyes, plunged into folds of a buffed silk advertised as washable. Her brown hair had grayed elegantly, prematurely, matched by her contemporary silver jewelry. Her teeth and gums looked, as her periodontist claimed, youthful, but as always she thought it was unfair that in order to display her best feature it helped to feel confident and/or be happy. Nevertheless, she knew how attractive she looked, because with a deliberate effort she had made a point to. She'd foreseen that being back in Boston after a dozen years as Bob's wife in Philadelphia was going to be comforting but also painful. And here she was, caught between these two emotions.

How could he so easily oversimplify as to ask, like some man after a first date, "To be continued?" Did he honestly still not know why she wouldn't let him see her in those years after the divorce? It had taken all these years in Philadelphia, and money, for her to consider herself a worthy enough investment. She'd made it back, pound by pound lost, so she could resemble herself, so she could remember herself. He must not know. Neither Margo nor Charlie must have told him.

"You're just as lovely as always," Gary told her, as if this were the proof.

This, though, made it all seem futile — "it all" meaning the good and the bad — and because she could neither hide nor help herself, Gale had to let him witness this sadness in her. Having come to Boston a day ahead of Bob to oversee the arrangements for this dinner, she'd driven directly to the brick Tudor-style house to which she and Gary had brought their two newborn babies home from the hospital. She'd sat a long time outside in the car with the engine running, filled with fresh grief.

"*There* you two are!" Charlie now discovered them in the hall. Of course he hadn't expected to find them in the same place.

∞

Sandra waved Gary over to her when he came back into the dining room, her fatigued good-sport smile conveying that Ed had run out of good jokes as well as charm. "I got Ed to tell me all about you as a boy," she divulged, "which makes Jason look positively angelic." Her now genuine smile meant it had been worthwhile, if only for this hard proof that her ten-year-old son was less of a behavior problem than Gary tried to convince her he was. "At least Jason hasn't been arrested," she said delightedly.

Ed said, "Pontiac thief," shorthand for the hubcaps Gary's father discovered in a shallow grave in the back yard.

"All my best-kept secrets," Gary replied with a contrite shrug, even though the old wound still pained him.

"But if you ever dare press charges against Jason —" Sandra threatened.

"I won't," Gary said, in order to avoid prolonging the conversation. He never would because, unlike his own father, he didn't believe parents should turn their kids in for petty crimes. Even if the police officer only pretended to write up an arrest, nothing had ever frightened Gary so much, so needlessly.

"Promise?" Sandra pulled him down to her by the leash of his necktie, then reached up for him with both arms, her already pushed-up breasts rising nearly right out of her dress. Ed looked away. Gary leaned the rest of the way, promising whatever it was Sandra wanted.

Because of air traffic and expressway delays, Gary and Sandra had been forced to arrive straight from the airport. In the foyer of the restaurant Cousin Ed had stood next to Margo and asked, "Who am I again?" To which Margo said, "Once removed," containing the implication that if he didn't behave tonight he'd instantly become twice removed. "No, who am I babysitting?" Ed meant. Margo told him Sandra, just as Sandra came through the door, which the maitre d' held open as he deadpanned, "Maitre d'or." Sandra answered, "Nice to meet you," thinking he'd introduced himself.

"She's the newest wife," Margo had informed Ed, as if her father were polygamous. "Not a hardship," Cousin Ed had replied. Ed could convince children they had coins in their ears, and some of his jokes were famous. He knew he drank too much, and since Sandra immediately appeared to be wondering where the bar was, he'd been able to help. "Gary does pick beauties, though," he'd said to Margo, but disinterestedly. Ed himself never married, and the older he got, the more he had to wonder why people did.

Back in August, Gary had suggested maybe going to the wedding alone, but Sandra had argued that simplicity isn't a goal when it comes to your children's weddings. The night was starry and it was late, the only time it got cool enough to go barefoot outside. "And anyway, Charlie's my stepson," she'd said, as if Gary had just told her this wasn't so, "so you can certainly imagine how I feel: if it was Jason's wedding, you'd skip it?"

"He's only ten," Gary lamely offered from the edge of the pool.

She was in the water, hanging on to his foot like a ladder. "You wouldn't, right? Say it."

"That I wouldn't skip Jason's wedding? Fine, I wouldn't skip Jason's wedding." He'd tried to get her to let go, but she didn't. "Charlie may not need an extra mother at his age, the way Jason needs a dad. That's all I meant." Sandra straddled his leg, sitting on his foot like a little girl playing pony, except that her breasts were full-sized, sort of floating. "Come in," she invited, tugging.

And so he did.

"Will she like me?"

"Who?"

"Your old wife." By contrast she was his young wife.

Gary hadn't wondered what Gale would think of Sandra, only what she'd think of him for getting married a third time, this wife younger by eighteen years. The water wasn't too deep for Gary to touch bottom — for Sandra it was — so with Gary finally in the pool with her, she wrapped herself around him, her arms and legs in tight sailor's knots he'd have to cut. Their nightly ritual once Jason was asleep was this quiet foreplay swim by starlight, the noise coming later.

"Let's leave Jason here with my mom," Sandra suggested, "so we can go to Boston alone and be even freer." She wasn't exactly inhibited, ever, but that night she helped him easily imagine the two of them throbbing like a pair of bongo drums, overheard by the entire fucking state of fucking Massachusetts.

Right this moment, however, Gary was stirred not by his present wife's breasts but by his first wife's legs. Back at his own table, while one of Beth's aunts detailed her life in Montclair, New Jersey, Gary was thinking about Gale, imagining her the nude who descended the staircase.

Having met Gale in the ticket line before a B.B. King concert, he'd had to wait several hours, even in the sixties, before she took off those jeans in order to wrap those legs around his slim hips. Never were the blues so unforlorn as all the rest of that night and the following day, when they both called in sick, as in lovesick. Gale's legs had been longer and stronger than Sandra's were, at least as he remembered his first impression of them clasping him, squeezing the life out of him. He was thirsty. God. Who was this chatty woman, Paul Gold's brother's wife? Eve's sister? She couldn't stop talking about the truck traffic on the George Washington Bridge. Meanwhile, Gary couldn't stop thinking of the time Gale was driving and, enough distracted by each other's bodies as to be a danger on the road, they'd pulled off into the breakdown lane. Gale downshifted from fifth to second, engine shrill like a jet landing, wheels touching down while going full speed ahead. He'd arranged the passenger seat — slid and lowered back — before Gale brought the car to a complete stop. They had sex in less time than it took to change a flat tire.

Gary knew it was his turn to speak, to offer gracious words to their hosts, Gale and Bob. It would be nice for everyone if he'd demonstrate how well they all got along, to set, if not an example, at least a tone. The woman seated next to him interrupted herself to make it easier, but he couldn't stand up to propose a toast without revealing for all to see the bulge in his tweed trousers. He gulped her water like a teenage boy, unapologetically.

∽

The bride's mother, Eve Gold, stood up instead, as, across the room, did Beth's father, Paul. Rehearsed like their sons, he and Eve alternated stanzas of "Thanks for the Memory," a tradition begun with the first of their three sons' bar mitzvahs. Because neither Beth's nor Charlie's name offered appropriate rhymes — "barley" maybe, but never "death" — in this version of the song they were simply called Female and Male, rhyming with "hail" and, of course, "Gale." Gary wasn't mentioned by name, perhaps because, unpromisingly, the obvious rhyme was "wary." Nevertheless, in order of appearance the complete cast of characters was assembled and arrayed in corny lyrics invented to convey unmitigated appreciation. Compared with Margo's ironic presentation, Eve and Paul were sweetness and light personified, so heartfelt as to be bolder. Everyone cried.

The feeling unanimous on this positive wrap-up note, all the guests began to depart. Gary had missed his chance, and reconvening the group meant risking more than he dared, which was why he decided to say something the following day. Anyway, he was also tonight's host, sort of. At least this thought served to nudge him to ask Bob whether he'd like to split up the costs.

But before he could, Gale quickly moved to Bob's side, and together they stood by the door saying you're welcome as people said thank you. Charlie gave Gary an alternative purpose by coming to stand next to him and telling his father it was here in his favorite restaurant that he'd proposed to Beth. Like Charlie himself, the Apple Pie was basic and trustworthy, and the menu so deliberately American it was Thanksgiving half the year and the Fourth of July the other. It was in the section of downtown that was deserted every night by the faithful suburbanites, the family men and women in their rubber-soled shoes, heading home to dogs needing to be let out and kids needing to be let in.

"So, Dad, how's Boston looking to you?" It wasn't a question, just a way of talking.

"Great, Charlie," said Gary, equally affably, "and how's everything been going?"

"Great too. Ideal. The big day's tomorrow," Charlie said with a gesture to indicate, by means of all the people, he knew very well how obvious this was. Charlie had lost enough weight for his shirt collar to be a little loose. "Looking forward to it. We're going on our honeymoon to your part of the world, to some ranch Beth found. New Mexico, that is."

Gary felt something like guilt for not having helped Charlie and Beth to find someplace nice. He knew all those places. "Which one?"

"Rancho Alto. Know it?"

Gary wasn't sure he did, and anyway, what would be the point of having a reaction this late in the game? Sandra would likely know it, but then she'd have to give her honest opinion, and no one needed that.

"I guess it's pretty small, for a ranch," Charlie said, his green-ish-flecked eyes — Gale's — squinting.

Then Gary surprised himself and Charlie by saying, "You're going to really love my part of the world. Can you come by?"

But Charlie hadn't meant to introduce the Southwest as a way to reject his father. He said, "Gee, Dad, the tickets —"

"Of course not," said Gary.

"Sorry." Now of course Charlie wished he'd kept quiet about their plans.

"My fault," Gary said, practically for the first time ever.

As if Charlie were in the insurance business, he quite automatically said, "No fault."

Beth came from behind the two men to slip an arm through each of theirs, a lineup like the good old days. Her watch was huge on her slim wrist, so there was no messing with her authority when she said it was time to go. Her tight black curls frothed around her face, whitening her skin except where she'd blushed it in triangles of pressed powder. Her naturally long and thick eyelashes had been lengthened and thickened with an ebony mascara wand, but not so as to look artificial. As for eye color, immodestly but also accurately Beth would call it mahogany.

This was also the color of David Haynes's skin — not ebony, mahogany — a version of brown more than "black" but still contrasting dramatically with Beth's literal "white." Sandra had David by the hand, maneuvering him across the room to Charlie and Beth, and now she released him as she proclaimed, "The best man has an announcement!"

As if it were the best man's job to keep everyone in motion, he suggested, "Let's check out the Transportation?" He was asking Charlie and Beth.

"Dancing," Sandra annotated.

Beth's watch face was so legible it was like a grandfather clock. "Thanks anyway," Gary answered quickly, so Charlie wouldn't get caught between Beth's wishes and Sandra's desires. It didn't work. "Come on, let's." Sandra appealed to the bride and groom, as if it were their duty to entertain the out-of-towners. "We should get to know each other. Come on, one drink."

"Sandra —" Gary cautioned.

"Hold it," Sandra stopped him, "we need to use up the two-hour time difference between Tucson and Boston. Otherwise, it's way too early for us."

Beth raised one nicely shaped eyebrow, so again Gary said firmly, "Another time."

"Oh?" Sandra turned to Beth to ask, "But wouldn't you say it's bad luck to assume there'll be another time?"

∞

Back at their hotel room at the Colonnade, Bob was picking up his phone messages long-distance, answering serious questions equally seriously, his back to Gale. She lay next to him on the bed, her hands crossed on her chest as if she could have died right next to him without his even noticing. The ceiling was low and seemed to be getting lower. Or was it her?

"One more," Bob said, "quick one." Not that the other two had been quick ones. Then he was lost again. Or was it her again, lost? She was aware for sure that her rings felt tight.

Gale admitted to herself that in that awkward moment when Sandra unsuccessfully tried to enlist Bob's interest in joining the Transportation party, she'd felt envious of Sandra, going dancing with Gary while she and Bob, like old folks, were retiring. She'd felt equally resentful of Gary's guest-like behavior all night, when he should have stood up to offer Charlie and Beth — or Eve and Paul, or even Bob and her — some kind of toast. But wasn't it rather that she resented Gary for making her feel envious of his wife?

Usually, in analyzing her own feelings, she was no more critical of them than of dreams. It wasn't appropriate to stand in judgment of the unconscious, and in her case especially, since she was professionally nonjudgmental. Why was she so irritated at Gary for not getting his wife to shut up? Or was it Bob she was mad at?

"There." Bob had completed his calls.

"Thank you," she said impatiently.

"Sorry. None of the messages were critical."

Because she'd also heard the sarcasm in her own voice, Gale said, "I'm sorry too." It was herself she was mad at, for not being more assertive, more like Sandra. Just because Bob said no didn't mean they shouldn't have gone dancing. It was Charlie's wedding — her son's, not Bob's — and she should have claimed her own authority, not blame him for his. In addition, she knew very well it was a doctor's job to return phone calls, as she herself had done earlier in the day. "Thank you for the party, Bob."

"You're welcome, my darling." In his relief Bob pivoted toward her, still keeping one foot on the floor as he touched her hip with his other knee. "I'm so pleased for Charlie and Beth," he said.

"I imagine them together always," Gale said. But this intensified her own regret.

Bob had already untied his shoes, so he slipped from them as from the grasp of needy patients and tipped toward Gale. He hesitated to ask her, but his curiosity overcame his natural reluctance to pry. "What was it like for you?" He knew she'd understand he meant seeing Gary for the first time in all these years.

Instead she said, "Did we just have sex? Did I miss it?" Horrified by her own response, though, she quickly apologized with, "It seems to have been complicated for me."

"Yes," he said, disappointed, "understandably." His own impression of Gary was that he was immature, so there was nothing complicated about that.

She started to say she'd expected Gary to seem like a complete stranger, but instantly she saw she'd only *wished* this, because it was easier to find a stranger irresistible. "He seemed young, but probably because his wife is." By this logic, she herself would seem old.

Believing they were talking about the same thing, Bob said, "She's not that young," sounding like a physician making a preliminary diagnosis. "Judging by her hands, she's forty."

Gale was genuinely surprised. "Margo tells me she's thirty-three."

"In my humble but professional opinion, she couldn't be," Bob assured Gale competently, good-naturedly.

"Well."

Sandra had made a fuss over Bob, telling him he looked like a younger Paul Newman, then changing her mind to an older Tom Cruise. Gale wasn't sure what it would mean even if it were true that Sandra was forty, other than the fact that she always felt superior to women who needed to lie about their age.

"Your age when we married," Bob said invitingly, "for example."

"You remember my hands that well?" She offered them to him, so he took her hands in his and pressed her arms onto the mattress straight out from her sides, like an umpire signaling him safe at home plate.

"Feeling better?" He unknotted his tie like an illusionist.

"Yes."

Bob didn't usually initiate — when they made love, it was mutual — but he slid his hands behind Gale's back and lifted her as he undid the zipper of her dress.

"I'm sorry it got complicated." She meant this sincerely, for her own sake as well.

"It's understandable," he said again. His first wife having died, his life was linear, whereas Gale's was circular. It didn't take a genius to observe the genital imagery.

∽

At the Transportation it was unbearably crowded, all the more with their arrival as a party of ten. Brand new, the club was on the edge of the old Combat Zone where, back when Gary still lived in Boston, on your way to the theater or for Chinese food you'd pass ticket booths with partial photos of what were proudly proclaimed as Nude College Girls. Now, here at least some of them were, it appeared: Live and In Person.

Not nude. Rather, they wore tubes of the fabric — not really cloth — called spandex. As if they were cyclists, you could see their carefully worked muscles pumping, pumping each other up. No matter what their race, their badly dyed hair was intended to look unnatural, so it was either an inch long or practically as long as their arms. All these twentysomething women looked uniformed by a skinflint, their stainless steel jewelry from a plumbing supplier, their chunky shoes designed by a cartoonist. Sandra loved them, even though she knew she looked like their mother. Her lipstick was red, for instance, instead of a purple that looked like licorice.

Beth and Charlie were such good sports they didn't seem to mind that — obvious losers, as if already long married — no one in the Transportation looked them over. Charlie's wedding haircut was his regular Boy's Regular, so he had little in common with the men his age who were all coiffed unisexly. Having inherited his mother's perfect teeth, however, he wasn't altogether without advantages. When he smiled he looked Transported.

Sandra announced this was her round, but was disappointed that their group was so unextravagant as to order just wine or beer. She herself went for a Sunrise, to see if they were genuine on the East Coast.

The all-business waitress nevertheless assumed it was Gary's tab, so Sandra reached past David and Margo, protesting, "My round." Her wrist brushed Gary's bottle of Sam Adams, which tipped onto its side like a dropped garden hose, spraying all around. "Whoa!" Sandra shrieked, but she caught the beer bottle with her free hand, an old bar trick she'd perfected. The waitress smiled admiringly, revealing involuntarily her orthodonture. "My treat," Sandra repeated, producing a crisp fifty-dollar bill.

Beth and Charlie waited while Sandra composed her tribute to them, gesturing for complete silence. Then, when she had it, she began, but as if right in the middle, "So there's this girl and boy who met in nursery school, if not before — right? — and who never screwed around in all this time, no doubt, so who, unlike the rest of us, got it right the first time — bravo! — and who are so, *so* — um — *cute!*" Because the music was so loud she had to more or less scream, "So here's to the perfect couple!"

Because Margo had been waiting all night to hear what Sandra might possibly say, she said, "Finally, somebody said 'perfect couple.'" She touched the rim of her glass to Sandra's and salt crystals fell into her wine. "I agree," Margo said.

"You do?" Sandra sensed she could be being mocked.

"Perfect," Margo reassured.

Now feeling encouraged for the first time since landing in Boston, Sandra demanded that Charlie and Beth dance together for her, and then in her unrestrained joy she barged onto the dance floor to join them. David Haynes commented to Margo, "Hey, you gotta watch out for those Sunrises or you could get too early a start." With equal good humor he asked, "Anyway, aren't they from the part of the country that's famous for spectacular sun*sets?*" The music made it impossible to say more.

Margo had visited Tucson once on a business trip, and her impression had been that Sandra and her father were ideally suited. She'd been at their wedding too, but it was different to see their daily life as around-the-clock positive reinforcement for her father. Sandra's self-acceptance extended to Gary, coating him like Teflon, prompting him even after years as a failure to become successful again. Similarly, her mother's life with Bob was predictable and safe, and so it fulfilled Gale's needs. In fact, Margo felt that if she'd met her parents separately, she'd never imagine they'd once been married to each other, so different — while each content — were they in their own lives. And yet at the moment this didn't seem to be quite the case.

Gary's disapproval of Sandra was obvious, but he also refused to get out on the dance floor with her and make an ass of himself too. So he went to find the bathroom, which was opulent with onyx-looking granite and so many layers of glossy black enamel it was like being inside a lacquered Japanese lunch box. He could practically see his reflection off the wall behind the urinal, but there was also a mirror hung there, so that everyone of average height could admire himself.

Unready to go right back upstairs, Gary glanced at his watch and then, seeing the pay phone, reached into his pants pocket for a dime. He had the number of the hotel on a card in the pocket of his jacket and, dialing the Colonnade, he asked for Gale's room. It was a gesture, just a small impulse he didn't stop to think through, so he was surprised when on the first ring, instead of Gale's voice, the phone was answered by a sleepy male voice: "Dr. Oakley." Like a nuisance caller Gary hung up the phone.

He checked his watch again to verify that it wasn't even eleven yet, then he asked a guy heading for the bathroom, "Do you have the time?" The guy pressed the side of his digital watch and a greenish-blue night light came on. "Twelve fifty-seven," he said, continuing efficiently down the hallway. Gary said "Huh?" because the concept of his having forgotten to change his watch seemed too simple. "Three minutes before one" was the conversion to more colloquial speech, but it meant the same thing. Gary said "Thanks," but the guy had disappeared behind the black door.

He liked to play practical jokes, and so he'd phoned Margo when she won the Disney commission, pretending to be Walt calling Margo from Formaldehydeland. But this urge to call Gale was purely, harmlessly, honestly, to chat. About? Maybe what a nice party she'd given, or how glad he was to be with Charlie and Beth, or what it was like to be back in Boston, in her company. Maybe even to admit what made it impossible for him to make a toast. Was it because it felt so natural to be back with her that it had seemed equally natural to call her? She was the shrink. Let her tell him.

∞

Gale had been wakened by something other than the phone, which rang a few seconds later. She and Bob had switched their usual sides of the bed, less because this was how they'd ended up after making love than for the more practical reason of his being nearer the phone. He always answered it "Dr. Oakley," on the mostly accurate presumption that it would be for him. At home her calls came in on a different line, a machine with unlimited space for messages.

"Who?" asked Gale, though since he'd been hung up on, Bob didn't know who. She'd been startled, and her breath felt tight in her chest.

"Expecting a call?" he asked.

"Aren't you?"

"For once, no," he said pleasantly, using the opportunity to walk all the way around the bed and to the bathroom, by her side. In the dark she listened to the serial running-water sounds — his stream, the toilet's flush, the tap, a sip from the glass by the

sink — before he retraced his steps all the way back — "Good
night again, darling" — into the same deep sleep from which
he'd come. Seemingly instantly, his breathing was as noisy as it
gets: adenoidal, Bob had diagnosed. He could sympathize that
Gale had to sleep with a partner who snored, because his first
wife did. The more she'd had to drink, the worse it got.

Often at home Gale would sleep through the ringing phone,
but here they hadn't remembered to turn the volume down, a
necessity in these hotels which treat every message as if it were a
wake-up call. Gale wondered how she would ever get back to
sleep, doubted she could, especially when she reminded herself
that something else, likely a dream, had first brought her awake.
She policed her unconscious so routinely she might as well be a
radar scanner, but nothing presented itself to her. She tried to
remember what feeling she'd had in the seconds before the
phone rang and, as if there were no difference between panic and
pleasure, she couldn't even say whether or not it had been a
nightmare she'd had. She felt amateurish since of all nights in
recent memory this was one time when she'd have wanted, even
expected, to be able to retrieve her dreams.

Gale turned away from Bob, her back to his as if they were
bookends. Since his snoring presented ample evidence that she
wasn't alone, why did she feel alone? It was possible that in her
entire life she hadn't ever felt so alone.

Something in his saying "Dr. Oakley" had caused it, but this
seemed odd because that was her own name too: Dr. Oakley.
Dutifully she'd changed her name twice, first to Gary's and then
to Bob's, making her full name Gale Stuart James Burr Oakley.
In reality she represented five entirely different families: Gale
her maternal grandmother's maiden name, and Stuart her own
mother's, then James her father's father's, going all the way back
in a straight line. Gale James was the only name she'd actively
liked, so, given these times when there's everything in a name, it
was hard to understand first why she'd given it up, and next why

she hadn't taken it back. She'd had two opportunities to take it back, but when she and Gary split up she didn't want Charlie and Margo to feel they'd been abandoned by both parents at once, and when she married Bob, because as he admitted he was from the wrong generation, he couldn't tolerate her keeping Gary's, even if her license to practice had been issued in that name. Charmingly, Bob had told her that he didn't want the only Mrs. Oakley in his life to be his aged mother. Anyway, he thought Dr. and Dr. Oakley sounded doubly mighty.

It fatigued her, all this good behavior of hers over the years, but what was the alternative, passion? That hadn't worked either.

Rather, it had worked, but not everlastingly, no matter that after meeting Gary — crashing into each other like cymbals — for their eleven years together she'd felt like a fountain in which the water is collected and recirculated over and over and over in an endless supply. From that first night's concert it was weeks before they saw the daylight of daily life, and by their third week together they had to enforce a trial separation of forty-eight hours in order to sleep through the night, twice. In addition to having no clean laundry at either of their apartments, they both had crazed looks, causing one of the principals in the firm where Gary was an intern architect to accuse him of doing heavy drugs, while Gale's supervisor at the training clinic worried that Gale had overly identified with those bipolar patients whose eyes, like Gale's, had diminished blink reflexes. Everybody was relieved when they turned out to be treatable.

Until that moment in her life she'd never been aware of using all five senses simultaneously. At the time she'd said that this alone was worth the price of admission, even though, in her case, it made her wonder whether she should switch her specialty from clinical psychology over to experimental. She was living proof of the stimulus-response theory at work.

So how could they have ended up just another stressed-out

couple in their early thirties with two kids, failing marriage counseling? Gale put her hands against her mouth as if to prevent herself from sobbing, and waking Bob, then having to account for feeling so bereft. The marriage counselor could have said, "Look, you two, obviously you love each other. Think of the anger as the opposite extreme of the passion. As reflective. As corrective." Instead, he'd played to her weakness, not discouraging her in her belief that in addition to being betrayed by Gary she'd been betrayed by passion itself, including her own. She'd vowed never again to give herself away recklessly, and never had.

It wasn't a marriage of convenience she'd settled for, but her relationship with Bob had no comparable internal fuel source. On a regular basis they'd get recharged with a few days in some pretty place with an agreeable climate, where they'd make love much like tonight, unrecklessly. The vacation was from the phone, freeing them to talk to each other and enabling them to remember what comfort there is in being compatible. Because Bob's first wife was alcoholic, Gale had learned from him immediately that her own restraint gave him a security he'd yearned for but never experienced. Similarly, with him she hadn't ever been frightened, not of him or by her own feelings for him. She could be confident with Bob, knowing she'd be neither betrayed nor scared by the power of a second forceful relationship. Things could be worse. Once they had been.

Her discovery of Gary's three-month affair felt at the time like attempted murder. As if to save her life by screaming for help, she'd temporarily injured her vocal cords, straining them, bellowing at Gary that he was killing her. It was at this moment that she'd seen she'd loved him even more than she'd been aware, which she found equally terrifying: what if she literally couldn't live without him? This rage she'd felt toward him matched in intensity the freedom she'd learned, with Gary, first to experience and then to express.

If she'd challenged him with "Why *her?*" she could perhaps

have seen that Jeannie could mean nothing to him. If she'd dared ask "Do you love her?" Gary could have said of course not. In fact Jeannie, in the childlike absence of any sense of the connection between actions and consequences, was using him solely for her own amusement. Gary was an experiment in married men: Jeannie had been wondering whether it was worth it to have an affair with one, or not.

Before going to sleep, Bob had put on his paisley pajamas, but she hadn't bothered to locate her nightgown. Lying on her side, her legs curled, she slipped her cold hands between her thighs like a letter opener under the flap of an envelope. Without a conscious intention to delight herself, and with the lubricant of Bob's semen already inside her, she very efficiently did. It was her pleasant discovery that all this time, evidently even asleep, she'd been on the near edge of orgasm, which now pressed itself, urgent and slippery, into being. Just before her pulse throbbed, Gale remembered the dream she'd bolted from just before the phone rang: Gary was drizzling jasmine-scented oil warmed with the heat of his hands, spreading it all over the place.

2

IN THE RENTED CAR GARY FASTENED HIS SEAT BELT BUT, sobered by his own stupidity and a double espresso, he resisted driving in the direction of the hotel. Because she was an expert at rescuing him while simultaneously getting her own needs met, Sandra proposed, as if they were in Rome and could see a sound-and-light show at the Colosseum, "Show me Boston at night," or, more like it, since she wouldn't get another chance to return to Massachusetts in her lifetime, "Show me the famous Harvard Square — or no, wait — show me Cape Cod. It looked pretty in Margo's slides, so let's drive to Cape Cod and watch the sun come up. What's the point of being so far east otherwise?"

"Sure," he answered. Caught in a riptide, as Gary already was, why not sit by the shore and watch the ocean at cross purposes?

If in principle it wasn't a good idea, it became a better idea by their already being a block or two from an entrance to the expressway. In no time they were passing the exit for the JFK Library, and though the sun also rises from there, they were a few hours too early. The traffic was moving so fast, Gary didn't have a chance to think about anything but his own second thoughts, little and big.

Being no dope, Sandra knew this. She recognized very well these confusions Gary got into. Luckily she was practiced at straightening him out. Sandra pulled off her pantyhose now, planting her bare feet on the dashboard, her short skirt shoved up like a sleeve. "There we go. That's better, more like home," Sandra said.

"Jesus, Sandra, this is fucking *Boston*, not Las Vegas!"

"What, you think the truck drivers will watch me in their rear-view mirrors?"

"Watch you do what?"

"Never you mind." But she got her skirt to cover the top third of her thighs. "Anyway, no trucks. It's not a work night." With her bare toe she turned on the radio and got Afro-pop. "Cool," she said, sounding like her ten-year-old son. "I wish we'd brought Jason, don't you?"

The only advantage Gary could imagine was that, in sharing a hotel room with her son, he could avoid sex with Sandra. So he agreed. Next he realized this was what he was accomplishing by driving around. Most men would tell him he was a complete idiot.

On the other hand, he had to wonder if it wouldn't be better in the long run to go back to the hotel and let her tease him into an erection. Sandra could sit on his chest and brush his face with her breasts, rub herself against him like that damn cat of hers. Unlike the cat, however, Sandra would lick him all over. And it would work. So was it already working? No, it wasn't.

She reached across the emergency brake to knead his thigh, as if he had a cramp. "I should have been born left-handed," Sandra proposed, "or else British."

He laughed, but at trying to picture her as British.

"So you'd be on my right, I mean." She reached as far as she could reach, and rubbed him there.

Not everyone would agree it was a hardship to have a wife this hot, but for him Sandra was her own kind of predictable. "Cut it out," he complained and pushed her hand away. "Back east, you're not alone on the road. Here, driving takes serious concentration." But he'd lost his, so that rather than bearing left to follow the big green sign for Route 3, which would double into Route 6 and go all the way to Provincetown at the end, Gary went right. Familiarly finding himself on the old highway to Falmouth, mid-Cape, he thought it was maybe perverse, sure, but she didn't have to know he was taking her to the town where he and Gale had rented that house Margo featured in her slide show. Let Sandra have her Cape sunrise. It was her idea, after all.

Damn it: now she had the hiccups. She gulped air and held it, closing her eyes as if making a wish. "*Woossshhh*," she let it out, and hiccupped.

It saddened him to remember the road so well. Sliding left across the four lanes of Route 128 — it was a quick exit left after coming in from the right — he also felt as if they were careening, and not just across a busy road, but in their lives.

"Are you okay to drive?" Sandra never was the designated driver because, no matter how much he'd had to drink, she'd always had a few more. "I thought we might roll over, you switched lanes so fast. Anyway, you got rid of my hiccups for me. Thanks."

"You're welcome." In addition, this stretch was unlit. It was like coming into a dark kitchen, blinded first by the light in the fridge and again, closing the door, by its absence. Gary had to ask himself if in fact he was okay to drive.

"Everything's so close here, isn't it? Not like home." This mileage was nothing. "So you could slow it down, hon."

"I'm okay." Out west, if you weren't speeding you'd get blown off the highway by the passing traffic.

"Not too sleepy?" She offered him a miniature brick of Dentyne gum, which he, as always, refused. Cinnamon was Gary's least favorite flavor, but she loved it so much she was confident she could change his mind one of these days.

If Gale were to interpret him, he figured it would go like this: having initiated their own marital problems, he hadn't anticipated being himself rejected by his second wife, so when that happened he overcompensated by picking — picking up, actually, in a cocktail lounge — a woman whose career aspirations were even more modest than his own. Sandra was a part-time realtor who was increasingly successful, but there was no danger of her abandoning him for work that mattered more. That is, she freely spent whatever she had to give on him, and if some days it didn't look like much, there was no denying the value in being told every night and every morning that you're the best. Jason's generous nature was the proof of Sandra's success, and the boy's ready devotion to Gary had demonstrated to him the power of security. For Gary the certainty was absolute, and for him this too had been a first. In other words, didn't Gale's interpretation talk him into appreciating the wife he currently had? Gary gave Sandra a second chance.

"All these thousands of trees I liked from the air, flying in, now look scary to me," she decided. "I only like them in daylight. I like them green."

"They're still green," he told her gently.

"You know what I mean. They make me uncomfortable." So she turned up the car radio, too loud to talk.

∞

"This is good," she said as they neared the Bourne Bridge. "Look how the trees are getting shorter."

She was right, they were. He didn't remember that about this drive.

"What are they, scrub pine?"

"And scrub oak." Little acorn lids underfoot, Gary recalled.

"Scrub everything."

He'd guess they were driving by a cranberry bog, but it was still too dark to see for sure. "See that? It's a cranberry bog," he nevertheless told Sandra as a way to describe the thrill it was to watch them harvested. The farmers flooded the bog, and the water shook the cranberries off the bushes so they bobbed like beads — like rubies — in narrow canals that became conveyer belts. Gary told Sandra how Charlie couldn't believe his eyes.

"Me neither," she said. "One of my clients needed to put in a new septic system, and guess what about the old one. There was a lifetime supply of those One-A-Day vitamins floating on the surface, round and red, like cranberries."

"Come on."

"Really. They'd gone right through his digestive system completely unabsorbed. I'm serious."

"His whole *life?*"

"That might be an exaggeration. Let's just say since the last time he got his septic system pumped out." She laughed as she said, "So much for truth in advertising, unless of course One-A-Day never claimed their vitamins could be absorbed." Her laugh illustrated what fun it was to be in real estate.

But Gary was thinking again about Charlie, specifically of the time Charlie phoned, so excited, to say he'd just gotten his driver's license. The only thing Gary said was, "Hit a tree, you die instantly." Compensating, Sandra congratulated Charlie and said she was proud of him. "I can't believe I was so cruel, telling Charlie, 'Hit a tree, you die instantly.' " Even Gary knew, though, that his cruelty concealed his hurt at not being the one who had taught Charlie to drive.

Now Sandra said, "I hope you'll tell Jason the exact same thing when he's Charlie's age." She turned in her seat to look at Gary. "Promise?"

That she was proposing an event six years into the future made Gary feel claustrophobic. Again he heard her ask him to promise, but he found it less dishonest to say, "Luckily for Jason there won't be any trees by the side of the road." Not in Tucson, Arizona, he meant.

"Then, hopefully, Jason won't get into Harvard" was how Sandra chose to end the conversation.

This made it worse, because he'd also missed out on helping Charlie choose a college. He was fourteen when Gale moved to Philadelphia, marrying Bob, and though Gary had objected to Gale's sending Charlie to the elite all-boys Chestnut Hill Academy — Bob's own as well as his two sons' school — Gale had informed him that he'd removed himself from the school conversation by having chased Chloe Fortunado around the world. Charlie had survived middle school without a father to help him with algebra, Gale pointed out. His ambitions for Charlie, Gale said, had become irrelevant, and sure enough, somehow or other Charlie had been guided to Wesleyan where, as it happened that freshman year, so had Beth Gold. "See?" This was what Sandra would say, he decided. But this was how Gary rationalized avoiding any involvement in Jason's school life, as if the lesson in Charlie were that Jason would no doubt be better off without him.

Continuing with her own train of thought, Sandra said, "Jason should get to know Charlie more than just on the telephone, don't you agree? And then if Beth could meet him, there's an even better chance that Charlie would get more involved, right? Let's invite everybody out. Seriously, let's. Don't you think?"

"They already are coming out, to Rancho Alto. Know it?"

"Rancho Alto, Rancho Alto," she repeated as if she could conjure it up, but, "No."

"No, me neither."

"When?"

"Now. Their honeymoon."

She hesitated, but then she said, "It would be nice to know that."

"Now you know it."

"It would *have been* I meant. Obviously." Sandra pulled her skirt down as far as it would go and covered her bare knees with her hands. She could tell by his posture that he himself must have been told this only tonight, but still she couldn't make herself sympathetic. "Even Jason's father stays in closer touch than you do."

It was the word "stays" that prompted his rhyme, "Not that he pays."

"So?"

"What do you mean, *so?* It's the fucking law! It's called child support." No matter what, Gary had always been in compliance, monthly, though what he'd really resented wasn't the money spent but the loss of involvement in his children's lives, given the demands of Chloe's career.

Sandra's silence communicated how many times they'd been through this argument. No, she wasn't going to let herself get trapped into making the false distinction between having married, or not, the other parent of your child. Not again, not here, not now. It had been an easy decision, since Jason's father was a loser, period.

∞

The dark was being diluted by oncoming day, but there were no other cars in this residential area. By the brackish pond Gary remembered to turn left up the hill, and he recognized the driveway as the one where he'd persuaded Charlie to let him remove the training wheels from his red bike. Gary pulled into that driveway, newly asphalted and shortened by the addition of a three-car garage, which ruined the lines of the old house. Straight ahead was the Sound, where he'd taught Margo how a tiller works.

"There's the Atlantic Ocean," announced Sandra.

"Nantucket Sound."

"Whatever. But let's get closer. Let's pretend that we own the biggest and the best, with a huge porch right on the water." In a made-for-TV bad-guy voice she suggested, "Let's trespass."

They already were trespassing, but there was still a little time before sunrise. He backed out and drove down the steep hill that gave Falmouth Heights its name. She hadn't recognized the house, but he almost hadn't either, reconfigured as it had been by profiteers during the economic boom. Like the garage, the square footage had been tripled, conspicuously consuming the entire yard.

"What's the matter?"

He'd suddenly pulled off to the side of the road and hunched around the steering wheel, collapsing with his recognition of all the time he couldn't ever get back. Because he couldn't tell her the truth, he said, "I missed out on the real estate boom." Now he wouldn't have to admit that his grief had nothing to do with being a failed architect. It had to do with that tiller, those training wheels.

"Oh, that," Sandra replied. "God, you scared me! I was worried you'd be having a heart attack."

"Sorry."

Sandra stroked his back, using her fingernails to remind him how much he liked that. "You know that doesn't bother me, hon. Anyway, you recovered: you're one of the top twenty-five architects in the Southwest. Just don't get sick, okay?" Chronic unemployment ran in her family, so she'd had a lot of experience making men feel better about economic difficulties. Time after time, scheme after scheme, her father lost everything, until finally he seemed to have permanently lost his own way home from the track. If not for her mother's odd jobs they'd have been evicted from the crummy temporary housing Sandra didn't recall from her childhood as having been that bad, although it was. So her first achievement as a real estate agent was to find her mother her own bungalow. Sandra was confident about everything but illness. She'd had no experience with that.

Gary wasn't listening.

"Okay? Just don't get sick."

"Sure." The chill morning air helped him to recover.

Gary drove through the town of Woods Hole, past the ice

cream shop beside the drawbridge over the narrow channel from protected water, where the little boats were anchored. Those summers they'd come here every evening for cones dipped in chocolate jimmies and they'd watch the ferries come and go, to and from the islands.

"Aren't there mansions?" If you asked her, this dinky place looked like something right out of the fifties. Root beer floats. Cherry Cokes.

"No, that's Newport." To this spot on foggy mornings he and Charlie came to hear the bells clang and the horns moan, Charlie calling out, "Ahoy!" He'd believed pirates could have hidden in these coves in that fog.

"I don't need Vanderbilts," Sandra reassured him as she pointed to the private peninsula called Penzance Point. "What about over there?" It was getting light enough to see that those homes were suitably handsome. She decided, "That's as close to the horizon as we can get."

Gary drove past the aquarium and turned left, following the shoreline. He stopped at the gatehouse, but, as the saying goes in the workplace, the Penzance Point security guard seemed to have stepped away from his desk. Now they proceeded past several driveways marked SERVICE ENTRANCE and stopped on a causeway that didn't seem to be PRIVATE. Though this was a summer retreat, Gary told Sandra that if this were his place he'd live here year-round. From the corner master bedroom of that yellow-trimmed house right there, he'd watch sunrises *and* sunsets.

Sandra's bare legs were cold, but it was worth climbing over the slick rocks to get onto the dock, which rested on pilings thicker than telephone poles. Suspended over the water, she and Gary could claim as theirs everything between them and the horizon, just as she'd wanted. She needed his jacket, so he gave it to her, even though he needed it too. "This is the life," she said, even though it went quite without saying.

Above their heads, hanging from the flagpole they were leaning against, an oversized Stars and Stripes undulated cinematically, and Gary felt similarly disembodied. Boston was such a small town that, if he hadn't moved on, he might possibly know whose dock this was, whose enclosed garden was abundant with dahlias in bold colors. If only his life had gone according to plan — Gary's own plan — instead of prowling these properties like a ghost, he'd own a house. He'd be in his own bed, asleep.

The sun came up looking like a lightbulb — both that shape and that white — then suddenly it turned round and orange, more like a tangerine. Relaxing against the flagpole, Gary announced, "Presto!" as if to claim credit.

Now the sun seemed to settle for being yellow, with rays. "Jason drew it like this when he was little," Sandra told him because he hadn't known her son when he was in nursery school.

"Everyone did," he said, thinking of his own from childhood, as well as Charlie's and Margo's. Gary shivered, not from the cold but from his loss.

Or from his own stupidity. For a long time he believed that he'd been entrapped — how else could his life have been reversed by a young woman whose name he couldn't even remember? — but he'd come to see the fault was his feeling entitled. This, however, was the mystery: how on earth could he have come to feel entitled? As a child he'd done so poorly in school no one thought he'd make it to college, much less to architecture school. His mother's favorite word was "disappointed," how disappointed she was in him, and as for his father, well, he had become, officially, a missing person. When Gale found Gary, unofficially a missing person himself, she was like somebody who knows CPR. Her very breath got him going. Newly self-confident, engaged, energetic, Gary had become a changed man. For the first time in his whole life he'd had a feeling of power. The trouble was, he abused it.

If he had only known she'd been just as insecure as he'd been

— hurt equally by withheld love in a childhood as sad as his — even if he hadn't been able to avoid having a meaningless affair, surely their marriage could have been rehabilitated. They had everything in common, including self-hatred.

Sandra hummed, recognizably, "Here Comes the Sun." The gold in her hair caught the light and, like good news, relayed it on. She yawned like a lion.

On the day of their births, he'd promised both his kids, no matter what, that he'd be an on-site father. He knew the importance better than anyone, even before Gale read to him from her textbooks. What a failure he was. He and his mother were right about that in the first place.

∞

Back in Boston, where this clear October morning occurred after a good night's sleep, Bob had gone for his run along a piece of the city's pretty Emerald Necklace. Gale wasn't a runner, so she'd showered and dressed in corduroy slacks and a slate-blue cashmere turtleneck. Breakfast was being served in a dining room with gray plush banquettes.

"Last night you were wanting cozy," Gary said to Gale as he approached her table. "May I join you?"

She'd been watching half-and-half marble her just-poured coffee, so she was enough absorbed in this that he startled her. Even though it was only a table for two, she answered, "Sure."

"Cozy as in plush banquettes, remember?" He poured himself a cup from Gale's pot. "Last night you and I agreed it's too bad the way our kids' generation is so unromantic." He took a sip of coffee right away, no matter that it was way too hot.

"I remember, sure." Gale was studying him, wondering why he was wearing the same clothes as the night before, and why he wouldn't at least bother to shave. "So where's Sandra?"

Sandra had spent the drive back to town expecting Gary to want to take a bath with her, since why else was there a Jacuzzi in their hotel room? She'd had the Do Not Disturb sign in mind. They would pretend they were in the master bedroom of that sunrise mansion on Penzance Point. She would make him feel less gloomy, more like the father of the groom.

"In the shower," Gary answered.

"And did you keep them out all night too?" She saw him dragging the bride and groom around Boston, dancing, bringing them to the top of the Prudential Tower so he could have the city below spread out like a skirt made of twenty thousand lightbulbs when he proposed the toast he hadn't had the good manners to offer earlier, when it was his turn to speak. "Did you think it was your job to convert them?"

"To romance?" Gary laughed. "No, we just went for a drive, Sandra and I."

"How nice," Gale said, like a mother. As if he could still read her mind, she was trying to conceal from him that he had been in her dreams.

"We went to Woods Hole." He took a breath because it made him sad to say, "The ice cream place is still there by the draw-bridge, only now it has more flavors."

"You can't get from there to Nantucket anymore," she informed him. In other words, Gary couldn't have it both ways.

"But remember that night?" he asked. Once, spontaneously, they'd boarded that last ferry to Nantucket. Margo and Charlie had slept the whole way on the worn green leather — yes, banquettes — while Gale and Gary stood out at the ship's rail. The sea was so calm it was as if they were at the porch railing back at the house they were renting with Eve and Paul. Gary knew at the time he would never in his life forget the feel of the balmy night breeze in their faces, and he hadn't.

Gale relented. This was a fond memory they'd held in common all this time, so — permanently joined — she recalled, "At the drugstore on Main Street the next morning we bought one toothbrush we all four shared. The kids had just discovered germs, so, along with their normal bedtime, there went another law broken!" As she turned to face him more directly, she could see that, still dressed in yesterday's clothes, unshaved, Gary looked like the same guy. If only this were that morning.

"Even then," Gary said, "they were more conservative than us." As he remembered it, Margo had been merely fascinated by germs, but Charlie was obsessed. Gary wished he had that toothbrush right now, to get rid of that same taste in his mouth.

"Charlie was so worried," she said. "He was convinced Paul would call the police and that there'd be a 'manhunt,' which would be quite 'tremendous.'" Gale knew Charlie was still capable of being simultaneously thrilled and terrified. For him and, as she'd have to admit, for her also, the fear was part of the freedom, and vice versa.

"His favorite word was 'tremendous.'"

"For a decade, at least." But as Gale said this, she also couldn't help thinking that when they split up Charlie was nine, so not even a decade old.

The fatigue didn't help, but as if having done the same calculation in his head, Gary's eyes watered enough to fill, and spill. And so did hers.

At that moment Margo appeared at their table, and she told her mother, "It's conventional to cry, but not yet. I'll point out the appropriate moment, if you like, during the wedding ceremony itself."

"Okay," said Gale, smiling at Margo's choice of the very word "conventional."

"And as for you," Margo cautioned Gary emphatically, "just because Charlie isn't making you wear a tux, don't think you won't have to change clothes."

"Okay," he said too. He'd missed so many opportunities to be bossed around by her like this.

Margo borrowed a chair from the next table and firmly set it opposite them. Ten at the time of their divorce — but so much more alert than her gullible nine-year-old brother — she'd taken on the impossible task of trying to make everything better. That other Saturday morning, in 1977, she'd peeled a tangerine for them, divvying the sections as if they were petals of a daisy, reciting "she loves me" and "he loves me" while skipping over the "loves me not" parts. Now, to chase away the only ghost Margo had, she told her parents, "Don't tell me you two are getting a divorce." Even at ten, she'd known this was what it meant to walk into the dining room and discover your parents crying.

∞

"Two for the buffet?" the head waiter asked Bob and Sandra as they entered the dining room, like a couple, together. Wearing a tuxedo uniform, the waiter looked overdressed compared with Bob's camel-colored Shetland crewneck and Sandra's designer denim skirt belted with silver and turquoise.

"We'll join them," Sandra said as she headed for the other three, requiring the waiter to say, "Certainly, I'll pull up another table for you."

"Hi," Sandra said. "Look who I found in the elevator." She indicated Bob, who would have been happy to sit alone with the day's newspapers.

The waiter brought two fresh pots of coffee and stood nearby as Sandra gave the table her firsthand impression of the Cape. She said it had no beaches, and nobody corrected her. "Just rocks," she said, as if they'd driven along the Maine coast instead.

When it became Bob's turn to speak he said, "Tea, please."

"I mean, I do know sand," Sandra said, pulling a croissant into thirds, "since I'm from the desert, after all."

Margo added, "Not to mention that your name is *Sand*ra."

"Oh, wow." Sandra checked to make sure Margo wasn't mocking her, then said, "So, see?" To the others she said, "Get it?"

Already Gary needed a nap, so he asked, "What's the schedule?" As an architect, he'd put in many a long night on charrette, but he was too old or something. He was wiped out.

Sandra made the question specific. "What time's the wedding?"

"Noon," said Gale.

"*Noon!*" Sandra glared at Gary, the source of her misinformation. "I was told evening reception. My dress is too formal for noon."

Blamed, Gary responded, "There are fifty stores within a three-minute walk from here, and there's time enough," although according to his watch, the stores hadn't yet opened. "So I'll help you find whatever you want to wear."

"You will?" Sandra was so surprised she threw her arms around Gary, now no longer needing to wear anything other than the dress she'd brought to wear. Turning to Gale, she said, "See? This is the conversation we should have had way back in the first place."

Margo, ever the fixer-upper, told Sandra, "You'll be fine, because even though the wedding's out in Brookline at noon, the reception is back here at the hotel and will go into the evening. Like a European village wedding," Margo said, implying dancing into the night, again.

But now Bob was feeling uncomfortable. In order to check in on his bypass patients, he'd have to fly back to Philadelphia that evening. It hadn't occurred to him he might miss something.

"And there's a brunch tomorrow, right?" Sandra hoped she'd brought the right thing to wear for that.

"Beth's grandfather's giving a brunch for the out-of-towners. Remember Herb?" Margo asked Gary. And from the brunch she and her mother would drive off, destination unknown. This extra time was a bonus opportunity for Margo.

"He's the little guy, right?"

"You men," Margo said, feeling superior that women don't measure each other by their height.

"Herb's generous," Gale said, because he was always inviting Margo and Charlie to come along. "One time he flew all six children to Quebec to hear French spoken and eat real *frites*." What would Bob's not being there mean, other than dancing with Gary — unlike last night — just like old times?

"Rich," said Margo, without acknowledging this was no better a way to measure.

"He must have been there last night," said Sandra, "so how come I missed him? No offense, but I'm sure I would have preferred him to Cousin Ed." She asked Margo to point Herb out, then returned the conversation to more immediate concerns. "Mine's already a dress I got specially for this," she said, though this was true of everything she'd packed for the weekend. "What color's yours?"

"For a change I'm not wearing black," Margo said. "Sort of red, I guess."

"Good, because mine's a yellow. Actually gold." Sandra then turned to Gale, with a smile to acknowledge the hierarchy: "And the mother of the groom?"

Gale had made a happy discovery the day before, and with obvious pleasure she said, "Mine's the color of the big maple tree next to Eve and Paul's house." Not that, consciously, she'd planned it that way.

"I remember that tree," Gary joined in. "It's a sugar maple," he told Sandra, who'd missed seeing it before the dinner last night. "We tried to tap it one year, and we boiled the sap a thousand hours and never got maple syrup. Remember, Margo?"

Margo added, "In fifth grade Charlie and Beth carved their initials in that tree, inside a heart that must have become enormous this many years later. It was the greatest climbing tree in the whole neighborhood, probably in the world." Margo had carved her initials too, but not with anybody else's.

The day before, Gale had seen that sufficient leaves had fallen for the skeleton of the tree to show like an x-ray through the bright veil of color, revealing almost diagrammatically the mature maple's primary and secondary branches. It was beauty and strength superimposed, orange leaves pink.

"What color's a maple? We don't have them." Naturally Sandra had seen pictures of whole valleys of changing color, but this meant Gale's dress could be almost anything.

"It's a blend."

Sandra wished there could have been a way for her to have thought up the idea herself, of matching a tree in the yard, but instead of admitting this and risking sounding envious of Gary's ex-wife, what she said was, "Then we all match."

∽

Sandra asked the waiter to bring her a Bullshot, saying, "'Dr. Bob' prescribes it — or could, and should — for the bouillon, since it lowers cholesterol, I'm pretty sure."

Bob smiled one of his tightest smiles, which caused Gale to suggest — otherwise somebody might tell the truth — there was enough time to tour the complex of Harvard hospitals. Bob had gone to medical school here, Gale told Sandra, who merely elaborately refolded her napkin.

Because he'd graduated from Harvard Medical School, he'd been trained to be the expert opinion no matter what medical community he might end up in. And though Bob's personality didn't require his making sure everybody at Penn's teaching hospital knew that he had gone to Harvard, he recognized every time he returned to Boston, including this time, how much he wished he'd stayed. He'd been invited to remain for his residency, but his wife Priscilla argued that a surgeon's hours entitled the surgeon's wife to reside where she could have a life too. For her this meant Philadelphia, where she descended from founders. Only in Philadelphia's Chestnut Hill could Bob's children — because they were hers — have unlimited advantages: Chestnut Hill Academy and Agnes Irwin, Philadelphia Cricket Club and Gulph Mills Country Club for the rest of their lessons, knowing for certain who was Registered, who was not. To that world Bob wasn't exactly a stranger himself, but unlike her, he easily could have left it behind him. He wished he had.

In addiction jargon, this life of Priscilla's functioned as her codependent. The drinking was ritualized — no matter how unhealthy it was for you, like a daily bacon-and-eggs breakfast it was the ancestral habit — so Priscilla could pretend it was sanctioned. Bob was helpless because, codependently, he'd pretended to be deceived by the full extent of her problem until, eventually, she'd drunk herself to death.

"Great idea," he said to Gale's suggestion, quickly signing the check before escape could be postponed. Bob felt himself panic in Sandra's company, which made him sympathetic to Gary, who acted helpless, the way he had. Needless to say, Bob was glad to have the problem wife behind him, the solution wife beside him.

"What, my saying 'doctor's orders'?" Sandra was alert to Bob's discomfort but misunderstood its source. "It was a joke, for God's sake." Her eyes were clear and so was she, about being condescended to by those with fancy educations.

Bob evaded this challenge too.

"I saw you cringe," she persisted.

"Drop it," Gary said like a master to a pet with something nasty in its mouth. "We need some sleep."

Nobody could argue with that.

With Gale, then, Bob felt safe, which helped him to understand how off balance he'd been for so long, and how he despised the feeling. To his relief, Gale even found it possible to live with him in Priscilla's own parents' house, where for centuries every chair had sat just so. An only child, Priscilla had made Bob promise to remain its custodian even if none of their own three wished to live there, in case a grandchild, or if not, a great-grandchild, might decide to. Because it was literally museum-quality — no place for children to play more than board games — in his gratitude to Gale for agreeing to live there with him, Bob insisted she pick out a vacation home. She did, in the Virgin Islands, so that at least on vacations Margo and Charlie could relax.

Gale's guilt endured, even right up to this minute, for having subjected Margo to a childhood that had been going smoothly in Brookline but which, among Agnes Irwin's all-girls, disintegrated into the cruelest of adolescent scapegoating. To this day, Margo would say she'd had not one friend in all those years, and only those few girls with nice mothers ever invited her when there was a party. As a result, Margo wouldn't consider applying to any college less than a thousand miles from Philadelphia.

Margo took a last sip of coffee and left them to their own devices. "Have fun," she told her mother, as if it were fun to tour hospitals. To Gary she said, "Take it easy," although she meant, "Easy does it" with the vodka. She'd caught her parents avoiding each other's eyes, like teenagers afraid of what would be revealed. She had a bad feeling as well: what if they ruined everybody's lives, again?

∞

In Bob's day, there weren't the blue H signs on every corner as navigational aids. Still, he would have known to make this left turn onto Louis Pasteur in order to go by the original entrance of the old Boston Lying-In, since replaced as Harvard's obstetrical hospital by the cylindrical Brigham and Women's. Could that be it? So old? So grim?

"I did a rotation here at the Lying-In," Bob said, which made that period of his life seem too long ago.

"I did two rotations there," Gale one-upped him, "fourteen months apart."

She'd never told him her childbirth stories, so he knew nothing, certainly compared to Gary, who was right there, hands-on. She said, "We used to tease Charlie that because he was late, he became fanatically on time from then on."

Bob wouldn't have been able to say when his own children arrived in relation to their due dates, which he knew enough not to tell Gale at this particular moment.

"And Margo was two weeks early. Always in a rush." Gale didn't tell Bob that Gary's excitement on the morning of Margo's birth was — like the sky or an ocean — uncontainable. In the delivery room, without taking off his paper mask he sang out loud the Stevie Wonder song that opens with a newborn's first cry: "Isn't She Lovely?" He was thrilled by Margo that first morning, on her birthday, and ever since.

Bob also sensed it wouldn't be a helpful thing just now to mention that he hadn't been on hand for the births of any of his children, because all three times he'd been in the middle of an operation he couldn't exactly interrupt to catch an elevator upstairs to Obstetrics.

Twice, Gale could have told Bob, Gary was Mr. Paternity Leave. With Charlie's birth devotedly compensating Margo for the insult she was clearly suffering in no longer being Mommy's only favorite baby, Gary consoled her while being none the less glad to have one of each kind, a daughter and a son. As a psychologist, Gale knew how delicate this early balance was, and consequently how important it was to remember not to hurry Margo out of her crib, away from her bottle, onto a toilet seat. The surprise to Gale had been Gary's understanding this intuitively, empathically. Although she was the professional, Gary was clearly the pro.

"Hospital entrances aren't what they used to be, are they?" asked Bob. They were passing something that looked like a luxury resort in a good climate.

Gale's "hmn" barely conveyed an awareness that he'd spoken. She preferred to think about coming through her own front door, stripped and repainted by Gary, holding Margo, holding Charlie, never happier. Their door was the red of fire trucks.

"Ambulance entrances were strictly functional, not what you'd call architecture," Bob continued, as if they were in a conversation together as equals, as they drove past an Emergency sign and a formal canopy with Corinthian columns.

When again she didn't engage, he let it go. It would be a topic to discuss with Gary during an awkward silence, such as while the photographer has everyone lined up but has to check the light meter one last time. "Who's taking the pictures?" asked Bob.

"What pictures?" Why couldn't he shut up?

"The wedding pictures." Of course Bachrach had taken his and Gale's. Like the bartenders who come with the caterers, Bachrach photographers knew what everyone liked. If Bob remembered correctly, the original Bachrach Studio was in Boston.

"I have no idea," Gale answered impatiently. "Not Bachrach, though, I can promise." But now she couldn't stop either. "Of all the pictures in Eve and Paul's house, not one has those artificially posed hands. Not one, pretending to be an oil painting, is stamped pretentiously with that gold signature."

"Darling, I have no need for it to be Bachrach." He defended himself, although he was surprised it was still such a sore point. It had taken Gale five years to tell him how she felt about that picture, but he thought she was over it. Hadn't she gone back to have another taken, to replace that self with this one? "And I'm sorry I brought it up."

"I wish you hadn't *then*, either," she pushed the point. Did she need to have an argument in order to release this tension in her? How ridiculous to argue about wedding pictures when Bob gripped the steering wheel like the captain of a small boat in choppy seas, keeping them, although barely, from flipping over.

"I quite agree." He'd just wanted to balance Priscilla's portrait, which for the sake of the children and grandchildren he'd felt obliged to display, as always, on the grand piano. In it, Priscilla looked more alive than she'd been for the decade before her death, whereas in Gale's — she wore a champagne lace dress that looked white in the silvery tones — the prospective bride seemed, in her own opinion at least, waxen. Bob happened to like the effect because he thought she looked serene. Unlike right now. Bob had been about to propose stopping to tour the newest hospital building, but this would be impossible. Gale's shoulders were hunched up around her ears, and her eyes were shut tight.

At the sitting she'd complained about the bouquet the photographer's assistant put in her hands, a spray of silk orchids she'd resisted as too conventional, not to mention patently fake. At Bob's request she'd gone to the Bachrach studio on Boylston Street, but she'd felt foolish — like an aspiring actress — bringing her costume in a zippered bag. She was an adult — a Ph.D. — made to look like a dowager.

That she would eventually become Bob's mother was what she'd feared most in marrying Bob. "Call me Mother Oakley," the old lady had invited Gale on that wedding day, pressing upon her an oval sapphire which had its own insurance rider because it was the size of a watch face. As it had turned out, however, by comparison to Gary's mother, not to mention her own, Mother Oakley herself had been a wedding gift. That is, there were worse things in life to become than the successor to a grande dame.

But Gale had to admit this wasn't what she was feeling right now, stuck in the mud of her own ancient resentments. She looked over at Bob's perfect profile and saw his jaw muscles working to prevent him opening his mouth, to let his last words to her stand, his "I quite agree." In spite of this — in spite of herself — Gale told him, "Then they made me sit against that ridiculous Bachrach background of wispy clouds, so that rather than looking like the wife you were about to marry, I looked like the one who'd died."

∞

They were stuck in Red Sox traffic and, worse, when they tried to loop around the Fenway they somehow ended up even closer to the ballpark. Kids with orange flags competed to wave stopped cars into costly parking, while baseball-capped father-and-son pairs of pedestrians cut between cars, hurrying to get autographs after batting practice, before game time. By the time they reached the Colonnade, Gale had become just as furious at Gary, for not taking Charlie to Fenway Park like all these regular fathers. Naturally she recognized this anger as a composite, but her real agitation deepened into the vividly pained expression witnessed by David Haynes, who was in the hotel lobby, ready early, like a professional best man.

As Gale hurried from the car and through the door into the hotel, David didn't know whether to tell her then or later that while they were out, Bob's daughter called from Philadelphia and reached Margo with this message: one of her kids has the chickenpox. He risked it.

"Tell Bob," Gale said, crossing to the open elevator. Bob was leaving the car with the valet parker, since Charlie had hired a bus to bring all the relatives to Brookline for the wedding and back here for the reception. She let the doors close behind her, and in their brassy reflection she had no choice but to watch herself cry. "So that makes three for three," she said aloud, alone.

The other two of Bob's children, his sons, had faxed Charlie their congratulations and regrets, no matter that Charlie would have come from the other side of the world if either of them were the one getting married. It wasn't as if they couldn't have arranged to come on business: they each made frequent enough trips back from Tokyo and Hong Kong to keep up their memberships in their clubs. "Poor Charlie," Gale said, even though Charlie himself would be the first to forgive them.

There she was again in the hall mirror and, full length, in the mirrored wall of the bathroom she locked herself into in order to start all over again. Was she weeping because of poor Charlie or at what she'd done to her children by having married Bob? Hot, hot water flattened her clean hair to her scalp, raining on her, the steam gradually making the mirror opaque.

What she'd done to her children, in giving herself the stability of a safe marriage, was to take away from them all of the comforts of home. In Priscilla's house everything was registered with Sotheby's, breakable and irreparable. Because ultimately everything belonged to Bob's kids, who were away at college back then, Charlie and Margo had bedrooms borrowed from his absent children. "Do you think Grant would mind," Charlie had once asked pathetically, "if I hang up my Red Sox banner?" Philadelphia's baseball team was in last place, so Charlie's actual worry was about whether Bob would think he was ungrateful for still being a Red Sox fan. More than anything, Charlie wanted a father.

And Bob tried to be a good one, despite the fact that his work prevented him from being any more available than he had been to his own children. No, Gale's guilt — this pained expression David Haynes had witnessed — wasn't about having given them Bob, but her recognition of the cost to them of their having lost Gary. No, this was her own grief. She was experiencing her own version of that loss of Gary.

When she emerged from the shower in the hotel's terrycloth robe, Bob was hearing about his granddaughter's symptoms, his voice in response completely sympathetic even though it sounded like a mild case. When he hung up he said automatically to Gale, "Jane sends her love."

Because Gale was silent, Bob suggested tolerantly, "But even if we think she could have, or even ought to have, by now it's too late to come."

This was factually true, so Gale left it at that.

"Should I call her back?" All he wanted was to do something to help.

"To tell her to come anyway? No. If it had been her impulse, yes, but obviously it wasn't." Gale watched Bob unbutton his barely worn blue shirt so he could change it for a fresh white one. "And it wasn't, was it?"

"No," he had to admit.

Gale hadn't been surprised by the "obligations" Jane offered as reasons why it was going to be impossible to come for the entire weekend. Bob had disputed Gale's theory that Jane had been counting on Amanda's being named — as if this were a pageant — the flower girl, but Gale supposed he'd said something to let Jane know to make a token appearance, for appearance' sake at least.

Equally objectively, Gale felt entitled to point out that Jane's live-in help might have freed her for a few hours, enough to have flown to Boston and back, the way working women are obliged to, even if their children are sick. She stopped herself short of saying it would never have occurred to Jane to make an effort like that.

Because Gale made it sound so simple, Bob agreed, "That's right, she could. Should I call her back?"

"Don't you *see*, Bob? It didn't occur to her!" Gale was sick of Jane's "sending her love" when the truth was, Jane was too selfish to love anybody more than herself. This had been clear to Gale from their first encounter, when Jane's agenda hadn't included wanting to learn about Gale, rather to make sure Gale knew all about her.

Now Bob felt forced to defend Jane somewhat too, so he said, "It's chickenpox Amanda has, not an imaginary complaint." His white shirt buttoned, he was knotting his tie, looking at her over his shoulder in the big mirror over the bureau. "I suspect you'd have stayed home too if Margo or Charlie were sick."

"Yes, you're right." She left it at that. Her intolerance of Jane was magnified by such clear memories of her own children as infants. How could she not feel she'd failed them?

Now Gale returned to the steamy bathroom to blow her hair so dry — with her head upside down, Margo taught her, to add volume — the blood would flow back into her face simply by virtue of gravity.

∞

"I see what you mean about Gale," Sandra said matter-of-factly, unfastening the fabulously crafted silver and turquoise belt she coiled like a snake. She let her denim skirt and pearl-buttoned shirt fall to the floor in a blue heap. "You two have nothing in common."

"Did I say that?" Gary doubted it, if only because it wasn't true. But as if to demonstrate their own compatibility, he abandoned his clothes the same way. Then he called the front desk and asked to be wakened in an hour and a quarter. The sheets had already been folded back, but twelve hours earlier.

"It's obvious." When she added "And *him*," it was clear what she meant. "A cold fish," she said anyway, yawning. "Not that there's such a thing as a warm fish."

Gary could feel his lungs slowly filling with air and emptying, unlike a fish.

"Aren't I right?"

"Hmn."

"She's too aloof for me, but she's perfect for him." Removing the Belgian chocolate wafer from its foil, Sandra asked him, "Can I have yours?" In addition to one-of-a-kind belts, mints with sparkles in them were another of her weaknesses, as she herself would be the first to admit.

Now it was too great an effort not letting go, so he let go.

She knew she should sleep too, but she was the kind who likes to run everything by one more time. It was one of her strengths, she felt, to give everyone, including herself, a second chance. After an inventory of ten or fifteen seconds she decided she wouldn't change anything so far. So that was easy.

Gary faced her, curled like a shrimp, but this position seemed designed to fend Sandra off with his knees, to protect himself, it could seem. Back home he was more natural, sleeping on his back, wide open. And look at those covers, pulled tight like a drawstring. He must be cold. Shouldn't she have insisted on that hot bath in the Jacuzzi? Well, right there was something to change.

When the phone rang, she was calculating how many hours remained until the plane, so she was able to tell her mother, "I was just thinking about you two." Sandra's cheerful outlook came straight from her mother, who believed that for every bad apple there's an entire barrelful of good ones.

Gary half woke, relieved to learn time wasn't up. He heard his wife say, "Bob's about your age, would be my guess, and he's really handsome, only in a Gregory Peck sort of way, you know? So not our type." Sandra and her mother had made it quite clear to Gary he *was* their type.

"Pretty, but cool, like him," Sandra said about Gale. "She's a psychologist or psychiatrist or something, so you can see her mind working all the time but without any idea what she's thinking."

Her mother seemed curious about everybody. "Beth? Adorable, curly hair. Margo's the only bridesmaid. Margo, right. Right, Disney."

Gary was in danger of waking up altogether, so he turned his back to her and pulled the covers over his head.

"Boston? Different."

It was Tucson he'd call different. What was different was them, from each other. He heard her say, "No, he's asleep. We

did the tourist thing all night, so I'm exhausted too. Cape Cod."
Evidently Sandra's mother had her own opinion of it but, as on
most things, they agreed. "Too crowded, yes." This was Sandra's firm opinion, even though all night they hadn't seen one
other person.

"Hey, honey!" This would be Jason. "How's my guy?"

Gary knew Sandra would repeat back every detail about Jason's school day: "Macaroni and cheese? Math test? Hold it,
hon. So Nana let you watch Jay Leno?"

Next she said, "I give up. Okay, one guess. Lifeguard?" Jason
had been planning for Halloween since the first day of school,
pestering them to guess what his costume would be. Gary had
been made to promise Jason a genuine pumpkin from a real
patch, silly as a pumpkin in the overhead compartment might be.
No doubt Sandra would want to persuade him to let her bring
dried cornstalks and a bag of fallen leaves. In a million years
Charlie wouldn't have thought to be a lifeguard. In Boston you
needed to wear too many clothes.

"I give up. Surprise me!" Sandra's enthusiasm was genuine
but noisy. "I know that whatever you pick will be perfect. Now
put Nana back on. Love you."

Charlie was a cowboy mostly, not a costume Jason thought of
as a costume in a state famous for that look. Gary heard Sandra
verify their arrival time, then tell her mother, "Love you." As a
girl, Sandra had been taught, along with brushing her hair a
hundred strokes, to say "I love you" at least ten times a day, even
if all at once, to one person. When Gary first met Sandra and her
mother, he'd been amazed people talked this way, but then he
became the beneficiary and understood that this — not the sixties — was the real meaning of free love.

Unlike her son, Sandra had no trouble at all getting to sleep,
and to prove it, in less than a minute, she was. Unlike Gary.

He'd been made too painfully aware of how many Halloweens
he'd missed out on, which forced this question: how could he

have believed there wouldn't be consequences? Gale had accused him — "Cheat!" — flinging the implication that he had cheated on tests and taxes too. But it was true he'd lied to her.

"I never lied!" he'd uselessly argued, since Gale then gave him three quick examples, proofs of his affair with Jeannie. He'd tried deflecting her by demanding to know how she'd found out, claiming his right to a fair trial, when she lunged at him like he was the enemy in a world war, ripping the breast pockets off his shirt and, for the only time in her life, roaring. It was this raw sound Gale's rage made that finished it for him — poof! Jeannie was all gone: he was no longer unfaithful! — but not for Gale. "Get out!" she'd screamed. "Go!" she'd ordered.

Now awake for the duration, Gary admitted to himself he'd had yet to learn proper respect by that point. By 1977 the concept had been introduced into American culture, but regrettably he'd been a little behind.

Not anymore. He'd paid off his debt, since in his second marriage, throwing himself into Chloe Fortunado's career, he might as well have been an employee. This was inadvertent overcompensation, but he'd learned that lesson all right, as well, eventually, as the one about what it feels like to have a spouse who has a lover.

Like a magician with the power to remake a moment in time, Gary now chose one: instead of predictably fleeing to the opposite extreme when Gale tells him to go, he stays.

3

GALE SCRUTINIZED GARY AS HE CAME FROM THE HOTEL: a pinstriped suit too nicely cut not to have been tailor-made for him in London, and on his feet matte black, new boots, which made his long legs into exclamation marks.

Just behind him was Sandra, whose dress came with a fitted matador-type jacket, embroidered and reembroidered with gold curlicues, like her hair. She was right about it being wrong for the middle of the day, but she surely looked like the answer, once and for all, to the question about whether or not blondes have more fun.

They were the last to board the Boston Coach bus hired to take the hotel guests to and from the ceremony. Sandra appeared to be speaking to Gale — "Love that color; can't wait to see the maple tree!" — then to nobody in particular — "I just realized I match the Gold family itself!" — as they moved to seats farther back. Sandra was already taking pictures, whereas Gale retreated into an examination of her own exposed knees and the intricate microscopic webbing of her stockings, tinted to be invisible. Needless to say, she recognized her escape into the pure geometry of woven nylon as a way to flee from her own feelings about Gary. Was she as distractable as he was?

This had been his charm once, but it was also what opened him to Jeannie's simpler charms, so it was ultimately the thing that ruined their marriage. Except that from another point of view — his, say — what finished them was Gale's inability to negotiate a truce with him. She knew she believed in truces, because she counseled her own patients not to quit until they had tried hard and failed. In other people's lives she was an expert at conflict resolution, advising them to take plenty of time, endorsing a caution she herself had been guilty of not being capable of. If it were appropriate to be a negative role model for her patients, she could tell them, "Do as I say, not as I've done," but what patient wants an unreliable doctor?

She glanced at Bob, who was resting, eyes closed, unaware how busy Gale was with her memory of that long ago Saturday morning when Eve's live-in babysitter, Jeannie, admitted having a three-month-long affair with a married man. Eve had told Gale she didn't want to know which married man it was, and especially when Jeannie told her it was Gary. *Gary?* Eve would never forget hearing the name because, as with a death, she'd had to have it repeated.

And although Eve had wanted to shout at Jeannie, "Get out," instead she'd had to say, "Come here," and let the poor dumb thing weep in her arms, since only then had Jeannie been made aware of the consequences. "I wish," Jeannie had lamented uselessly, "I'd told him to find somebody his own age." As if this were the worst of it.

Nevertheless Eve firmly told Jeannie to find another place to live, and by that afternoon   "Children, say goodbye" — all Jeannie's few possessions were driven off. "Say goodbye to the children" was what Gale told Gary too, as if there were no serious difference between parenting and babysitting.

Gary banished himself by volunteering to oversee a complex renovation project in Australia and, self-imposed punishment, missed summer altogether that year. When he returned, it was to the perpetual winter of divorce proceedings.

In that same year she'd buried her own bones in a weight gain so dramatic she could have been her own distant cousin. Gale made no excuses for herself, which wasn't the same thing as her mother calling it — and her as well — inexcusable. Her minuscule mother weighed herself each morning to know how much or how little to eat that day. And Gale's only sister, Kay, was the mother of twin fashion models who looked like plastic flamingos.

Gale cupped her kneecaps with her hands, never taking it for granted that now they fit, like caps on jars. For that awful period of her life she'd lost touch with her own infrastructure, believing her bones had returned to dust without bothering to wait for her death. When an x-ray was required after a fall on an icy patch, that fractured bird-sized bone proved she still existed. In other words, when Gale hit the sidewalk, she'd also hit bottom.

Or this was what she'd told her kids, who didn't need to know the full effect of their grandmother's controlled death that year, when, refusing to die by more ordinary means, she took her own life. It amazed Gale even to this day that, like a snapshot in a wallet, the image of Gale that her mother carried off to her death so little resembled the person she'd been before or since. Now, again, she wore her flesh with the ease of a sundress, no longer puffy in the down-filled parka of her desperate overweight. Her fingers were slender, manicured nails pearly, rings an extra thin platinum band overwhelmed by the fine oval sapphire Bob's mother awarded her like a political endorsement.

On their own wedding day Bob had taken that hand of hers to hold in both of his, putting into deliberate words the difference she'd made to him, bringing him a lightness of heart he'd last experienced as a preadolescent on the first day of every summer vacation. To describe the depth of his love and gratitude there was no appropriate word, but he'd chosen "devotion," even though it sounded too religious. What he'd meant was that when she filled him, he'd seen how empty he'd been.

Bob's hands had been softened by the routines of scrubs and

latex gloves, and like vegetables grown in earth mounds they were unnaturally pale. Seeing them now, folded passively in his lap, saddened her because Bob's hands did more good in a single surgical hour than her own ever had. "Oh, dear Bob," she said, but which sounded like "Dear God," as in "Help me."

The bus glided to a stop next to a fire hydrant and a dozen white balloons tethered with frizzy ribbons. At the front of the bus, Margo touched David's tie to make sure it was silk; that is, to make sure her baby brother hadn't bought rayon ties for his best men. At the curb, in matching ties, stood Beth's three brothers and Charlie, who suddenly had visible age lines in his face.

Though they'd boarded in pairs, they got off one by one. Of Beth's relatives, the men were all as well groomed as the women, whereas Charlie's relatives — Cousin Ed wore a bow tie, and a younger cousin's blond mustache had no personality at all — had that self-made Protestant look that never asks professional advice. With the exception of Gale and Margo, the women on their side wore dresses that are good travelers, thanks to busy patterns and the tiniest amount of a synthetic in the fabric. By contrast, the Jewish women all wore vibrant colors with deliberate lines. Such confirmed stereotypes made David wonder what he looked like to them.

"Pink!" shrieked Sandra. Never before in her life having seen such a tree, she was thrilled to have it in the family now, so to speak. "Red and yellow make pink!" No one contradicted her. She wasn't wrong exactly, only exaggerating.

Sandra told Gale to stand in front of the maple tree so she could take her picture in the dress that was the same color. "Don't worry, you don't disappear," Sandra said and took another one just in case. "Now both of us," she told Gary, and handed him her camera so she could pose with Gale. Gary felt a rush of relief that his mother wasn't here, since the last thing he needed right now would be her opinion of his two wives.

From the front porch, decorated like a bandstand with garlands of white mums, the professional photographer took her picture, of the three of them. Near Gary, Charlie stood next to David, of whom he asked, "Ready?" with a good imitation of a ready smile. Because David had never seen Charlie look this unrelaxed, he put his arm around him like a brace. It would have made a nice picture if Gary had thought to take it, but at least with her close-up lens the professional got the shot.

∞

Inside, Beth had sensibly insisted on having rented chairs so that everybody would be able to see. Her little cousins surrounded their grandfather like tugboats, and berthed him in his place of honor.

"You must be Herman," Sandra said to Eve's father, Herb. One of Beth's brothers had seated her next to him, so she introduced herself as Sandra, the groom's stepmom.

Herb responded, "How come ever since the sixties nobody has a last name anymore?" Then he said, "Herb Fleischman."

"Sandra Burr. I'm real happy to meet you."

Herb smiled, showing expensive teeth. "Since Aaron Burr comes to mind, in your case I'm more sympathetic."

Between Sandra's eyebrows two creases represented her effort to remember why that name sounded familiar, but before she could come up with it, another of Beth's brothers apologized. "Sorry, Poppa," he said, "it seems I put Sandra in the wrong seat." In the front row were six chairs, two by two by two, for the parents and stepparents.

An oboe and a violin played a particularly melodious suite, and once everyone was seated, a collaborative silence signaled the start. This being a Saturday before sundown, already the ceremony was liturgically incorrect, and yet there were reasons, the most fundamental being that, by definition, intermarriage means inclusion. Herb had protested the violation of the sabbath, but his daughter had responded that she'd learned from him to always value the spirit of the law more than the mere letter. Then Beth and Charlie together reassured Herb that their future children were already Jewish, because Beth was.

"But no *chuppa?*" he'd asked. "How could anybody get married without a *chuppa?*" Herb had consulted his rabbi, who patiently instructed him in the crucial difference between theology and cultural symbolism: "Have a *chuppa* if you want, just don't expect any decent rabbi to take part in a Saturday wedding ceremony at noon." The compromise candidate was a Jewish justice of the peace who'd been asked to do stranger things than read from Psalms.

He entered now, robed like a judge, carrying a black leather folder that looked like it contained a diploma in Latin calligraphy, not a marriage license. The musicians filled the silence with a single sustained note that was at once grave and hopeful.

The silky white *chuppa* symbolized the roof over the couple's heads, while on the reverse of the double-sided fabric — Beth would have it both ways at once — was the ancient symbolism of the stars against a night sky. Beth's schooling in market research meant that in planning her wedding she'd taken nothing for granted, counting down from ages ago so there'd be time enough, once the hotel was booked, to redecorate the living room in case her parents agreed. And it looked great, the teak of their entire marriage replaced in a day by overstuffed taupe sofas and stone tables the same color. The loosely woven wool curtains on wooden rings had been replaced by microblinds in a color called Burmese Cat. The rug cost as much as a car.

Without knowing how recent the transformation was, Gale was content to envy Eve's freedom to get rid of the Fifties Modern and start over. This would be impossible in her life with Bob, because Priscilla's fifties were the *eighteen* fifties. All the furniture was catalogued, so Bob's children could know its value without having to wait for him to die in order to divvy it up. As if

Bob had just then whispered in her ear "A penny for your thoughts," Gale shook off a chill, appalled to be thinking about Bob's death.

∞

Directly overhead, in Eve and Paul's bedroom, Margo was calming Beth, who finally had a tiny case of the jitters. Charlie and David took sips of cool water and checked the shoulders of each other's dark suits, David verifying for one final time that the rings were still there in his pocket. David then took Margo's hand and they went down the stairs, cuing the musicians, who played something lovely by Beethoven.

The musicians' job was to chase shadows from the corners and clear all minds of their preoccupations, which was why it was another minute before the piece ended. It wasn't necessary for a clerk of court to call "All rise," because all did.

Eve's unmitigated and wholly apparent joy divided her age in half, into Beth's age, and even her pure black hair looked natural. Paul too, for this one moment, entirely forgot that he was employed by a university president whose contempt for him was equally matched by his own. Paul's normal posture was a slump — at an impasse his whole career, he was tenured but without real academic freedom — but now he looked tall, even compared with Gary.

Gary clamped his trembling lips between his teeth and his mouth became a short straight line, reinforced like a buttonhole. His fatigue had given him such a headache that lines of sweat on his forehead indexed the tension inside his skull. He wished he were Charlie, and he wished Beth were Gale, so he could get married again for the last time.

Sandra pointed her camera at the massive polished hardwood staircase. No doubt it would be a selling point in this real estate market, but because most of the Tucson houses she sold were on one floor, she thought of stairs as wasted space. Even these spiral balusters and the fluted newel post, while unique, were hardly necessary. Still, it was interesting to get into one of these merrie olde New England homes, even if the foyer came straight out of a Charles Dickens movie.

Now there was a cellist bringing notes like dolphins from the depths of the sea to the surface for air. As if also raised up, by the sound, Gale took Bob's arm to keep from sinking back down. Contemporary, classical, the music's power was in being both at once, and unfamiliar. Listen to this, it demanded. Pay attention. Look up.

On the landing at the bend in the stairs, Beth and Charlie stood together, pausing — posing — so the sunlight coming through the window washed them with the combined colors of the sugar maple. Beth had doubtless planned that effect, as that from somewhere came noon bells one after the other, all twelve.

Charlie's teeth were dry, so long exposed to the air. This amused him, remembering how as kids he and Beth would rub their teeth dry with their fingers and fold their upper lips under, in order to look more like eager beavers than they already were. He told Beth, "I love you I love you I love you," knowing everybody there was reading his lips. Beth said, "Those are my three wishes," and he said, "Then you get two more."

Against her white dress, Beth's black hair looked almost like patent leather, as shiny as a limousine. She was carrying white lilies and white freesia, whose combined fragrances spread across the space like syrup. Her dress was a convenient length for not tripping on it while descending the staircase, and from beneath the wide skirt her narrow feet looked like origami cranes in shoes that appeared, like those of a goddess, winged. Now that they'd stepped from the pink glowing window light they appeared even less earthly. In such a theatrical moment, hope hangs suspended along with disbelief. Beth knew this was the desired, transforming effect, but until now she hadn't fully understood this was the heart of the human heart, not fantasy uplift, that she and Charlie were helping people to remember to believe in.

An inaudible sob escaped Gary, so Sandra took his hand. Gary had moments with Jason when he'd suddenly feel grief-struck at having missed Charlie when he was Jason's age, and ever since. Gary believed he could remember the imprint of Charlie's body against his own, even though he was capable of admitting it was probably more because Jason was, like Charlie at nine, a lanky kid with unusually long arms. Jason would cling to him the way Charlie once did, and Gary would pretend to forget what Charlie had told him: most of his memories, the undiluted happy ones, stopped at nine.

The only other person Charlie had ever told this to was David. Freshman year, when Charlie discovered Beth was in their class at Wesleyan, he told David he was going to marry her as a way of bringing his parents together. He was joking, sort of, and he sort of wasn't, which David saw but never once teased him about, not even when Charlie gave him permission to.

David reciprocated by trusting Charlie with what it was like, not being white, to never feel entirely comfortable, always ready for some challenge that he didn't belong, wasn't welcome, always having to push through that in order to claim his own rightful place. Without presuming equivalency, Charlie provided uncon-ditional comfort by telling David what it had been like for him to strive to disappear when his mother moved them to Philadel-phia, so afraid was he of making some huge mistake he wouldn't know how to avoid. The rules of that restrictive society were so firm it was a surprise they were unwritten, which was what made that life so tricky. It went without saying that David understood, even better.

So David winked at Charlie as if to blink away all their com-bined self-doubt. "You're free, man, home free," David signaled, so certain was he that Charlie had found in Beth not only a perfect match but his other half.

Gale sat between Gary and Bob, but because Bob sat in the exact middle of his chair, their shoulders didn't touch the way hers and Gary's did. Or was she the one leaning toward him? Gale sat straighter — no, it was him — in order to concentrate on Charlie and Beth under the white canopy, looking royal. Beth was no mere consort, however, since she'd been first in her class ever since nursery school. Her authority shone the way a light does, from the inside out. Everything she knew about self-doubt, in other words, she'd learned from other people.

There was nothing Gale wished for them that they didn't already have, since this absolute confidence they had in themselves and in each other was the one thing that seemed always to be missing in her own marriages. According to her children, "I'll have to ask Bob" had become her standard answer to their questions, as if in marrying him she'd forfeited her spontaneity all at once, as if she'd been pickpocketed. To them, "ask" meant "ask permission" — Bob as boss — so, following her example, they too were on their best behavior. It was a misunderstanding — by "ask" she only meant "discuss" — but by the time they got it all worked out, her kids had a lot of good examples they could point to. For instance, when it was only the three of them, when school was canceled because of a winter storm they'd improvise an adventure, which was why Margo and Charlie held it against Gale for neglecting to mention that in their move south to Philadelphia — Bob verified when Gale asked — they'd be losing their snow days altogether.

Hadn't they been navigated safely through their early adolescence by a single working parent? This was their fair question, and the correct answer was that this woman had been traded in, though in the bargain she also got a partner. Without regret Gale gave up the burden of solo authority, not intending, however, to give up power altogether. Was it her own power Gary was returning to her simply by reminding her he was there, by touching her shoulder with his? She let herself feel him from that shoulder to her elbow, which she pressed against his. When his silent sob made him lurch like that, she had wanted to be the one to take his hand, to admit out loud she'd lost something equally precious, to allow this grief to exist even in the midst of such joy as they each felt. This, Gale remembered, is freedom: whatever happens is by definition true.

"Do you freely take this man to be your husband?" the judge asked Beth. It looked easy to answer yes, as Beth quickly and firmly did. "Do you freely take this woman to be your wife?" To which Charlie answered, "Yes, freely," knowing it would be more accurate to say "Yes, involuntarily." An involuntary act, that is, such as breathing.

∞

Sandra was annoyed. In letting go of her hand, Gary interrupted, even ruined, her memory of Jason in his miniature white suit. The ring bearer, he had walked down the aisle ahead of her, and never ever had she been so proud. Since it was her one and only wedding, she had packed the chapel full of friends and family, who might not have been all that sure about her being somebody's third wife but who nevertheless gave Gary the benefit of the doubt. Which is more than she could say about these people.

She hated easterners for acting superior, making her feel like some cheap date. They had a nerve pretending to have good manners. Bob, for one. He didn't hear a word she said, and he looked like a stunned animal paralyzed by headlights whenever she opened her mouth, which must be why she provoked him with this "doctor's orders" line she could see made him really uncomfortable.

She looked at Gale's hands, clasped in her lap, that sapphire ring equal to Princess Di's crown-jewel engagement ring. Sandra could see Gale checking out hers, too, no doubt having an opinion about pear-shaped diamonds.

Deliberately making the best of Gary's letting go of her hand,

Sandra took a picture of Beth and Charlie, and another, her automatic camera whirring between frames like a toy train around a track. Anyway, why wasn't the photographer taking these pictures? Sandra had had a video made of her wedding, including their on-camera vows.

The only disagreement she and Gary had beforehand was over whether to leave in or take out the ritual references to "the gift of children." She'd argued that the "if it be Your will" language was only symbolic, but he'd convinced her that since they both believed conception was an act of nature, not God intervening, they really ought to leave it out. As it turned out, the last thing he needed was God's will in their lives, given that at the time Gary's own will leaned toward a vasectomy.

"Don't be jealous," Gary had said when she said she was, of Gale, for giving birth to Gary's children. It wasn't that she was desperate to have his baby, more that she would have liked at least the possibility of changing her mind. "I'm jealous of her for having had you longer," Sandra told him. For having had him when he was younger, was what she partly meant.

But wait. "Don't be jealous"? Oh, sure. Look at Gary with his shoulder against Gale's, as if the chairs aren't wide enough for him. "Mr. Universe," she'd called him the first time he took off his shirt, and you know what? For a second he didn't seem to know she was teasing. In truth, for fifty-one he wasn't in bad shape, but the fact was that she'd gone with a lot of men who had better bodies, who worked at it, who cared. It was only in this last month and a half that Gary had joined a fitness center and worked with a personal trainer, as if — well, Jesus Christ, she sure was a fool after all — Gary only wanted to look good for Gale. So much for remembering Jason in his white suit.

The judge joined two fragments of psalms Beth and Charlie had selected. " 'It is good to give thanks to the Lord, / to play in honor of your name, Most High, / to proclaim your love at daybreak / and your faithfulness all through the night / to the music of the zither and lyre, / to the rippling of the harp.' For, 'The word of the Lord is integrity itself, / all he does is done faithfully; / he loves virtue and justice, / the Lord's love fills the earth.'"

Finally the judge pronounced, "Now, by the power invested in me, I pronounce you husband and wife." Beth's grandfather chimed, "*Mazel tov!*" as Beth and Charlie kissed. The music resumed, but with a picked-up, less penetrating pace.

"Nice idea, that umbrella effect," said Cousin Ed. "I've never seen it before." His bow tie was crooked.

Sandra fixed it with one hand, like the propeller of a toy plane. "It's Jewish," she said.

"That much I figured out myself," Ed assured her, shaking Gary's hand as he said, "Congratulations to the father of the groom." Secular tradition had its own requirements.

"You're right," Gary answered, as if Ed had chastised him for failing to play his role sufficiently. And here was a tray of tulip glasses filled with champagne the color of honey.

Before Gary could change his mind, he tapped his glass with the silver key ring Sandra gave him when they married, to hold the key to his own new front door. He had everyone's complete attention, so he began even without knowing what he would say. "Thanks to you two," he said, "and I mean thanks to *you*, the rest of us get this chance to say *thanks* to you." Gary could feel his voice vibrate with the fright of knowing, if not what he would say, what he wished he could say. Suddenly Charlie looked worried, so Gary looked at Beth instead.

"Beth," and as Gary addressed her, he got the idea to say, "remember how you rode a two-wheeler precociously, and taught Charlie how to?" The image of Beth flew into his head like a sparrow through an open window. Now what? Would it circle frantically and crash into a mirror and break its neck?

"I saw that driveway just last night in Falmouth Heights," he continued, "so it's still there."

Sandra nodded, confirming that she'd seen it too.

"And Charlie, remember Sammy?" Charlie nodded too, but only tentatively. "Sammy was a kitten Charlie and I rescued from Jamaica Pond, the only one that survived of a litter someone tried to drown. We buried the other three —"

"Four," Charlie corrected.

"— and you gave Sammy to Beth."

"But Beth had parakeets," Charlie said, "so —" But what he meant was, "So? What's your point, Dad?" Was it necessary to describe dead kittens ten minutes into their marriage?

As Gary remembered it, he'd rented a rowboat that Saturday instead of raking the lawn. Charlie's orange life jacket made him round like a buoy but, hanging overboard from the bow seat, his arms turned out to be too short. Charlie saw the plastic bag half afloat by virtue of trapped air and told his father to bring it aboard because it was making that sound Gary could still hear in his head. In a rush he said, "So you brought Sammy home and said you'd wait for the birds to die — 'Cats outlive birds, right, Dad?' you asked me — and my answer was, 'Young cats —'"

"'— outlive old birds,'" Charlie recited, letting himself relax a tiny bit.

Gary looked at Beth to see if she was getting with this or not, and he was pleased to see she looked like she trusted him. "Now then, what's a two-wheeler got to do with Beth's parakeets and Charlie's Sammy?" Gary ventured a gaze around the room, startled to find that everybody, including all the kids, looked to be quite engaged. "Pragmatically — that is, as deliberate and skillful as she was in teaching Charlie how to ride a bike — Beth offered a trade: if he took her birds, then he could give her Sammy, right? So he did."

There was a catch. He didn't know for sure which ended up

outliving the other. Gale would remember, so Gary looked to her, taking the approval flashing in her eyes to signify he'd guessed correctly. Anyway, it's the law of both nature and averages that young cats like Charlie are born to outlive old birds like himself. But now the catch was in Gary's own throat. Raising his glass, he managed to offer, "Long life."

"Long life," all the others echoed. This was the one thing Beth and Charlie didn't already have.

∞

Like teams, they were being posed for family photos, Beth's varsity lineup outnumbering Charlie's, even though his only cousins, the models, knew how to fill a lot of space. Their mother, Gale's sister Kay, gave them their careers as babies, as if her kids were cuter than anybody else's. As a result, they grew up believing they were wholly blameless, which made them unreliable. For example, they'd just arrived.

"All smiles!" the photographer requested. And because Gale realized the wide-angle lens would make them all look like fish, even those two, Gale smiled nicely for the camera.

Sandra took advantage of the opportunity to ask a question she'd always wondered about: do professional models say "Cheese!" or what? The answer given was that they say whatever the fuck they want.

"Oh," Sandra said, making her mouth really fish-shaped.

"Look at the camera!" the photographer issued, but as a plea, not an order.

"Cheese!" the two young women said in mock unison.

"Hold it." This was Gale, who held up her hand like a traffic cop. "You two may *not* be rude to Sandra. You got that?" Gale waited for them to acknowledge her with a nod. They finally did. By now the photographer had to read the light meter again.

Although Margo was the first granddaughter, her cousins outranked her with their larger advantage of growing up — off and on, depending upon their mother's fortunes — at their grandparents' address on Ononta, in Cincinnati. It was an advantage, that is, until their grandmother's unexpected death. Margo was thirteen at the time, and with the exquisite moral clarity of a newborn adolescent, she was opposed to suicide by any means, by anyone. All Gale could offer Margo by way of explanation was that her grandmother had resented, to put it mildly, being obliged to grow old.

Her mother's refrain during Gale's adolescence was what a shame it was Gale wasn't as pretty as her sister Kay, whose photographs throughout childhood looked so much like their mother's, *they* could have been the two who were sisters. What a pity Gale had the James chin instead of the stronger Stuart chin. She could always cover her large ears with her thin hair — although too bad it wasn't a better brown — but there was nothing to do about those big bones. And size eleven shoes? On a *girl?*

Gale had permitted her mother to steal her soul, which was the real, abiding shame. Ultimately Gale came to see her mother as her own victim: she couldn't tolerate herself as she grew old, and the more she couldn't, the more she grew to resent Kay, whose beauty, perversely, paled when compared with that of her own two daughters, whose astonishing faces were hired to decorate glossy magazines. Unable to embrace her remaining daughter, what could she do but kill herself? And, in the note the police found, blame Gale for abandoning her. But this was the total lie that also freed Gale.

Not surprisingly, Kay dismissed Gale's interpretation as typical shrink talk. Less convolutedly, Kay preferred to believe it had been their father's passion for golf that did her in, to which Gale had replied, most amiably, "That too."

Margo relaxed now that the group photographs were done. Beth's family was so large and welcoming that all Charlie's relatives could be taken in by them like foster kids, which made it matter all the more to Margo that Charlie have a real family too. Margo wasn't losing a brother, she was gaining a sister. And because they wanted babies, she would have nieces and nephews while her parents got the grandchildren that would make them friends again. It didn't seem too much to ask.

In the living room a pianist played jazzier music than any composed for oboe and strings, and from the kitchen the caterers brought more champagne and trays of one-bite assemblies: miniature wild-rice pancakes with roasted duck and mango-and-kiwi chutney, that sort of thing.

"Bourbon? I'll see," said the pleasant young woman in a white dress shirt and black trousers.

Sandra told Eve, "Hope that's okay," then said, "I really like your house. I'm a realtor, but I don't much see colonials."

Sandra's genuinely gold hair contrasted effectively with Eve's, but it was Sandra's that looked artificial despite the fact that Eve had been coloring hers for a decade.

"I really like your yard also," Sandra went on. "Meaning the trees. They're the main difference between Boston and Tucson." Then she said, "Oh, thanks," taking a glass from a tray. "Sure you don't mind? I can wait until the hotel. It's just that I don't do champagne." Sandra pointed to her forehead and said, "Headache."

"Me too," Eve said, glad to have found something to say.

"So, what's the story, then?" asked Sandra as she took a sip. "I mean, you're a doctor, aren't you? How is it I can get trashed on this stuff and function just fine the next day? Like today," she admitted with a little embarrassment in case Eve had heard about the four Sunrises she'd had at the Transportation.

"I'm a pulmonary specialist," Eve said, almost apologetically.

"Oh." Then Sandra said, "So? Shouldn't you know why, though?"

"Why champagne gives headaches?"

"Actually, they say fine champagne doesn't, but either I've never had it or it couldn't be true."

"You're right, I should know that," Eve said.

"Maybe Bob does." Sandra's mother always told her she could lead a horse to water and be the only one in history who could force it to drink. Before moving to approach Bob, Sandra coyly asked Eve, "Aren't we always supposed to get a second opinion?"

∞

Gary put himself in Eve's way, specifically because she'd been avoiding him. Taking in a now-or-never breath, Gary said, "Nice wedding, Eve."

"And what you said was sweet." Then she said, "Welcome back."

At croquet, he and Eve always beat Paul and Gale, though just barely. "Thanks for having me back, partner," he drawled in a western accent.

"It mustn't be easy."

"I appreciate that. I sincerely do," he said, sounding like himself. Eve was making it easier for him to say, "I've owed you an apology."

"Yes."

"Because I don't even remember her name." But he wasn't asking to be told it, either. "That's how stupid it was of me."

"Yes," agreed Eve. At the time she and Paul both felt violated, but Gary wouldn't have known how threatening it was for them to witness the immediate unraveling of a marriage they'd each considered to be stronger than their own.

"I dreaded this so long I can't believe it's already over." Already too, though, as if Eve were treating an injury, he felt much improved.

But she was trained to pick up symptoms without needing to ask the obvious question: are you feeling better or worse? Gary proved that it was surely worth it to have stuck it out with Paul, but Gary wouldn't want to hear this from her. Nor did he need to know he'd been a valuable object lesson. As they moved toward the dining room Eve said, "But it's not over. It's just beginning."

The large table was draped with a Russian tablecloth embroidered with male peacocks, a fourth-generation wedding present from mother to daughter. It was "old" and "borrowed," and the eyes of the peacocks' tail feathers were every "blue" ever invented. The "new" would be Beth's to have created by the time she passed the tablecloth on.

By now Sandra had discovered that Beth's grandfather had gone to Arizona every winter for the past ten, and hated Florida. "Too many old people," Herb complained. "Unsafe roads, with them on it."

"I've never been," Sandra admitted, "but now that Margo's a Disney architect, I'll be bringing my son Jason to Orlando, definitely." Gary had only contempt for what he called the Disneyizing of the whole world, and in Sandra's opinion this was why Margo had become wildly successful and he hadn't.

Herb told her, "Stay in Arizona, if you want my advice. Take him to see Taliesin." In response to Sandra's blank look he elaborated, "Frank Lloyd Wright. Now that's real architecture."

"So I've heard," Sandra said, glad that, thanks to Gary, at least she had. "Thanks for the recommendation, too. I've been meaning to get there." She spun the ice around the inside of her glass and suggested brightly, "When you come this year, let's go together, okay?"

He'd already moved on. "What's the other guy's name? Also Scottsdale. The bells." On their last trip, Herb's wife bought a dozen of them, telling him the wind ringing the bronze bells would keep him company.

She didn't know what his name was.

"Oh, boy. I guess I'm losing it." Herb scanned the room for the red dress. "She's in the red, the architect, right? What's her name again?"

"Margo."

"Bring me the bridesmaid, the girl in red," he told a grandchild, and, to Sandra, "Who ever heard of red on a bridesmaid?"

As if he would care, she told Herb, "Mine wore lilac."

Too impatient to wait for the expert, he remembered, "Arcosante! Okay. It's an Italian name. He's Italian." He called across the room to his daughter, "Evie! What's Arcosante's name?"

"That's it."

"No, that's the *place.*"

"Then I don't know," Eve replied, content to not remember.

"Don't get old," Herb advised Sandra with a smile. "It ruins your life." Then he laughed, and his energy was like lightning discharged across the entire sky.

Sandra's ready consolation was, "But look at me. I'm young, and do I know the answer?"

"I like you," he told her. "You're good for me. Are you, by any chance, married?" But then he quickly moved away. His dear wife had been dead a year, and as a widower he had no business sounding like a pathetic old flirt.

How could she have not noticed Herb the night before? Plus, how could they think she'd have preferred Cousin Ed? Sandra said yes to a refill without having to say she was drinking bourbon. Things were beginning to look up; she was finally starting to feel comfortable among these strangers. For instance, Beth.

Sandra told her, "Your grandfather's adorable," just as he shouted, "Soleri, that's the name! So now I can relax." Only Sandra knew what he was saying. "Hey," she told Beth, "speaking of names, we're both Mrs. Burrs now: Mrs. Garrett Burr and Mrs. Charles Burr! Let's have a picture of us two!" Sandra looked around for the photographer, but didn't find her.

And anyway, Beth told Sandra, "I'm keeping Gold."

∽

Bob decided now was the time to give them his wedding present. David Haynes had finished reading from a stack of faxed congratulations, and perhaps because a shiny curled-up fax is the modern equivalent of the flat yellow Western Union telegrams of his day, Bob felt like announcing, "In my family we have a tradition — quite a few of them, as a matter of fact — which began back in the days of the horse and carriage."

He looked shy, even self-deprecating, his hands in his pockets. "At any rate, on his wedding day the groom and his bride are given a traditional present."

Gale was standing by Bob's side. She was confused, having thought they'd agreed that their wedding present was the washer and dryer Charlie and Beth requested and which — not that Bob would know this — were already installed. It wasn't like Bob to compete, but more to the point, she felt he should be gracious enough to let Gary's tribute stand unchallenged by the reality of his own role as Charlie's stepfather. Or Bob could have had the last word last night, when it was his party. Gale looked across the room to where Gary stood, Sandra by his side, and noticed that Bob had Sandra's close attention while Gary's eyes were on his son.

Charlie and Beth were framed by the dining room window on the front side of the house, poised confidently, their matching faces open to receiving yet more of the world's best wishes. But before they — or Gale, or Margo — could guess what Bob was about to do, he brought from the pocket of his suit jacket a key he gave to Charlie.

Bob had expected they'd shake hands, but instead Charlie

gasped, and he cried, "Oh my God!" as he threw himself into Bob's arms. He was weeping more like a boy from whom something had been taken away rather than given to. "Thank you. Oh my God," he said a half-dozen times.

Clearly, since Charlie had yet to look out the window, his reaction had less to do with the car parked at the curb than that in Bob's family tradition this gift was made by the father to the son. Charlie was being made Bob's son. Not even Beth was included in this moment.

Bob's older son had been married before Gale had entered their lives, but at the rehearsal dinner the night before his younger son's wedding, she and her kids had watched Bob present to Grant — who'd acted neither surprised nor, in Gale's view, sufficiently appreciative — a new car. Charlie, fifteen at the time, had been so astonished he apparently still hadn't quite recovered. It simply hadn't occurred to Gale — nor, obviously, to Charlie — to expect this. Yet in spite of the fact that for Charlie this gift was momentous, for Gale it was a disaster.

Now Charlie looked out the window at the black convertible — derived from that first carriage — which had been delivered sometime during the last hour. "A Saab Turbo!" Charlie could tell without needing to get closer. *"Ideal!"*

Bob didn't expect Gale to leap into his arms, but he thought she might at least smile. Instead, though she couldn't have been happier for Charlie — really — on her face was what resembled horror.

Beth followed Charlie out the door, as nearly everyone else did. Because Bob wasn't going to be sideswiped by Gale, he let himself be pulled to the curb by Sandra, whose enthusiasm resulted from having been given a fabulous idea: Gary would give Jason a car on Jason's wedding day, too.

The top was down, so the saddle-colored leather interior could be adequately admired. Charlie opened the door for Beth and got in on the driver's side while the back seat filled up with nieces and nephews who now thought Bob was the most impressive grownup at the wedding. At Bob's suggestion, Charlie turned the key in the ignition, and the antenna appeared like a magic wand. The music cued to play was every bit as deliberate: "Ode to Joy" blared from the best CD player money could buy.

Sandra used all the rest of that roll of film because, without this proof, who at home would believe such an expensive car could be a wedding present? Herb had been invited aboard for a test ride, and from the back seat of the Saab he waved like a politician in a parade. Like the Secret Service, Sandra trotted alongside while Charlie stayed in first gear, and she smiled reassuringly when Herb asked Beth, "Tell me about the other grandfather," worrying that by comparison to Bob, he might look stingy.

Next to demonstrate the back seat were Beth's photogenic brothers. "Evie," Herb asked, "who's the girl taking pictures, in the yellow dress? She seems very friendly, but should I know who she is?"

"Gary's wife," Eve said.

"No, I remember *her*. Not the one with the silver hair, the other one. The blonde."

"She's Gary's wife," Eve repeated. "Sandra. Gary's new wife."

Herb's confusion was made legitimate by the fact that Gale and Gary stood together, watching from the front porch. "So what happened?" Herb asked. They looked good together, like a couple. "No, don't tell me. I hate to know these things."

Because Herb spoke in a loud, hard-of-hearing voice, Margo heard him from where she stood, by Bob. It was a good question — "So what happened?" — and in fact Margo had only recently asked her mother how it had been left with Gary. "It was left unfinished," Gale had answered, as if talking about last night's dinner. In Margo's life, because she traveled so much, leftovers

always got thrown out, or else would spoil. Now Margo understood that what her mother must have meant by "unfinished"
was more like a symphony when it is a composer's last, greatest
work.

Jolted by this discrepancy, Margo felt dumb. She and her
mother were capable of having opposite experiences — in their
new lives in Philadelphia Gale seemed relieved to start over,
Margo never unhappier — but this didn't mean they'd stopped
communicating. Margo and Gale always read between each
other's lines, or at least so Margo had always believed. But right
this minute, if Margo had to describe Gale's feelings, she'd say
she couldn't. Wouldn't want to. Didn't want her intuition to be
correct.

"No big deal," Gary said and shrugged. He had no interest in
seeing the Saab up close, and held the porch railing with a kind
of death grip.

"No, I mean it," Gale insisted. "I had no idea, or else I would
have talked Bob out of it. Or warned you." Gale touched Gary's
arm. "I feel horrible for you. How could Bob think this wouldn't
make you look —"

"Even worse?"

"You're *laughing?* Don't you understand what just happened?" Gale felt infiltrated with a nausea greater than her
body's ability to contain it.

"I've been upstaged before," Gary said. For a while, with
Chloe, it looked as if he'd made a career of it.

Gale could see there was more to this than he was willing to
display, because he couldn't bring himself to look at her. Despite
a jutting chin, his profile seemed to be collapsing in on itself, so
that his hyperextended jaw, Gale saw, was Gary's way of prevent-
ing his chin from trembling. Anyway, it wasn't her job to tell
patients they were in even worse shape than they knew, so why
would she tell Gary he hadn't been upstaged by Bob but, even
worse, preempted?

"The music's a nice touch," Gary said, "so it seems you married a real classy guy." Gary bit his lip and nodded in appreciation, like an imitation John Wayne cowboy.

"If I were you, I'd be outraged," Gale said, as close as she could get to telling somebody else what to feel. It was certainly Bob's right to have fulfilled Charlie's wildest dreams, and Gale knew that her second reaction would be sympathetic, even grateful. But — here was her first reaction, still — did Bob's theatrical advance planning have to remind everyone that Gary had been unable, in making his toast, even to have selected a few sentences ahead of time? By comparison Gary looked so pathetic, it was as if he'd been rendered utterly harmless, as if he couldn't ever have had the power to hurt her. What if she'd been mistaken in thinking he could have had such power? Urgently, angry at herself, she admitted, "As it is, as me, I'm outraged."

He said, "I appreciate that," with the irony of Paul Simon in his song about failed love.

Gale just shook her head. If he wouldn't protect himself, how could she? Then of course she saw he *was* protecting himself.

4

BOB FOLLOWED GALE UP THE STAIRCASE AND DOWN THE hall to Eve and Paul's bedroom, where the thickly padded white carpet, installed for bare feet, added to their sinking feeling.

The full-length mirror on the back of the bedroom door scanned the room as Bob shut the door behind himself, and made the densely patterned William Morris wallpaper dizzyingly kaleidoscopic. The king-size bed was dressed all in white, a down-filled duvet puffy with coziness, a half-dozen pillows in large square eyelet shams invitingly propped against the bleached oak headboard. Gale sat on the near corner of the bed, so Bob remained standing, balancing himself by widening his stance and not crossing his arms.

He began, promisingly, with, "I won't be made to feel guilty for having made Charlie happy."

"You could have told me," Gale said. "At any point this morning while we drove around, you should have *said* you'd secretly arranged to have a car dropped off."

"*Secretly?* What am I, a spy?" Bob leaned against Paul's closet door for the stability as well as for the effect of being backed up. It would have been his preference to present the car at the rehearsal dinner, but it got complicated when the Saab salesman advised against leaving a brand-new convertible unattended like that, at night, downtown. What if the CD player got stolen, if not the whole car? So Bob got talked out of it. Yes, sure, he'd have preferred not to undermine Gary — and surely not to appear to steal his son, if that was what Gale and/or Gary thought he'd done — but since when was his generosity a fault? "Anyway, you weren't available this morning. You were —"

"And last night?"

"— preoccupied. Having breakfast with Gary."

"And last night?"

"I don't know."

"You don't *know?* You got close enough to have sex with me last night. For a minute." She could hear how punishing this sounded — beyond her intention — but she couldn't force herself to take the words back.

Nevertheless he waited to see if she would, and then, when she didn't, he realized this made him more powerful. "Charlie and I have our own relationship, Gale. And we don't need your approval." There was no need for him to say, "I rest my case," but still, he did.

This time she tried to choose her words. She didn't come up with any.

So he went on, "You're making a fool of yourself, you know. A spectacle." He pronounced the word, judgmentally, in three very distinct syllables.

"Stay out of it," Gale warned. All she'd meant to say was, "I'm not going to talk about it."

"Maybe you're not going to talk about it, but you're the only one who isn't talking about it." Bob could have said, "Your sister Kay, for example," but he saw this wouldn't be to his advantage, even though it was true Kay had asked him when Gale had last seen Gary, a question he honestly couldn't answer. It must have been this moment of self-doubt that prompted him now to summon one of his own. "I'm so glad Jane didn't come."

"*Jane?* What's Jane got to do with it? What the hell does your daughter have to do with any of this?" But was Bob right? Was it so obvious that people were talking?

"She would be appalled." Jane would be on his side for sure.

"She always is. Ap*pall*ed." Gale stood, ready to leave the room. "Because Jane's better than everybody." Needless to say, Gale knew better: in Psych 101 you learn to look behind what appears to be superiority for the inferiority complex.

"Wrong." Bob made Gale meet his earnest gaze as he said, "Jane admires you enormously, as you know. She admires your precision and control. She's grateful for your capacity for moderation. If she hasn't made this sufficiently clear to you, she should have." The truth was, Gale had been endlessly patient despite Jane's initial refusal to welcome her. Who could blame Jane, at first, for not wanting him to have stepchildren who had all the advantages and, with Priscilla dead, none of Jane's own disadvantages? Because this went without saying, so too did the extent of Bob's gratitude to Gale for being generous with Jane. Still, Jane was beside the point here.

"That's correct," said Gale, as if she were a teacher, "she should have been grateful." Now, unfortunately, like spilled fuel Gale's own large resentment caught fire. "And I should have been more honest with her as well. *I* should have been the one to tell Jane how inappropriate it was for her to want Amanda to be in the wedding. A *flower* girl! Don't get me started," Gale said, but she could see she already was. "I could tell Jane right now I think she's a narcissist, and I'll never forgive her for not being nicer to my children. Who the hell does she think she is?" Now Gale fixed him with a righteous glare.

These would have been her last words, except that before Bob could respond, Gale took several steps toward the door, catching her heel in the deep carpet and, in her rush to escape with at least this technical victory, lurching forward. Bob reached out, grasped her by the wrist, and perhaps he saved her from falling down. They'd never know.

She shook her arm free and, although at a disadvantage, attempted to keep the advantage by challenging, "Why aren't your children here, Bob? Instead of Jane, Grant, or Robert showing up, showing Charlie some support, you buy Charlie a fifty-thousand-dollar car." If Bob had stolen the money, her tone might have been appropriate.

"Don't use Charlie's car as a way to punish me. Or blame me for Gary's failings."

Because she refused to hear him, even while knowing he was right, with a vengeance she returned to Jane's faults and their consequences. "Instead of Jane sharing anything with Margo, you redecorate the third floor. Margo gets the *attic* while Jane's off at college! Jane made Margo's life a nightmare, in fact, and so did you, by your passivity."

"You don't mean that," Bob said, so quickly the words were sucked in with his intake of breath. "You can't mean that." Bob poked his head forward, as if to jab at the air between them, to make the final words his own. "Look, this has gone way beyond Charlie and the car. God knows, I wish I'd consulted you, but aren't you capable of imagining I wanted to surprise you too? It's understandable that this — reunion? — wouldn't be easy for anyone, least of all you. But that doesn't give you the right to ruin it. Or scapegoat me."

Gale flung the blame right back at him. "I didn't ruin the wedding, *you* did. The car. Making Gary look like a fool." Making her want Gary to be Charlie's father, instead of Bob.

"To ruin everything, I meant."

In the living room below, the pianist was improvising transitions between show tunes about love. Beneath their feet "Blue Moon" turned itself into "Over the Rainbow" while they listened to the echo of having said "ruin" three times.

Bob went into the adjoining bathroom and shut the door behind him, in a way hoping Gale would be gone when he opened it, also partly hoping not. Many nights when Priscilla was alive he'd lock their bathroom door, escaping her rampages by bracing himself against the sink, disbelieving that this could be his life, cursing his wife, despising her, wishing she would die, or he would.

Priscilla would have accused him, again, of ruining her life, abandoning her to three demanding babies she had never wanted to have, stranding her with the shipwreck of their bad marriage, forcing her to drink because what the hell else was there?

He'd tell her this was unfair — as unfair to her as to him — and he'd tell her she needed help. And he'd plead with her to get it. This would be when she'd throw something: her shoe at a mirror, or his briefcase at him. Then he'd retreat to the bathroom, locking the door, holding himself upright by gripping the rim of the porcelain pedestal sink. Because their children didn't dare to be near her after sundown, when Robert left Chestnut Hill Academy for Princeton, the younger two, Grant and Jane, went away to boarding schools, a full-scale evacuation. This meant Priscilla had the whole house to herself, so she'd careen around the ancestral mansion cursing Bob and their children, finding the right couch to collapse on. "Coward," she would scream up the stairs at him. "All four of you are shits!" Then she'd pass out. Before leaving for the hospital each morning, he would find her to see that she was still breathing. It was the housekeeper's job to take it from there.

Gale had this same power? Bob's heart ached. He pressed the crown of his head against the Golds' bathroom mirror to keep himself from falling into it and smashing it into pieces so small they would be beyond smithereens; they'd be dust. And he would be dead, dust too. Did a perfectly nice man like him deserve this, twice?

Bob ran water to muffle these words he couldn't keep inside him, so which were spoken out loud: "My heart aches." "I'll die." "I don't deserve this."

He hadn't locked the door — Gale wasn't violent — so she opened it and turned off both faucets and put her hand on the back of Bob's neck in order to say she was awfully, horribly, terribly — truly — sorry.

∞

When they finally emerged from the bedroom, at the top of the stairs they met Charlie coming from the other bathroom, where there were five differently colored towels hung on the hooks of a bentwood coat rack, like topheavy foliage on a slender tree. He was whistling, the way he used to as a child when he was pleased with everything. "Isn't the car spectacular, Mom?" he asked obliviously. "Thank you both."

"It's Bob," Gale said, but in a spirit of crediting, not blaming, him. "It's Bob's generosity, and yes, love, it is spectacular."

"Don't let anybody do the Just Married thing to it, promise?" Charlie asked Bob for this, as if Bob had such power he could prevent anything that shouldn't happen. "I don't trust her brothers," he said jovially, to indicate he really wouldn't mind all that much.

Charlie's nervousness before the ceremony had been exchanged for a balanced, energetic calm he exhibited, skipping down the staircase like Fred Astaire. From above, his grace made Gale hold her breath, not because she feared he'd trip and fall, but admiringly. From below, Gary also watched Charlie, who shouted, "Hey, Dad, how about that Saab Turbo? Pretty Turbiffic, huh?" Reviving an ancient game from car trips, as if no time had passed since they'd played it last, Gary came back with, "It Saabeauty, all right!" Gary looked to the top of the stairs so he could salute Bob with a wave. Bob waved back politely.

When Bob and Gale reached the middle landing, where the staircase angled and where Beth and Charlie had stood to be washed with natural light just before being married, Gale felt both sadder and wiser. "Look at how the maple sheds its leaves beginning at the top."

"Like balding," replied Bob, smoothing his own thinned-out hair. "It's genetic."

"Really? Trees have inherited traits?" First at the top, then the sides. "Pattern baldness?"

Bob wasn't a botanist, nor did Gale's question need a scientific answer. "You're lovely in this dress. You exactly match the maple."

"I don't disappear, as Sandra put it."

"Please don't." He put an arm around Gale's waist, wanting to implore, like Charlie, Promise?

"I won't," she said, sparing him the indignity.

On the front porch David Haynes was protesting that his to-do list as the best man wouldn't under any circumstances include turning a stallion of a car into what looked like a prom queen. With an older-sisterly shrug — her job was to strew rose petals — Margo also denied both participation and approval. "It's the Golden boys," she said, "as usual." To Margo, they'd always be the boys.

The hood of the car had been frosted with shaving cream to look like a heart-shaped cake, and right away Beth knew it had to be Sandra. Beth could tell from Charlie's clenched jaw that he was worried about the aerosol can's chemical propellants damaging the paint job, so — every good manager has studied conflict resolution — she suggested, unromantically, they could swing through a car wash on their way to the reception. Already they saw themselves telling the story fifty times, every wedding anniversary.

Out by the curb, Sandra was telling Herb, "Back home, we can't do this, it's too sunny. We'd be afraid the shaving cream would melt and get in the engine. Plus, nobody has black cars in Arizona. So," she confided, "I just couldn't resist the impulse, could I?"

Herb didn't have a position on this issue. "No rice, is all I was told," he said. "On account of world hunger." Although he didn't approve of hunger, he disapproved of confetti, except for New Year's Eve. Still, he took some from the basket Margo offered, not wanting to bring on bad luck.

Margo agreed with Herb, although for a different reason. She wondered whether confetti bestowed an equivalent fertility. Throwing rice was about wishing abundance, whereas paper was just litter, even if each piece was heart-shaped.

Like alumni at Homecoming, Gale and Bob watched from the sidelines. It was lucky there would be a change of venue, since they'd just had by far the ugliest moment of their marriage. As if Margo knew this and it scared her, she stood by them, with them. And hundreds of pink-bordered paper hearts rained on Charlie and Beth as they made their way from the front porch of Beth's old house to their new car, en route — with only two more stops, the car wash and the wedding reception — to the marriage all the rest of them had not only witnessed but each vowed to support.

∞

Although for a while Sandra stood next to Gary in the receiving line at the entrance to the hotel ballroom, when for a third time somebody assumed incorrectly she was Chloe Fortunado, she told Gary he'd find her at the bar. Bob had the advantage of being familiar, so he was able to greet the guests with pleasure, at Gale's elbow. Gary was encouraged in making the effort, because enough people recognized him for him to feel at home. Even better, these former neighbors had grown tolerant with age, so they greeted one another like survivors of the same wreck.

The guests' joy was so pure, Beth and Charlie could feel they'd done everybody a huge favor, as if validating elementary school romance had come to be in the public interest — talk about manipulating core values! — with their example of young love leading directly to marriage. It was ridiculous, this happiness, but Beth and Charlie weren't complaining about acting the parts of Romeo and Juliet with a nice happy ending. This was a dream they weren't the only ones to have.

"What a beautiful bride!" Though her dress was noteworthy on its own, it also functioned, like its built-in push-up bra, to showcase Beth. What you noticed were the features you'd always appreciated, such as her dark eyes, so deep-set there was no doubt they were directly connected to the brain. The intimacy in her greeting of each guest was as genuine as Beth herself, and the real pleasure of the guests, although momentary, would be memorable. Here again, as when she was poised on the staircase landing of her parents' house, she manifested — the way the gods and goddesses of ancient religions embody virtuous attributes — the best in us.

"You lucky man!" If this was the theme, then the variation was "You lucky woman!" Not that every wedding wasn't to some extent a triumph of hope against odds; still, this one seemed to represent a quorum, of hope joined to more hope and fulfilled. The impression it was possible to have was of a straight line from birth to marriage-until-death. Or, in other words, an optical illusion.

Charlie would be the first to admit that the flame flickered frequently at Wesleyan. Coming from an all-boys school, he overcompensated in his enjoyment of the smart young women at the head of the class, and he and David were famous for their party time. It wasn't until spring that he realized Beth was watching him from the other side of the room, but skeptically, and when he first felt judged by her to be disappointingly slight. Since Beth's had been a less extreme social adjustment, for her the step up was academic: for the first time, she'd found she had to work to be the best. Their relationship was as normal as they were — off and on — while term after term they made painfully slow progress. Their straight line had many corners, even if none was visible from here, from now.

Altogether obvious, at least to Gary from his place in this line, was that the majority of couples his age and older looked comfortably mated, like swans, for life. As with synonyms, there could be an aptitude test to arrange them in pairs, and if there were such a test he'd rank high on it. His only mistake would be in matching Gale with himself, not Bob, but this would be a trick question.

"Gary?" An unfamiliar face recognized his, and turned out to belong to a man who had worked with him on a housing design Gary never saw built. "What are you doing here?" the man asked, which was why Gary claimed, more strenuously than necessary, "My son's the groom! How about you?" The answer had to do with a recent kitchen renovation for Eve and Paul, as well as that their yards adjoined. "Well!" Gary said merrily. "Nice to see you again." At least Gale didn't appear to remember him either.

Bob checked his watch, telling Gale he'd be back after a quick phone call. His eight P.M. plane, he could already see this far ahead, was unrealistic, but so, he immediately discovered from a public phone in the corridor, was trying to change it without precise enough information about the flight he was booked on. This was, of course, why he had a secretary, who would know which airline it was, which he didn't, as well as what options there were for his return. At the moment his preference was to catch an early morning flight, to be with Gale another night, to fully recover. And/or to play it safe.

Not even the concierge could help without more information, so Bob had to go up to the room for his ticket. There, though, he had detailed phone messages waiting, signaling complications in every case, including even his granddaughter's mild chickenpox. In addition, he discovered that the only early morning flights to Philadelphia included intermediate stops and a change of planes at either Newark or National. Because of the brunch hosted by Herb the next day, Bob knew it would be unfair of him to ask Gale to fly home with him at midnight — there was a flight through La Guardia — so he couldn't. Anyway, this was his own fault.

When the wedding date was first set, Gale had sensibly suggested to Bob that he not operate on that Friday — yesterday — to free today from the necessity of his routine post-op hospital visits. And though he'd agreed this was a good idea, since he would never delegate such a crucial piece of patient care, unfortunately he'd forgotten to tell his secretary in time, until it became too late to reschedule those patients already booked. Surgery can't exactly be postponed by the same doctor urging immediate intervention. Everyone knows that with the heart — the organ, at least — the alternative to good care can be fatal.

∞

The band called Eclectic Guitar hurried people through the receiving line by making it impossible to talk, easy to dance. Musically, there was something for everyone: trademark Nirvana songs for the twentysomething majority population; for their in-between parents, one of the band was a Jimi Hendrix lookalike whose red guitar was as fierce as the female vocalist's imitation of Janis Joplin; for the elders, a crooner sang old tunes with predictable rhymes. In other words, this was no place for one of those self-important band leaders who took it upon himself to behave, insultingly, like a TV talk-show host, ordering the groom to kiss the bride better than that, longer, deeper. This band was a band of few words that weren't lyrics.

"Hi, I'm Charlie's sister," Margo told a guy about her own age who was a Gold cousin she hadn't noticed either back at the house or the previous evening. "Win some, lose some," he said with a compensatory smile, gliding off. "Hi, I'm Charlie's sister," she repeated to each unfamiliar face as she worked the crowd. Lose some, win some.

Margo recognized most of their former neighbors, but it made her sad to see how many of them, as couples, had remained on track. Going by appearance, their marriages had been a balance of "better" and "worse," but wasn't the value, even the purpose, of a railroad track the security of a predetermined route? The engineer doesn't have to decide every trip which valley to cut through the Rockies, or which side of the Hudson River to travel. A train, like a marriage undivided by divorce, can just admire the scenery. If she were to marry, she'd want one of these, where the track is nailed into the earth.

She and David Haynes danced to a Sinatra song, and he told her the red of this dress made her skin look browner than against the black the night before, when she looked pale. He could appreciate each of Beth's friends who, like Beth, were perfectly wound — like the kind of watches no longer made — but he'd always prefer Margo. Always unrequitedly, he'd hoped she wouldn't treat him like her little brother's brother, which was why he hadn't brought a date to Charlie's wedding. "I love you, Dave," Margo told him as they danced, and though this was what he'd wished for, incestuously, like a Cub Scout he replied, "I love you too, ma'am."

In fact, though, there was a sister for him, somebody Beth worked with but who hadn't been invited the night before: Sondra. "As opposed to Sandra," Margo noted with approval when he pointed out the one he had his eye on. Next to Sondra, Margo would always look pale.

"So what's your story?" he asked, because the song had more verses to go. "How come?" He meant: had she scared everybody off?

"You sound like my mother," Margo complained, even though

she looked forward to Monday, the extra day she and her mother had each taken off, when Gale would ask her, "How come you don't seem happy, honey?" But at least for the moment Margo could answer David, "How come I don't find Mr. Right? I'm always looking left."

David gave Margo's hand a supportive squeeze, by which she'd know he was saying, "I know the feeling." During the planning for this wedding it had struck David that it's like an interracial marriage when the Jewish bride wouldn't want a church wedding and the groom doesn't want to get married in a hotel ballroom. David figured that in the end he'd take his grandmother's advice and marry a girl from a nice middle-class African American family just like his own, with a pastor and a big Baptist church and dozens of relatives on both sides who'd make the trip from Memphis or Baltimore, New Orleans or Chicago. He wondered where Sondra came from and decided to ask. One of Beth's brothers was dancing with her, but ineptly, so David glided Margo over to them and, though he was too young to know the name for it, they double cut.

By now Sandra — as opposed to Sondra — had managed to drink herself into a bliss that was contagious, and which Gary seemed to have caught from her. They were sitting at the opposite end from the music, at one of the cozy café tables with one of Paul Gold's faculty colleagues and his much younger wife. "So I guess you didn't get run out of town," Sandra said gaily, adding, because none of the three knew which of them she was talking to, "for sleeping out of turn." She made it sound like speaking out of turn, so they all laughed loudly.

When Sandra asked, "Former student, or what?" the other woman attempted to portray it as more "collegial" than that, to which Sandra charmingly said, "Cut the crap. Take my husband here: he fucked the housekeeper."

"Nanny, wasn't it?" the other man asked.

"Oh, pardon me," Sandra feigned.

All he meant was that he remembered hearing she'd been an undergraduate. His own situation, in those same good old days before sexual harassment lawsuits, didn't result in quite the complete mess as Gary's.

"Graduate student," Gary offered, for the record. For the record, he felt ashamed, so he poked a toothpick into a Mediterranean olive and put it into his mouth, swallowing the pit.

"Okay," the other woman relented, admitting to having been a graduate assistant.

"See? I just mean we're all in good company!" Sandra widened her eyes so they could see there was no hidden agenda.

Next Sandra was asked what field she'd done her graduate work in, and she exploded with pleasure. "That wasn't *me!* Because that would make me *old!* The point is, you two men are much older than us women. Than *we* women. Sorry." She sucked an ice cube from her glass, vacuuming it into her mouth and eating it almost as noisily as a penny.

"Us," the other, now offended, woman said, "not we." Her expression conveyed that she felt manipulated into looking like some old floozy.

"I never keep that one straight. A million pardons." Like an angel Sandra brought her hands together, all ten fingertips aligned, in a totally enforced contact.

Gary knew to walk her, like a racehorse, until she had cooled down enough to stop saying, "Who do they think they are? Who the *fuck* do —" and he succeeded in getting her to shut up by professing to her that the other guy always was arrogant. "So it's not me?" she asked Gary, and when he reassured her it wasn't, she cried, "Thank you so much."

The photographer, not intruding on this delicate moment, was shooting almost randomly, figuring Beth and Charlie would know when they saw contact sheets which pictures to choose. From her point of view it had been very helpful to gather just the relatives for the wedding ceremony, so she could identify them

without guessing. For example, she would never have guessed
Gale and her sister hadn't only just been introduced.

∞

Bob returned to join Gale as she stood next to Kay, who was
trying to compare her fashion-model daughters' hourly rate with
Gale's. "Not too many professions get paid by the hour," Kay
analyzed, making Gale feel like a hooker.

"No luck," Bob said. "The best I could do was midnight."

Kay asked, "You have to leave tonight? How come?" Since
she'd never worked a day in her life, she had difficulty with the
concept of being essential.

"Bob left two patients in the recovery room," Gale explained,
making it sound like Bob was a hit-and-run driver.

"Too bad," Kay said. "I always prefer the party after the bride
and groom take off." But at the same time her expression conveyed that she couldn't imagine anyone being good enough to
marry her daughters. Spotting them in their perpetual haughty
slouches, Kay made for them.

Gale would have disagreed anyway, but in truth she dreaded
that unchaperoned moment: after Beth and Charlie take off and
Bob goes home, then what?

"So midnight's my backup, at least," Bob said. "And I made
you a reservation too, in case, although —"

"But what about Margo?" Margo rushed into her brain as if to
report a fire, even though she'd forgotten entirely about Margo.

"Oh, right." Bob flashed the good-sport smile he used when
he lost, infrequently, at tennis.

"Margo's counting on me," Gale reminded Bob. She knew
this was manipulative, no matter that it was also the truth.

"Of course." What else could he say, after being accused of
making Margo live in the attic?

In partial compensation, she suggested, "Let's dance," which
was a relief to Bob, because as a young adolescent in dancing

school the reliable rule was that the boys lead and the girls follow.

And the band cooperated with a Beatles song, the usual mix of sentiment and up-tempo, reinforcing the virtues of blending. Bob guided Gale with the flat palm of his hand against her back, hinting with subtle pressure when he was about to turn her. This synchrony was a lovely thing to observe in a middle-aged couple who appeared to have danced together since the invention of ballrooms.

Margo watched them and decided it was her fault that neither of them looked relaxed. She was to blame for not being able to leave well enough alone, which would have meant sticking with the seating plan the night before and, before that, not going out of her way to convince Gary he shouldn't skip the wedding no matter what second thoughts he had. "Ask your mother what she prefers," he'd told Margo when he got the invitation, but Margo had been emphatic in reassuring him that Gale would want what was best for Charlie. This was quite true, but a more accurate response to the question of Gale's *preference* might indeed have led Margo to recommend that Gary consider staying home.

Had Margo betrayed her mother? They'd conspired together all the overweight years when Gale didn't want Gary to know he still had that much power, but apparently Margo now believed Gale had made a permanent recovery. So was it her father she'd intended to see disadvantaged? Or — ah — was it perhaps Bob she was betraying, paying him back for coming into Gale's life at the wrong moment? Margo knew enough about bad intentions to recognize them by their consequences, but she was too inexperienced to understand hers was still a childish perspective. Gale could best answer these questions, since she knew the most about unconscious motivation. Nor would it hurt for Gale to remind Margo again — again — that her parents' divorce hadn't been her fault.

Still, even Margo would have to admit she'd turned her flaws into advantages. By never staying in one place, she avoided the restlessness that drove her peers into deeply compromised lives, whereas all her systems were go. She was among the twenty-seven-year-olds on whom, every generation, the future relies. She was — unless there was a newer word — chosen. It wasn't supposed to be fun.

And to emphasize that fun isn't even fun, Sandra's laugh pierced Margo's concentration. With a one-two punch Margo saw that although in general Sandra might be having a far jollier time, her laugh suggested that she could just as easily keel over. Margo watched Gary lead Sandra away from the bar and check his watch, as if to see how much longer Sandra had. The music stopped too. Margo followed her mother, who was escaping yet again.

In this bathroom there were swans on the wallpaper, swans embossed on the paper towels, framed Audubon-like swan prints that were almost life size. This was Swan Boat Boston, fair enough, but still, weren't these birds, in addition to being monogamous, known to be vicious? Both of these attributes felt to Gale like personal criticisms.

"Mom?" Margo didn't know whether they were alone, so she didn't want to ask if Gale was all right. "Can I help you?"

Gale flushed her toilet to give herself a second. "I'm fine," she said. Coming out from behind the closed door, instead of looking at Margo she checked her face in the mirror. At least there was truth-in-advertising in the waterproof mascara, or else it would be streaked.

"You sure?"

"I'm sure," she said in a tone she thought sounded motherly.

"Well, I've been watching you. The photographer, you know, asked me if something's wrong. She says that every time she frames your face she feels she shouldn't take your picture." Margo's voice was nonjudgmental.

Gale splashed water on her face and hid behind a paper towel, blotting. "I didn't expect this sadness." There was moisturizing lotion on the counter, and in her bag was enough makeup to improve herself. "Starting over," she said with a grin-and-bear-it familiar grin.

This was all her fault, Margo thought. When Charlie said he wished he could have them both here, she'd been only encouraging, and gone behind his back to both Gary and Gale, persuading them in advance of Charlie's own more timid request. So now was it also her fault they weren't ready?

"I'm sorry," Margo said.

Gale put some color back in her cheeks and said, "Presto: Institute of Health poster girl." Lipstick helped too. There was nothing makeup could do to restore her eyes, but to make them appear bigger she drew two thin black lines across the eyelids. "Need anything?" Gale extended to Margo the zippered cloth case, then changed her mind. "I would say you're perfect as is."

When Margo laughed at this preposterous idea, she flung her head back and displayed, as Gale already knew, that she had never had a single filling.

∞

The waiters were lighting candles on the larger tables, now that the unseasonably sunny late October day was revealed by an early dusk to be closer in the calendar to the winter solstice than the summer's. Through the windows, curtained in sheer billows, the darkening sky was opaque. Dinner was served.

Seated next to Sandra, Gary gave himself an all-form-no-content expression. She was able to be left alone in her discussion with a young broker from Fidelity. They were comparing Arizona's embarrassing former governor with all of New England's governors, and primarily because Sandra had persuasive personal gossip to tell, Arizona easily won. "Honest!" she swore. "Top that!"

Gary escaped into himself, wondering whose life his own had

been. It was hard to claim as his a three-month romance without enough significant substance to sustain it, given that it was substantial enough to wreck a marriage he had mistakenly believed durable. He'd flattered himself by overindulging — like a guest at a banquet — in the flattery of a sweet young thing who was too immature to know enough about consequences. Everything she'd done up to that point in her life turned out just fine.

"Earth to Gary." Instead of hearing this, he felt Sandra's elbow.

"Huh?" She reeled him in like a trout that ate a fly tied to an invisible line. Before he could know what happened, she had him in the frying pan.

"Weren't we the forty-eighth?"

"State," supplied Sandra's companion in this conversation.

Sandra teased Charlie's cute colleague, "You aren't old enough to know there used to be only forty-eight stars on the flag, are you? There did! Up until nineteen fifty-nine. Then Alaska, then Hawaii, but the last state to become one before that was Arizona. Nineteen twelve, like the Overture." Sandra turned to Gary, "Right, hon?"

"Right."

The young man from Fidelity appeared never to have met anyone so prepared to tell him literally everything she knew.

Without transition, Sandra said, "Now tell us all about Charlie. What's he like around the office?"

For this part, Gary was obliged to look alert. Also, as his mother would say, his dinner would get cold if he didn't eat it.

It was a meat-and-potatoes meal, but the potatoes had been cut into sticks, deep-fried twiggy nests containing a spinach soufflé, and the meat was a tenderloin. Shiny grilled halves of tomato, zucchini, and eggplant were the vegetarian options, and because they also looked appetizing to Gary — but this was before he lost his appetite — he'd helped himself to them too. His plate was impossibly full. Not unlike his personal life.

Worse, the image of his mother stood in the middle of his mind like sheep across a country road: he could honk his car horn all he wanted, to no effect. She'd always existed to tell Gary to come to a full stop, but he couldn't take her advice any more now than when it was her full-time job to get him to clean his plate. He couldn't keep his thoughts off Gale, thoughts his mother would call impure.

Gale's silver hair gave life to her face instead of draining it off, showcasing her like an Elizabethan collar in a museum portrait. Another thing Gary noticed was that by candlelight Gale's dress was the same color as her skin. Smiling, she could be wearing, like a strand of pearls, just teeth.

"Honest. Ask my husband." Gary was afraid of this: Sandra was telling the young broker — as if she were a prospective client of his — how much money she'd made this year. "Half again more. See, my boss had me on salary, so the better I did, the more money he made. One day I said screw this, my commissions are mine, or else. You work on commission too, right?"

The young man said he did.

"See? I told him it's un-American not to. *Individual incentive.* Since that day I've sold more houses — more and bigger — than I ever dreamed possible, and now I make more money than my husband here. A lot."

A salad of commercially grown baby greens was served, artfully heaped, as Beth and Charlie strolled like troubadours from one table to the next. The band was coming back from an extended break and, slowly, softly, one instrument and one voice at a time, began to play the Jimmy Cliff song that Charlie and Beth called their theme: "You Can Get It If You Really Want."

They danced to it, alone, while it increased incrementally in volume as well as speed, until Beth reached a hand to her father and Charlie to Gale, bringing them out onto the parquet dance floor. After this, like cell division, a multiplication occurred. According to protocol, Beth danced next with Gary, and Charlie with Eve, leaving David and Margo, Beth's brothers, and eventually Bob and Sandra to fill in the blanks. They switched and switched partners as if this were a square dance, not reggae, and they were photographed in each of their pairs before being outnumbered by those regular guests they'd inspired. Gary and Gale ended up together, and Jimmy Cliff's upbeat message wasn't lost on them: to really, really try to get it.

After that song, "Love Me Tender" slowed the pace, and Gary and Gale gave themselves the next dance too, a cheek-to-cheek, like the several generations prior to their own, for old-time's sake. His hand on the small of her back stayed there this time, because he was leading with it deliberately, pressing her against him while signaling his moves. She knew his moves. What was new were his suspenders.

"Did you used to wear suspenders?" she asked, patting the place between his shoulder blades where they crossed.

"Not in my youth, no, but often in middle age." With Chloe he'd worn black tie frequently enough for her to give him suspenders for everything, although these he wore were his own purchase, in red.

"What are you now, old?" Gale pulled her head away to look him in the face, which arched her body against his.

They kept their feet moving in synchronized patterns that required no concentration on their part. "Do that again," he said, but he achieved the same effect by leaning into her.

Once she'd had a professor whose lectures had a transforming effect, calming a room of undergraduates into a meditative state. The professor herself would arrive at the podium with her substantial stresses visible for all to see, but as she presented her material, her drained face would fill like a wine glass with beautiful color and the obvious strains on her body would release their tight grip. Her shoulders would relax. She would smile with pleasure at the information she gave to her students, and at their desire to have it. The interaction was a dance, so that by the end of the hour, the very air in the lecture hall was less thin.

Gale too was being changed in appearance by the process of becoming herself at her best instead of her worst. Being formally partnered with Gary, even for a dance, she knew the angle of her head conveyed her interest in him. Her silver hair swished like water as he turned her, and her mouth moved into such wide smiles that all but her molars showed. Even though they were technically on display, the other dancers provided camouflage, giving them enough privacy. The copycat Elvis at the microphone pushed "Love Me Tender" nearly to its full potential — "love me true" — quite convincingly.

"Did you forget?" he asked.

"How much we liked to dance? No. Did you?"

"Yes."

"Did you know your wife is watching?" asked Gale. "Not to change the subject, but —"

Gary took three or four dramatically long tango-like steps in the opposite direction from Sandra, who'd been returned to their now mostly empty table by Beth's middle brother, the family's nondancer. The broker had used the interval to escape.

And Gale stayed right with him. "What's going to happen next?" She didn't mean to sound so objective, since she wasn't asking for a weather forecast.

"Sandra started drinking way too early, too hard, starting this morning. Or really since last night." But he sounded unworried. "In fact, she's holding on uncharacteristically well. Under less demanding circumstances, she'd already have become a menace."

"A menace?" What a word for Gary to have picked.

"Or else passed out. She can be lots of fun." His disloyalty wasn't very nice either, but he let it hang in the air over their heads like something sprayed from an aerosol container.

"Did you know Bob's leaving tonight?" Gale's face was close

enough to his to make it seem like a secret she was telling him, only him. But the second she said it, she felt that she'd betrayed her best friend.

"Good," he said, qualifying, "as long as you're not."

She didn't respond right away, then said, "I'm not," as a point of information. If alcohol could be blamed for Sandra's bad behavior, why not also her own?

"Me neither, then." Now he laughed as if at a joke she'd just told him.

The lead singer finished the song with a melodramatic "Never let me go," slower even than the original version. Some couples, anachronistically, dipped like seesaws and thus nearly tipped right over, but Gary and Gale stood so still the effect was cinematic.

"Meaningful look," he mocked himself, though so was hers.

"You and I have to talk," she invited, although insistently.

"It's a date." It would have been too crude to ask Gale what time Bob's plane was, but then he did, crudely. She said she wasn't sure which one, earlier or later, he'd try to make.

The Eclectic Guitar made another schizophrenic break of a transition, this time to a heavy-metal sound that could have been a car wreck. Only the contemporaries of Beth and Charlie were able-bodied enough to keep dancing — here came Margo and David, looking like MTV superstars — so it went without saying that Gary and Gale had no intention of moving around to something with no discernible lyrics at all.

"Time's up!" Sandra was bearing down on them like an ambulance, her siren blaring. She shouted, "No more for you two!"

∞

Gary held Sandra's hand, but by the wrist. As they rushed toward the door, people moved out of their way as if she were about to vomit. In the elevator, innocent bystanders witnessed his hand over her mouth as if he were an armed robber. For once

Sandra couldn't strike up a conversation with the other passengers. Needless to say, neither did he.

Housekeeping had already been by, but for extra protection he hung the Do Not Disturb sign on their doorknob. Turning back to face Sandra, he caught her as she landed against him. "I hate this," she wailed. "First they think I'm Chloe, then you're dancing with Gale. It's like I don't even exist! Meanwhile, I'm bored out of my mind having to think up things to say to these people, so then, when I turn around and see you dancing — with *her!* — well, I'm sorry, but —"

"You don't need to apologize."

"I'm not!"

"I understand," he offered, about to say he was sorry for not having danced with her.

"No, you don't get it." Sandra pressed her face against his chest, tucking her head under his chin, which nested like a bird in her golden curls. "Usually you can, but believe me, you're not understanding my situation. *N*obody, no longer only Bob, will take me seriously. Except for that really cute grandfather, everybody smirks all the time, notice? How would you feel if this was happening to you?"

"Horrible," Gary admitted as he gently stroked her arm. So Sandra wasn't angry at him?

"See?" She exhaled, letting go of more air than she'd have thought she had left inside her. Then she replenished the supply.

He felt Sandra's body slacken. "Let's come lie down." He led her to the turned-down bed, sitting her on the edge. She was no longer wearing the matching jacket — he'd have to remember to look for it downstairs — so it was uncomplicated to unzip her jumper-like dress, which fell forward to her waist. She unhooked her bra, and as he lowered her to the pillows she said, "Here," handing him the gold-lace underwire bra like a pair of eyeglasses.

She raised her hips and he easily pulled the dress the rest of the way off, also slipping his thumbs under the straps of her gold shoes. All that was left was pantyhose and matching gold-lace bikini underpants, both of which he turned inside out as he slid them off. When he pulled the covers up over her she uncovered herself and told Gary, "Oh, no you don't."

"You need to rest," he soothed, because it was quite true.

"No, you need to come inside me," she counterbid.

"I really can't." Even if he technically could, he couldn't.

"Yes, you can." One thing she was expert at was coaxing him when he played hard to get.

Because he was serious — no, he really couldn't — he pre-empted her by putting a hand on her belly, the other on a breast. "Here, let me," he proposed, but like a clinician.

"Okay," she gave in, "but kiss me." This was assured, since she pulled Gary down to her with his necktie.

So he kissed her, but sat back up and stepped into the bathroom for the miniature complimentary Crabtree & Evelyn hand and body lotion. "Damask Rose," he said.

It wasn't her favorite fragrance, but at least it wasn't Sandalwood or Cucumber, like some hotels have. She always traveled with their own massage oil, but she thought he probably was right, too oily for just a short intermission before the wedding cake is cut and Beth throws the bridal bouquet. Damask Rose made her feel, well, rather ladylike. "A white-gloves scent, perfect for this behind-the-times, out-of-it town, huh?"

"Right," he said, turning off the bedside lamp so the only light was indirect. "Relax, just pretend you're at home." It helped him, too, to think about worries draining away with a swim in the dark, floating like a water lily but unanchored. Every night their sheets would also be fresh and cool, so it was a pleasure to get into bed with Sandra and sip a cognac harsh in its effect while at the same time calming their surfaces with oil, as if they were a pair of squeaky wheels wanting, and getting, grease.

When again he said, "Relax," he could see he'd already accomplished that for her.

Never completely incapacitated, Sandra was nevertheless worn out. He touched her so familiarly they could have been her own hands fanning the lotion concentrically. She didn't have more energy than to receive stimulation, so, as usual, Gary was right: she needed to calm down and stop feeling insecure, and he was helping with this. Her nipples responded like satellite dishes relaying messages to earth, from which place in her she arose like an idea being expressed. Having been on standby status for twenty-four hours, she was ready to fly, joining these mixed-up metaphors into the single image of a rocket launch. "Countdown," Sandra said, then, "Liftoff."

With his fingers inside her, Gary could feel her pulsing like time passing from second to second, sixty times to make a minute. After about that same amount of time, he could tell by her breathing that she'd fallen into a welcoming sleep. As he covered her again, this time she turned onto her side, to where Gary would be if he were coming to bed. He heard the end of her sentence: "— a little nap?" But she hadn't made him promise to wake her up.

This was what he was expert at, even without taking off his jacket or tie. His second wife had instructed him that sex doesn't always have to be a mutual event. More to the point, instead of it always being the man whose orgasm is assured, why shouldn't it be her own? Chloe always knew just what she wanted, also how to get it, so when he was first with Sandra she had been amazed, especially for a man of Gary's generation, by his capacity to regulate his timing in accord with hers. He was capable, in other words, of behaving like women, even to the extent — though Sandra couldn't guess this right this moment — of just getting it over with.

5

As Gary came from the elevator he was intercepted by David Haynes, who said it was time to cut the cake, "So don't disappear." By which he meant don't disappear on me again. It was a *job* being best man, like what he imagined it would be to direct a movie. No, worse, because there at least you'd get to do it over until you got it right.

The cake table had been wheeled out like a gurney, and the cake itself was in seven tiers, engineered to impress an architect. From where Gary stood, he could see there was something other than a bride and groom on top of the cake, but he couldn't tell what it was. Then he and everybody else got a closer look by crowding in. What, an angel? An ecumenical angel? No, it couldn't be an angel.

Charlie had the microphone in his hand, so all the guests heard themselves being thanked for coming to the reception. Naming names, he had a long list most people wouldn't have attempted without a real list, for fear of leaving someone out. Evidently Charlie knew that if he did miss someone, when it was her turn to speak Beth could cover for him.

Gary was still distracted by the cake: where there might be frosting roses, there looked to be petals scattered like fallen leaves — not petals, leaves — which were surely symbolic. He looked to Gale for interpretation, but what he noticed instead was that Gale stood next to Bob, with Margo between them, locking them together. Gary had no way of knowing that Margo was employing her arms, holding on to Bob and Gale, as a way not to catch the bouquet.

Beth had told Margo it was intended for her, but Margo said that would be insider trading — which, as Charlie knew, was punishable by law — and anyway, both her mother and Sandra had tossed theirs at her, so obviously — thanks anyway — it didn't work as a way of breaking the "always the bridesmaid" spell. Margo was "never the bride" because, so far, no man could seem to tolerate her tendency to claim credit, although from Margo's point of view, she felt entitled to taking whatever credit was due her, in order to balance the often excessive blame she took on.

According to Gale, Margo blamed herself falsely. But what Gale didn't understand was that Margo's standards for a relationship were set artificially high, so she wouldn't be tempted to couple with just anybody. If her marriage were to survive, she'd have to be better at it than her mother, and needless to say, her husband would have to be bigger than life.

Margo pointed out to Gale and Bob that Beth was noticeably taller than Eve, who was in turn inches taller than her own father. "It's upward mobility," Margo said, notwithstanding the fact that Herb made more money every day in his retirement than the rest of them put together. Herb's management gene had been inherited by Beth, bypassing her recessive mother: a physician, not an entrepreneur. In her pulmonary practice, however, Eve's job was to help patients with damaged lungs in the fundamental exchange of oxygen for carbon dioxide.

Flanking Herb and Eve were her husband Paul and their three sons, making tangible — all their good looks combined — the great potential in Beth's own dark beauty. The red dress she'd chosen for Margo could have been picked from a paint chip of the nail polish Beth wore. David Haynes called it Affirmative Action Red because it gave them both the benefit of any doubt. With red fingernails and lips it was Beth's intent to be photogenic.

And the photographer was ready for anything, once having documented a food fight that ruined both the wedding veil and, ultimately, the marriage too. The photographer's guess was that Beth and Charlie would share a polite taste of their cake. That is, if these speeches would ever finish.

"A short word about the cake," Charlie continued, "which has on the topmost layer a bird with a twig in its beak. This symbolizes the building of our new nest and, because the bird is a dove, every kind of peace."

Margo smiled, wondering how many kinds of peace he thinks there are.

"Domestic and foreign. World peace," Charlie clumsily improvised. "So this is an olive branch, and every piece of cake will have a leaf from that branch, which means *shalom*." He didn't want to sound like a UNICEF card, so he didn't say "peace" in all the languages he knew it in. He just gave Beth the microphone.

Ah, thought Gary, peace. He liked it. Sandra had gone for the regulation plastic bride and groom, and Chloe had insisted upon an unfrosted summer fruitcake. He couldn't remember his and Gale's wedding cake, though, so he looked across the empty half-circle and saw she was looking at him with a strange grin. Gale was trying to remember why she and Gary had key lime pie instead of a wedding cake. All she could recall was that the preparations were made in haste and without sufficient forethought. Their wedding pictures were snapshots, making it look like some impromptu jamboree, except that there wasn't a tent. And so if it had rained that day, would they have had to postpone it? They hadn't thought that far ahead, so rushed were they to be married. Compared with Beth, Gale felt frivolous, which was a funny feeling, since her major self-criticism, and Gary's, was that she'd been way too earnest.

Talk about earnest: Beth began with another list, of all those who weren't there. Her maternal grandmother, Herb's wife, had been dead just over a year, and neither of Paul's parents was still living. Of Charlie's five grandparents, Gale's mother had eliminated herself, her father had a bad heart, and his stepgrandmother Oakley had just had her hip replaced. Gary's father was long since missing in action, and his mother — though of course Beth was more polite — was too uncooperative. Beth wouldn't know the truth, that Gary had talked his mother out of coming in order to spare himself the aggravation. His labor-intensive mother was a burden, but Sandra was working on him to be nicer to her. Was it his mother's fault that she'd been abandoned by his father? As Sandra pointed out, no doubt his mother would have preferred a husband who could have set Gary a better example.

Gary felt selfish, and guilty, when Beth mentioned his mother, even though all Beth said was that it was too bad she couldn't be there. She was alive at least, whereas others — two of their contemporaries — had died, one in a fatal car crash, another because of breast cancer. Beth didn't go so far as to mention public figures who had recently died — Jacqueline Kennedy Onassis in eternal, absurd juxtaposition with Richard Nixon — but as in religious services there was the moment of silence for remembering your own.

Margo was too irreverent to be comfortable, so she squeezed Gale's arm when Beth echoed Charlie's *shalom,* bringing them back to wishing peace for the world. Wait. Would she prefer they love war?

And the photographer was right: two polite bites. The surprise was inside, a moist cake so densely chocolate it appeared to be black. Since she did weddings all the time, she'd learned to be choosy. Not all wedding cakes were worth the calories.

While the cake was being cut, before it could be distributed, Charlie got back on the microphone to announce, good-humoredly, "We're so politically correct we're both going to throw the bouquet — needless to say, there's no garter — and both men and women are eligible to catch it."

"Oh please," Margo whispered to her mother, who merely smiled.

Now the band came back together, playing something rahrah, like the soundtrack for a silent movie. Beth and Charlie turned their backs to everybody and, holding hands around the flowers, threw them quite high although not far. The little cousins acted like it was a baseball hit into the stands: you could scramble for it only if your seats were in that lucky section.

Margo's reluctance was doubled as the bouquet sailed right at them.

So Bob caught it.

What was he going to do, let it fall at his feet and get trampled by the children? He just put a hand out and there it was, like a pass successfully completed. Now what?

Margo vanished from between them, so Bob did the expected thing, which was to present the flowers to his own bride. He was in no way a candidate for marriage, because he already possessed the perfect wife. In fact, he couldn't wait to get back to Philadelphia in order to continue their life together.

Gale accepted the bouquet graciously, but her sharp guilt derived from the fact that she couldn't wait for Bob to go back to Philadelphia, alone, so she and Gary could talk the rest of the night and try to make sense of their lives. What had been the cause of their rush to get married? To have one child and another? To own a house? What could it mean that such conventional choices seemed so reckless? Why did it make her want to weep, over and over, that she couldn't ever be this free with Bob, not once in their twelve years together, and not now. In the bouquet Gale clasped, the white freesia had rows of buds along each slender stem, buds that would keep on opening in a straight line, like the pale inner arms and synchronized legs of Broadway showgirls.

Bob elegantly kissed Gale on each flushed cheek, and as if they had just publicly reaffirmed their own wedding vows, there was applause. Because the kiss lasted a second too long, she had time to feel like a total fraud, which was why she put her arms around Bob, releasing him quickly because he would be uncomfortable on display.

Bob's blue eyes looked cobalt, his gaze was so intent with its longing. "Come with me, please," he said, and made it easy for her by adding, "Up to the room while I pack."

"Where's your cute wife?" Herb asked Gary, but without his having noticed that Sandra hadn't been around since before the cake was cut. "Where's everybody?"

Gary scanned the room, but he was looking for Gale. From the back of Sandra's chair he retrieved her little gold jacket like the father of a child whose coats and sweaters always end up in the lost and found.

"Your wife's the only one who's got any life in her," Herb asserted flirtatiously, no threat whatsoever.

Gary could have said, "Not at the moment, Sandra doesn't," but instead he told the other truth, which was, "She said the same about you."

"And how about those two? I feel like I'm at some ADL fundraiser with all the *shalom*ing." And then he winked at Gary to show how very proud he was of those two.

Gary watched Herb make his way back across the room, greeting so many people along the way he could have been mistaken for a politician. His own obscurity permitted Gary to search out the place — more like a cop — looking for Gale.

He couldn't be sure how long Sandra would stay asleep, so he was in a hurry to take advantage of whatever time there was. Now he felt like the child of that parent, about to break the rules.

∞

Parallel to this impulse of Gary's was Gale's, but she had the professional, time-consuming handicap of needing to study the relationship between motivation and behavior. In other words, while going forward she looked back. Specifically, while helping Bob pack she was retracing her steps all the way back to her childhood, when she'd always been the good girl.

Because her mother had so clearly preferred Kay, as a child Gale's effort to please was always greater, and useless. At Barnard she'd fallen in with the wrong crowd, according to her father, whose term for the social sciences was "soft sci." When nevertheless she applied to Tufts for a graduate program in clinical psychology, he told Gale he'd already paid her last tuition bill. Enforced independence qualified her for financial aid, but more, it released her from this pattern of good — although unrewarded — behavior. She was no longer the good girl, and Gary blew through that open door like a, well, not unlike a gale-force wind, blowing her door off its hinges.

Bob zipped shut his monogrammed canvas garment bag and the small matching carry-on. Gale had stuck the bouquet in a glass of water, and only Bob thought to suggest, "Shouldn't you unwrap the tape from around the stems?"

"Good idea." Gale was aware that he wouldn't have had to tell Priscilla that, since her one reliable area of expertise was flowers.

"With those in your hands you look like my bride a dozen years ago." Bob came toward her, but he'd given her the excuse of a necessary task, so her hands weren't free. "Have you forgiven me?"

Gale couldn't imagine what for.

"For not telling you about the car for Charlie. I wanted it to be a nice surprise for everyone, even for you."

She stuck the flowers back in their water and held her arms out to him. "No, Bob, I'm the one who's sorry. And I apologize." "No need. It was selfish of me. The more important thing is that Charlie's happy." With this advantage he pressed on. "Gale? Thank you for having given me your children. I so want them both to know how very grateful I am."

She couldn't speak, but Bob seemed not to need her to, as long as she held him tightly.

In the years before she met Bob, she'd come to understand that falling in love with Gary had been a mistake accompanied by an explanation, the way flunking out of school signals an adolescent crisis. Because Gary was such a liberation for her, she couldn't call him a mistake, but — more like flunking out — a lapse. Her mistake was her own moral superiority, as if Gary had been a white-collar crook she had caught red-handed. Her second mistake was in not daring to see Gary when his marriage with Chloe was over and he asked if, when he came to Boston for the kids, she'd see him. By then she'd agreed to marry Bob, so she'd told Gary no.

Now she knew why she'd refused this invitation, but how could her conflict have been more extreme — if, say, he'd coaxed her not to marry Bob — than the conflict she felt now? She was as open to Gary now as ever because, now as ever, he held the key to the things she kept locked.

"So," Bob asked, "isn't it your plan, after the brunch tomorrow, for you and Margo to drive partway and spend the night, and get home on Monday?"

"She needs the time with me." Actually it was entirely mutual.

"No, it's fine. I just need you to reassure me. I need to know you're coming home." Bob held Gale's face between his hands and looked directly into it. "Promise?"

"Promise."

"Call me," he said.

"I will, don't worry."

"I'll worry."

So when she said, "I wish you could stay," she meant it.

"When Margo gets married, I'm planning to take a lot of time off. Tell her, okay?" Bob's most endearing expression came into his face from within.

Just before they left the room, Gale noticed the gold-foil-wrapped mints on their pillows. "Here, take these to Amanda and say we hope she's feeling better." As far as Amanda was concerned — she said as much — Gale was her real grandmother. This offering was an appeasement, not to a little girl but to her own conscience.

"I'll still worry, just so you know" were Bob's last words before the elevator door opened onto the next event.

∽∞

Now Beth wore a cloak-like amethyst Kashmir scarf and gray trousers, and Charlie, to prove their compatibility, a heather cashmere turtleneck and gray flannels. Their look evoked Edinburgh more than New Mexico, but they were very definitely a couple. It was Charlie's idea to fly west into a different time zone as a way, with extra hours, of extending their wedding day just a bit longer. They were going to spend what was left of this night in Santa Fe because, as Charlie said, "*Fe*'s Spanish for fidelity," which was meant as an endorsement of his company, not a criticism of his father.

According to this generation, marital fidelity wasn't a goal but a given. So many were children of parents whose own "open" marriages had been closed down that they opted for contracts worthy of old-style arranged marriages. Also, so many of them were lawyers — David Haynes was Charlie's lawyer, for instance — that the law became an extension of their self-confidence. It was too soon to tell whether their insurance policies could protect them against "acts of God," but they firmly believed that lawyers had made theirs a safer world.

Gale and Gary hadn't been ruined by lawyers because Gary felt so guilty, Gale got it all. On this basis they'd gone the cheaper and quicker no-fault route, no matter that the fault had been clear. Their only problem was that, there being no time for second thoughts, Gale wasn't permitted any. Their anger didn't smolder like an eternal ember kept viable by the periodic breath of their attorneys, it simply flamed and burned out.

The car had been restored to its beautiful black, and anyway, Sandra wasn't there to note the bride and groom's disapproval of her idea of decoration. Most of the guests remained upstairs, but the families gathered at the curb like groupies.

Beth and Charlie got into the back seat while David Haynes performed his last official act as best man by loading their bags — including Bob's too — into the trunk. It hadn't been Bob's intention to ride with them to the airport, but when the situation became clear to Charlie, he insisted on it. In the passenger seat Bob felt like a car salesman no one wants to come along on a test drive, especially when Margo produced more heart-shaped confetti everyone showered on the bride and groom with best wishes.

Gary wouldn't let himself think Bob could be leaving town, because such wishes, his entire life, had never come true. But Gale had kissed Bob as if to tell him goodbye for longer than just the trip out to the airport and back again. And didn't it seem like Bob was telling Eve and Paul to come to Philadelphia soon? And Margo that he would see her Monday? Gary couldn't believe his eyes, or ears. Or luck.

Beth's oldest brother, the driver, raised the convertible top against the suddenly chilly night air and honked the horn twice as they drove off. Because of recycling there were no tin cans to clatter along after the car.

∞

Improvising, but like an athlete with the unexpected chance to score a goal, Gary suggested they all cross Huntington Avenue to enjoy the Christian Science Center's reflecting pool behind the Mother Church. Compared with the open bar and the band still playing in the ballroom, however, none of the others seemed to find this idea irresistible. "Well, we won't be long then," Gary told Margo in case Sandra should materialize.

"I must have put her jacket down again. Sorry," he said, as if Gale would have worn Sandra's jacket. "Here." He gave his own suit jacket away for the second time in less than twenty-four hours. Once again he needed it too, but he wanted Gale to have it so he could be surrounding her. She took it for the same reason.

"I forget so much," he said. "I forgot how tall you are, for one thing. My height." The only way he could rest his chin on the top of Gale's head would be to have her sit down.

"Forgot?"

"Sorry, doctor. What's the word, blocked?"

"Repressed. Repression's my specialty too." By which she meant she'd repressed just as much about Gary.

"Then what's *sup*pressed?" Anybody listening would think they were talking about her work.

"Stifled. Urges, for example." An embarrassed smile acknowledged neither of them was doing a very good job stifling urges.

"You're right, I don't know a single thing about that."

"I can't teach you, either."

"That's good," he said.

Water in thin sheets fell over the rounded lip of the block-long rectangular pool bordered by trees in the shape of lollipops. The water's surface was fractured by bright lights. Gale slipped her hand into Gary's as she told him, "Charlie said his favorite wedding present was us."

Across the plaza were arches supported by columns lit to enhance the pure architectural lines, fulfilling Gary's hopes so thoroughly he felt — he wished! — they could be in front of one of Europe's best cathedrals.

"Dick's Last Resort." Gale read the name on the awning in the next block, a restaurant with a lot of empty outdoor tables but plenty of noise coming from within. She could have played with the implications of "last resort," but she let the words stand unadorned by sentiment or wit.

He didn't. "Pathetic, huh? Pretending we're taking a walk?" But for once, he didn't feel at all pathetic.

Gale had her other hand in his jacket pocket, and, like reading braille, she felt his room key with its code punched into the plastic card. Their rooms were no doubt identical, with one distinction: her room was empty, his not. So she had to agree, "Yes, we are pretending, aren't we?"

A damp wind blew them toward the lights of Dick's Last Resort, a red-tablecloth sort of place where the food played backup to a big beer menu. The other patrons wore name tags, first name legible from across a convention center, with the company name — Hasbro, Mattel — even bigger. Dick's was around the corner from the Hynes Auditorium, and these toy salesmen were raucously intrusive but, unlike their toys, nonviolent. All men, some watched the Celtics in preseason play, but mainly they seemed to be bragging about the fish they landed, or else the ones that got away. The waitress was experienced in dealing with such out-of-towners having a few, or even a few too many.

Gary ordered a Sam Adams because there didn't used to be a Boston beer, and Gale ordered a Heineken, remembering their bare-boat charter in the Antilles one year with Eve and Paul, when they chilled their beer overboard in a nylon mesh bag used for snorkeling gear. Now these tall frosty glasses came from a freezer, but they were both so thirsty they each poured the beer out much too fast and had to wait for the foam to settle back down. "Apt," Gale said, "as images go."

"As images go," Gary bluntly answered her, "you don't fit mine. I imagined you matronly."

"Is that what you heard about my life, that I'm a matron?"

"Margo told me about the Garden Club, said you call yourselves The Weeders." Gary worried that he was betraying Margo's confidence, and God only knew what Margo could have told Gale about his own life.

"No, that's not me," she responded defensively, "it was Bob's first wife's family's famous perennial border, which has belonged to the Garden Club of America since its founding." Then Gale realized she protested a bit too much. "Priscilla had a real genius as a gardener, though, so in inheriting the garden I suppose I got the membership too. It was Priscilla's best time of the day, mornings, but the growing season sadly wasn't long enough to keep her busy all year round." Gale didn't know how much he might have been told about Priscilla's death, but no matter what, this wasn't the time. "Anyway, I've found the Garden Club women nice, civic-minded in that old-fashioned way that went out of style during the Reagan eighties. I can't get to very many meetings because of my practice, but gardeners are tolerant, flexible people, which I've learned now that I've become one too, so —"

"So?" Gary waited for Gale to finish what sounded like a run-on sentence. His beer was half gone. "Enough about you. Let's talk about us."

Gale took a long sip. "You first."

But first the waitress needed to know if they'd be wanting dinner, and as she exchanged that menu for the all-nacho snack menu, she seemed to have confirmed her own guess about them. "You just holler," she instructed, "like them." She gestured with a thumbs-up. Gary asked her to bring them another round, but not right away.

"All I meant was, imagine my surprise. You're not a matron. You're more lovely."

"Than you imagined?"

"No, than you already were."

"Enough about me," she imitated him, not wanting to hear a detailed comparative analysis. Fueling herself with a large breath, Gale told him, "You are too, to me." She left it there.

It was true about him as well, that at fifty-one he'd become more of what he'd always been, more deliberate. His hair was no longer threatening to thin prematurely now that it had fallen out on schedule, so his forehead, doubled in size, had real power. And when Gary rolled up his shirtsleeves he demonstrated that his skin color — forehead to forearms — was wraparound. Her own summer color, such as it ever was, had long vanished.

As if he had all the answers, she asked, "What are we going to do?"

His best answer was to place those same brown hands on either side of her paler face and to pull their mouths together, where they stayed without being held.

∞

"You two give me hope," yelled one of the toy salesmen from the bar. The waitress placed two bottles and another pair of frosted glasses on the table and said that this round was on him.

"Hey, thanks," Gary shouted. "Our son just got married, so we're celebrating."

"And may he have just as good luck as you!" That guy wore a wedding ring too, but it had squeezed the life out of his chubby ring finger.

Since she'd become invisible in this dialogue, Gale knew she wouldn't be missed if she went to the bathroom. While Gary answered the question about where they-all were from, she learned how unsteady her walk was. It wasn't because of the alcohol in her blood.

As she pushed through the door marked REST ROOMS into an airless corridor, Bob came to mind, unhelpfully, and had to be dismissed rudely. It was more his habit than hers to seek refuge in a bathroom, but wasn't this her fourth or fifth time in these twenty-four hours? Besides, this one was pine-paneled like a rec room and overbearingly scented with a balsam spray that made her feel she was lost in an artificial forest. Yes, in the mirror she looked lost.

She pressed a cool, damp paper towel against the back of her neck, tossed it away, and left before things could get worse. Perhaps they got worse anyway, but it also felt like everything got better, because Gary was outside the door in that small hallway, waiting. He said her name in order not to startle her when he pressed himself against her, but apparently she felt safe, because she grabbed him with the same possessive force. Like teenagers at the mercy of hormones, they could easily have been mistaken for a pair of cannibals.

They interlocked like stitches in a sweater, their hands flying as fast as a knitting machine. One of them knocked the pay phone receiver out of its cradle, so it swung on its flexible metal cord sounding a shrill alarm for something like half a minute. In the resumed silence the passion was noisy.

Their first sex together, after the concert the very night they met, had been like rolling downhill, influenced by both gravity and the terrain. Because of the Pill, there was no need to stop in order to start over again, so they spun in place like prayer wheels, tossing into the air wishes joined with blessings. At one point she'd joked, "What did you say your name was?" which they both found so funny they could have been stoned.

"Who are you again?" Gale asked him now, remembering that first night.

"I'm your long-lost, *long*-lost —" and then he silenced them both with his tongue.

"— love?"

The toy salesman must have felt part of the family, because when he opened the door into the corridor he didn't go back to the bar but said, "Hey, hey, hey! Go for it," as if he were their personal trainer. "Here, I'll just hang up the phone for you," he said as he narrowly squeezed by them. "Honest to God, you give me hope." He could also have mentioned that they'd given him an erection.

When the salesman disappeared behind the one door, locking it for his own privacy, Gary pulled Gale into the women's bathroom and pressed the metal button in that doorknob too.

"No, I can't," Gale told him. "I can't."

"You mean, not here?" As long as she didn't mean no.

Yes, that's all she meant at this point, just not there.

"Okay, fine." The last thing Gary wanted was to ruin things again.

"It's too —"

"You don't have to explain." Even their first time, it had been in Gale's own bed. If he'd thought about it all day long, he never could have come up with such a location as this. "We can do better," he said with reassurance. While panic filled his stomach like too much food, he had to add, "As long as you don't change your mind."

He made it sound more like a threat than a worry, so they clung to one another and to the knowledge that they could already have had sex, already be dealing with consequences. Gale asked rhetorically, "Gary, what have we done?"

In this interval since their divorce, she'd known both friends and clients, men and women, whose spouses one day abruptly left their long-standing marriages. Always, Gale noticed, they would assume Gale knew exactly how it felt to have been rejected, and because she knew rejection intimately — taught from childhood by her mother — she never felt inclined to dispute their belief that they held this thing in common. In fact Gale felt more fortunate because of a crucial difference: Gary never said he was in love with Jeannie. Gary never said, "I don't love you anymore."

The irreversibility of such cruel words regularly reminded

Gale that her life could have been harder. At the same time, though, the irreversibility of such words had often caused her to wonder whether her own situation with Gary might not have been, by comparison, reversible.

∞

Gary again found Sandra's jacket, and this time he carried it up to their room. The light on the lock switched from red to green when he inserted the disposable key, and he opened and closed the door as quietly as a thief. It didn't appear that in his absence Sandra had moved even enough to breathe.

He put her jacket down on his side of the bed, and from the bureau he picked up the leather folder containing hotel stationery. Then he sat on the upholstered chair next to the skirted table. It would take a minute to figure out what message to leave her, because he felt neither guilty nor not-guilty. If he could admit to himself he was about to be unfaithful to Sandra, why was it he could tell himself this was different from adultery? Because this time he had no choice?

In his affair with Jeannie he'd definitely known at the time he could have made a different choice, and the proof was that to this day Gary better remembered his act of rationalizing than he recalled their acts of sex. This was because — typical male that he was at the time — his investment in excusing himself was greater than anything else, including loyalty to Gale. The rationalization? He pretended that what was a solution for him wouldn't have been a problem for Gale because there was already another, preexisting problem in their marriage. The saddest part was that he could no longer remember what that original problem had been, other than the normal stresses of a marriage with young children who daily sucked all the oxygen from the air.

It hadn't occurred to Gary to notice, for instance, that Paul Gold had twice as many kids, plus a wife whose twenty-four-hour-a-day job must have made her even less available than Gale was. And apparently Paul had chosen not to have sex with Jeannie, even though she slept right upstairs and was obviously eager. If perhaps Gary had had a men's group to confide in, the others could have confirmed his as a universal problem, while telling him he was a fool to believe he would be excused for acting out like a spoiled child. He was a fool. It didn't take a roomful of men to tell him.

Sandra's lips were parted, and in a way he wished she could talk to him in her sleep. Her advice was always smart and, for sure, she'd tell him to come to bed right now, no matter what. Nevertheless, on the hotel stationery he used the other available truth and, in the stylish lettering architects use on their blueprints, he wrote, YOU'RE SLEEPING SO SOUNDLY I DON'T WANT TO WAKE YOU.

When he and Sandra first got together, in fairness to her son she'd made Gary leave each morning before Jason awoke. For this reason he saw more sunrises in one month than previously in his life, but as a result, both Sandra's motivation and his conscience had been kept clear. The trouble was, in these short nights there was sufficient time only for talk and sex, or sex and sleep, never all three.

Finally, because having a lover can be as sleep-depriving as having a newborn, they'd become "engaged to become engaged," mainly for him, for the stability of sleeping in one bed per night. Unfortunately, now with time to talk she'd only wanted to make plans and more plans, which wasn't the same as getting to know each other might have been. In other words, before they became engaged to become engaged, she'd never used the excuse of his sleeping this soundly as a reason for not waking him up. And why? Because, as he'd come to see, it suited her overall plan to have him be the one pushing for an expanded commitment.

HERE'S A PIECE OF THE WEDDING CAKE, he wrote, though

it wouldn't be bringing her good luck by the time she woke to find it. Was this his fault? No, it wasn't. And now Gary could see he'd succeeded in making it Sandra's fault that he felt free to be attracted to Gale.

There was no way he was going to miss this opportunity with Gale, period, so there was no point in making up excuses, was there? He could go back and forth in his own mind, but this was one situation he wouldn't be talking himself out of. Gale was the mother of his kids, not like Sandra some sexy nobody he'd met in a bar or, like Chloe, on a concert hall project or, definitely not, like Jeannie, your basic conscience-free graduate student. In fact Gale was all three of these put together when they first met — a sexy graduate student at a concert — which might mean his subsequent relationships with Jeannie, Chloe, and Sandra were his acts of reclamation, if all he had ever really wanted was Gale.

All he'd ever wanted was Gale? Then what else could he write next but I'LL BE OUT LATE. With any luck, in case Sandra went searching for him, she would think a group of them had gone on to someplace like the Transportation. She wouldn't know Bob was on his way to Philadelphia, so she would believe, just like last night, Gale and Bob had opted for early retirement.

The trouble was, Sandra trusted him, with reason. Still, was it his fault Bob left early? Bob was an even bigger fool than Gary, as Sandra herself would have been the first to agree.

At his own dumbest, he'd never be so stupid as to leave with the bride and groom just because he might have given them the new car. Sure, Bob likely hadn't intended to end up in that front seat, but did he think they needed a chaperon? Did Bob think he was their personal physician?

Under other circumstances Gary and Sandra would have laughed at him, and Sandra would have felt it served Bob right for not taking her seriously. Watching Sandra sleep, her face twitching into and out of a frown, Gary could pretend that in her dreams she was getting her own revenge against Bob. She was a powerful woman, but he wasn't afraid of her. At least not yet.

Sandra's power over Gary was the same as her ability to trust him, consisting of her having given him all he could ever want, including her own only child. When they met Gary was in crisis, and soon his gratitude to her was so large it had seemed everlasting. He had completely forgotten the importance of being loved, and because this was the area of Sandra's greatest expertise, she'd brought him back from the edge of despair to the circle of hope. He'd known Jason half the boy's life by now, but instantly Gary had become devoted to this entirely sweet boy who wasn't embarrassed, even at the age of ten, to be kissed by him in public. Jason's open round face was right here in the hotel room, in the picture Sandra propped against the travel alarm, and in checking to make sure Sandra hadn't somehow managed to set the alarm, he nudged the picture of Jason, which fell face down.

"Sorry, honey," Gary wanted to apologize. The charcoal-gray and silver "laser" backdrop had been Jason's choice for this school picture, so he looked like a kid who was caught in a lightning storm, despite his freshly ironed shirt and parted hair. One day Jason would understand, the same way Charlie had come to.

Gary righted the photograph and wrote I LOVE YOU to both Jason and Sandra, because this would always be true, no matter what might happen next. All these years he'd continued to love his children as best he could, and, no matter what, in giving Jason his own name in the legal adoption he'd made Jason a commitment. No matter what, he'd fulfill it, too, although he couldn't help but notice that this was the fourth time he'd used the phrase "no matter what" in just these few minutes, the first in what would have been Sandra's good advice to him to go to sleep. Did this mean he thought he might die?

There was no danger of that, since adultery wasn't a capital offense. And anyway, Gary told himself as he brushed his teeth, it's not adultery when a man has sex with his own wife.

∞

Margo asked her mother, "Have fun at the Christian Science Center?" Her tone could afford to be bland; the irony was already implicit.

"Oh, hi," Gale answered evasively. She had been caught in the act of looking around for Gary.

"Actually, it's goodbye time. Herb just went home." David Haynes had found another dancing partner but had tried to convince Margo to join a group about to head out to a club. She'd declined, claiming fatigue, though it wasn't that.

"We'll see Herb tomorrow," Gale deflected, "won't we?"

"You tell me, Mom," Margo replied, hurt. This wasn't unlike high school, when girls felt free, if they got a date, to cancel a preexisting plan.

Gale couldn't tell for sure what was behind Margo's sarcasm, so she merely said, "I thought that's what we had agreed, going to Herb's brunch for all the out-of-towners — which includes us — and taking off from there. Is there a change of plans?"

"If you're sure you can spare the time."

Gale guided them to a table cleared of everything but flowers, green glass globes of showy dahlias. "Let's sit. Tell me, what's the problem?"

"How would you feel?"

"Maybe you could say how *you* feel," Gale suggested instead.

Margo hesitated, too close to her own fear to see what it looked like, unable to tell her mother what it felt like.

Here Gale observed the first rule of therapy: wait out the silence.

Margo placed her elbows on the table, her forearms angled like the legs of a tripod, her hands holding her head steady.

"Here goes. In my honest opinion, Mom, you behave like you're about to — this is what makes it so freaky — elope."

"Elope?"

"Take off." Margo had never been too conscious of consequences herself, so it was odd that she added, "Never mind the consequences." Just as uncharacteristically, she folded her hands now, like a parent.

"By myself? Without you, you mean?"

Margo regarded her mother with an I-wasn't-born-yesterday expression. "Of course not. With Gary!" She could have called him Dad, since it was what she called him, but she didn't.

"Take off with *Dad?*" The thought hadn't occurred to her.

"You see?" Margo pressed. "You're thinking about it, aren't you?"

Gale recognized that Margo's fear wasn't about being left out but about opening herself to feel a difficult mix of dread and what amounted to hope. It would have been easiest to tell Margo she needn't worry, but this wouldn't have been the truth.

"No," she said, since this was the truth. "No, I swear, I'm not planning to run off with Dad." Gale wished one glass of water had been left on the table, for her. "But are you trying to tell me it looks like that?"

"Kay thinks it does." Margo leaned back against the gold metal bamboo chair. "But —"

But Gale and her sister Kay were the kind of opposites that don't attract, so Gale couldn't be too concerned. However, she and Gary were examples of the kind that do.

Margo went on, "I don't know about the others, but my point is, you've been divorced half my whole life." Now her complaining tone was involuntary. "No, more than half."

"I'm so sorry, honey." Gale covered her daughter's hands with her own.

"I made the adjustment, I mean." Margo took in a breath, needing the energy.

"You did. And it wasn't easy, I know. Thank you."

"No problem" was the purely reflexive answer, signifying generational code for "You're welcome" rather than that it had been no problem.

"Actually, it was, wasn't it?" Now Gale could smile.

So could Margo. "God. Yes." She took advantage of the opportunity to ask, "Mom, may I ask you something?"

The musicians were packing up their instruments, and the remains of the wedding cake were wheeled through a double door while other waiters continued to fill their trays with cake plates and empty glasses. They weren't alone, that is, but yes, they were alone. "Sure, go ahead."

"Did you marry Bob because you loved him? Or what?"

"Such a question requires a considered answer," Gale said quickly, "so I'm glad we're going to get some time tomorrow and the next day. For now, just let me say —"

"No, Mom, please answer the question right now. I've never dared ask it before, and now's when I need to know the answer." Her courage felt quite permanent, surprisingly. "Did you marry Bob purely because you loved him? Or did you think you were doing the right thing for Charlie and me?"

Gale had to let Margo witness her discomfort because there was no hiding it. Yet she did manage to reply. "But it wasn't an either-or situation. Yes, I loved Bob, and yes, I hoped it would be a good thing for you." But what she heard was that past tense, having loved Bob. "I still love Bob."

"No, I know *that*. What I'm asking is if you got married *for* us."

"As opposed to not marrying? That wasn't an option. Bob couldn't have done that." Then Gale added, "Nor would I have given up my practice here unless I'd thought it was a good move. I hoped not to move it again." Now Gale was no longer sure of the question, and as a result she squeezed her clasped hands too tightly together. All ten knuckles turned white.

"Did you think we might not make it? Because, you know, Brookline High's a good school, and there's always UMass. In a million years I wouldn't pick a place like Agnes Irwin. Charlie too, you know, Chestnut Hill Academy was a setback. Not such a major one as mine, but still."

"Are you wondering if I married Bob for his money?" Gale had never had this conversation with anybody but herself.

"Did you think we couldn't make it on our own? That's what I asked you."

"I couldn't know. Perhaps I wanted to make sure." And now Gale offered the other motivation. "And to provide you a father. And to give myself a partner."

"We already had a father, Mom."

"I know that. Jesus Christ, I *know* that, Margo, but you couldn't depend on him in that period of his life."

"How do you know?"

Gale's whole body ached from the strain of the tension in those clasped hands. She released them and, like a supplicant, grasped one of her daughter's. "I didn't, because I couldn't."

"Or you wouldn't." But Margo's tone wasn't the least bit accusing.

And Gale heard it as intended. "Fair enough. That's true, I wouldn't."

In the second year of her relationship with Bob, Gary had called to say he'd be coming to town on business and, with Margo's encouragement, he'd asked Gale to let him take her out for dinner, an invitation she'd refused. Gary had known she would, so he'd said, "Actually, I've got B.B. King tickets. How about it?" Gale could recall now the way her stomach felt then, tight like a knot in a pine board, hard like the knob on either end of a big bone. No, she wouldn't, no, she couldn't. Hadn't risked it.

"Dad asked me again today how come you wouldn't ever see him, and I said, 'Oh, you know, she was pretty angry,' but I think you owe him the truth."

"I don't like to admit the truth."

"No kidding, Mom. Who does?"

Gale had to shake the blood back into those fingers, shaking her hands as if she'd just burned them. "I'm so sorry, Margo."

"It wasn't your fault, though." But she didn't mean to imply it was Gary's, either.

"I'm sorry for your sake, I mean."

"Oh, well. Me too." But Margo was able to laugh. "This is all I'm really saying: I'm feeling sorry for myself." Such an oversimplification had to be expanded. "And in addition, you should know I'm watching you closely this time. Don't fuck it up."

"You mean *again*," Gale lamented, laughing at the role reversal. "Some role model I am."

Here was another of Margo's points. "No, but you are! Look how you taught me to succeed as an independent woman. I'm a big shot, and at this rate I'll probably be a mogul when I grow up. I sure didn't get that from Dad. Or Bob either."

"I appreciate that, but," and now she said it once and for all, "it was such a giant mistake I made. If I'd gone to the B.B. King concert, what's the worst that could have happened? To forgive him? To get on with my life, finally?"

"I thought you'd be worried about falling in love with him again, wrecking your plans with Bob. Or is this what I wished?"

"Is it?"

"Isn't it my job as the child of divorced parents to always wish them back together?"

"Well, here we are."

"But the thing is, Mom, now I can see there are huge consequences."

"There were then, too. Exact same ones." This wasn't true, though, because there wasn't Sandra then. She herself barely knew Bob's children, and Jane's daughter Amanda, for whom she'd become Grandma, wasn't yet born. There were many more people now, lives poised, as her own children's had been at the time, to be ruined.

"True. Sad and true." Easing up, Margo said, "So let me get this straight. We're still on, you and I?"

"Absolutely." Gale refrained from telling Margo how sad it was.

"Okay, that clears that problem up." Margo guessed it didn't matter for the time being that this hadn't been the larger of her two problems. The other one was implicit: the potential chaos of her mother's and father's marriages. "So I guess you're on your own, huh?"

"No curfew?"

Their shared laughter was so unrestrained it served to help David locate them. "*There* you are," he told Margo, as if she'd been in hiding. He rushed toward their table, and though David wasn't including Gale, neither would he have intended to exclude her. "I insist. So come on, let's split."

"Have fun," Gale said, to make clear she wouldn't have been a candidate. In the doorway stood a dramatically dressed young woman whose earrings tossed off light like arrows shot from twin bows.

"That's Sondra," David said, "as opposed to Sandra," although there was no comparison, only contrast.

"Any others? Or just us three?" Margo had been the matchmaker, as usual, and was used to being third wheel.

"No, a real crowd. Including some guy who says his sister went to school with you at — what was it called? — Miss Agnes's. You're ignoring him, he tells me." David indicated with a wink that this was the game these two had played so long, he'd never ever give it up.

Margo shrugged her shoulders. "All right, but only this once. Only for you." She kissed Gale good night and hurried to catch up with David and anybody else under thirty. At least her generation was the correct chronological age for irresponsible behavior.

6

"GARY DIDN'T GO TO BED ALREADY, DID HE, GALE?" PAUL Gold asked. They were in the lobby, and the remaining guests were in the final stages of leaving.

"No, I don't think so," she answered. Quite unlikely. Impossible.

As the glass doors closed behind the last of the relatives, Eve turned back to Gale and Paul and a carved pumpkin smile filled most of her face, lit up as if by a candle. "I think the four of us should have a last drink together, to take credit for having introduced the bride and groom." Eve was the only one of the four who'd managed to drink little enough to make it sensible to have one more. "Now that I can relax," she admitted, by which she meant "as a favor to me?"

"Sure." Gale was unable to muster much enthusiasm.

Eve asked, "Gary didn't go to bed already, did he?"

"Quite unlikely," Gale said. Impossible.

"I'm dying to know how you've been." But Eve meant "how you are."

Gale positioned herself to face the elevators. Of such a long story, no doubt the most recent installment was written in her flushed cheeks. What more could she tell Eve? That Gary had gone to check on Sandra to make sure she was still asleep? That she herself hadn't quite told Margo the entire truth when Margo accused her of thinking of running away? The impulse had run through her like a chill.

It seemed Eve had been preoccupied by the simplicity of her daughter's joy, so she appeared to be unaware of any undertow beneath the still surface of a wedding that had gone according to plan. Eve seemed entirely, unnervingly serene.

Near where they stood, by the window onto the street, was a grouping of overstuffed cartoon-like chairs with rounded arms and backs, looking like pairs of Volkswagen Beetles. Paul sat in one, and almost as soon as he did, Gary appeared and Paul intercepted him. "We're having a drink."

"Good!" said Gary, like a good sport, though it was surely the last thing he needed.

"Like the good old days, I suppose, but," said Paul in his upbeat voice, "good enough reason for me."

"Me too," echoed Eve. She looked the most like herself from those same good old days, even though of the four of them she'd had by far the least beauty sleep.

In those days, before doctors wore pagers like banded birds, it was possible to get too far away to be reached. People would "keep trying" if the phone was busy, or eventually they'd give up. Eve and Gale could sit in blissful ignorance on a beach, or on a bench, while their children took turns at whatever it was they played. Things would happen one at a time. Unlike today.

Eve and Paul preceded Gary and Gale down the maple-paneled hall to the bar, which that same morning had been the breakfast room. Gale felt layered enough to be fieldwork for archaeologists: Gary rested his hand on the back of her neck, pressing his index finger against her brain stem. Gale refused to look into the mirror on the wall straight ahead of them, but she knew that in these twelve hours since morning she'd either aged permanently or shed decades. Gary removed his hand, but only in order to lick her neck — not wetly like a puppy — sharply, like a snake.

"This is a nice place," Eve enthused from the doorway.

That's what Gale meant: instead of just being a cozy hotel bar in the evening, it was the same place she and Gary, on that gray plush banquette across the room, made each other sad with memories of ferrying to Nantucket.

"Fine," agreed Paul as the headwaiter indicated the table in a corner, "and we'd like the champagne list, please." He'd already had sufficient champagne to launch a ship, but individual glasses didn't seem festive enough to mark this moment.

"You choose," Gary said when Paul insisted on being second-guessed, and in the meantime Eve kept the waiter standing by because she asked, "Oh, and do you know why you don't get a headache if the champagne's really good?" Inclusively, Eve told the others whose question to her this had been.

Paul interrupted his deliberation to say, "Hey, that's right, where's Sandra?," making it clear he'd forgotten all about her.

"Too much champagne," Gary said.

"Personally, with regard to headaches I don't myself experience a difference, but," and then the waiter posed a hypothesis he made sound more like a theory: "Ask your doctor." He glided away with their order.

Gary asked Eve his own question, which had to do with the effects of adrenaline on fatigue. His more pressing question was about the influence of his fatigue on sex drive, but with polite attentiveness he listened to Eve's answer to the question he'd dared ask. It was his own fault for not getting any sleep the night before.

The waiter interrupted this thought in order to perform the ritual opening of the champagne, so the question became why the actual sound champagne glasses make isn't the *ting* of popular mythology, but an off sound. No one asked this. Their four tulip glasses made a bouquet.

Paul had a long, "latest outrage" story to tell. This was his standard opening line about university gossip, but it didn't occur to him that Gale and Gary had each moved on from caring about every tyrannous act the despotic university president got away with. Those were Paul's words: tyrant, despot.

Now his "latest outrage" monologue threw Gale back against the wall of her own memory, of choosing Barnard College because she'd been raised in Cincinnati — neither north nor south nor east nor west — and needed to get out of Ohio and be someplace — Manhattan! — that couldn't be mistaken for anyplace else.

How was she to know Columbia would become the role model for upheaval? When her father put a stop payment on her tuition, Gale was pretty sure she'd seen her conservative parents for the last time in any familiar way. Her parent-pleasing sister Kay couldn't be bothered to broker negotiated talks, so the next few years Gale devoted her energy to getting her doctoral degree. "Incommunicado" was what Gale's parents told everyone, as if she'd been struck dumb by lightning. But what they meant was "finito."

Not even a wedding, not even a grandchild, could tempt her mother to relent. By mistake Gary once persuaded Gale to write, offering to visit them with her husband and their infant daughter. Gary's firm had been a finalist in the competition to build a theater in Cincinnati, but, true to form, Gale's mother replied that it was better not to open old wounds. Anyway, Gary's firm lost out to another young group of architects, Hardy Holzman Pfeiffer, whose national reputation rocketed from that very spot beside the Ohio River.

Gale noticed Gary's stifled yawn, but he did such a good job of hiding it, Paul didn't seem to. Eve did, so she changed the subject, but gradually, in one long sentence bringing Gary and Gale back into it, finishing with, "Then, when Charlie told us you two hadn't even seen each other in all this time, I was worried. I couldn't believe it."

Paul asked, "Weren't you both at the Wesleyan graduation?"

"No, I couldn't make it," Gary said. Nobody needed to be reminded that he was on his honeymoon that day, their wedding plans too far along to change by the time he and Sandra were told the date of Charlie's graduation. "Margo always seems to graduate in December, in private," Gary said, to change the subject.

"True," Gale said, unable to come up with anything else to add.

"Literally," Gary added.

"I know. That's what I mean. It's true." Still, Eve was right. It seemed impossible.

"Nobody died?" asked Eve.

"Right," said Paul, "there wasn't a funeral you both went to?" He took an assertive sip and said, "I'd come to Herb's funeral."

"Of course you would," Gale said, "but that's because you've known him thirty years." She'd been about to remind them all that her mother died, but in accordance with specific instructions there had been no service.

"Don't be so sure," Eve joked, not that it was funny to speculate about her father's funeral.

"Now it's on the record, though: I'm coming to it." Paul took another sip, as if to close the deal.

"Me too," Gary said. "So we'll come together." His jaunty tone made it seem like they were only talking about Herb's brunch the next day.

There was no burial either, because Gale's mother had asked to be released, like a balloon filled with helium, into the air. Before killing herself she'd moved her husband from Cincinnati to a South Carolina all-season golf course condominium, where he could play daily until, one afternoon of his choosing, he could drop dead in the clubhouse after a round. The ashes sat in a cupboard for a few months while Gale's father thought about what to do with them. Gale had suggested taking a boat from Charleston harbor — the impulse to go as far offshore as the horizon, let the ashes keep on going — but her father preferred scattering them on land. At five-thirty on the morning of the birthday for which Gale and Kay had gone there to be with him, without warning, he invited his nongolfing daughters along for a ride in his new golf cart. The first golden-green light of that day was pristine, and the first tee time wouldn't be for another hour. From the middle of his favorite fairway in the world, their father dispersed his wife, and when the automatic sprinklers came on, the ashes vanished.

"Where will you be?" Eve asked Gale, as if, along with weddings, the dates of funerals could be set in advance.

Gale was already wondering the same thing: "That's the question of the hour." Even one hour earlier, before Dick's Last Resort, it wouldn't have been such a tricky question.

"She'll be here too," Gary answered for Gale, turning the conversation around from point of origin to destination.

∾

"Remember the bare-boat charter that was so bare there were no charts?" It was Gary who both asked this question and had proposed visiting the island whose name he liked, Saint Eustatius.

Eve teased Paul, "To keep us from running onto the reef, you hung off the bow like one of those carved wood ladies on whaling ships," and she flung her arms back on the diagonal, lifting her chin.

"We used *road* maps!" Gale remembered, disbelieving still that they hadn't all been lost at sea that week.

"I prefer to think of myself as a prow dragon on a Viking ship, if you don't mind." Now Paul posed, holding his hand like a visor above his eyes.

"Whatever," said Gary, sounding like their children.

Paul had taught himself to sail by a *Sports Illustrated* booklet, so it was irresponsible indeed for them to have been permitted a boat without a hired captain on board. And yet like a pro — actually like a mermaid — Gale dove and resurfaced with conch or giant tropical crayfish. Never farther offshore than what they stupidly believed a swimmable distance, they were so naive as to completely relax. Their hilarity all these years later was the laughter of the survivors of an accident.

"In pale water it seems deceptively easy," Eve said.

"We're just lucky there was no wind." As Gale remembered it, they always had a gentle breeze behind them, nudging them from cove to cove like a fat bee from flower to flower. Sated, they flew home, as ignorant at the end of their week as on the first day.

"Innocence."

"Dumb luck."

"Paradise." But immediately Gary wished he hadn't evoked paradise, having himself later been banished for eating forbidden fruit.

It was unusual for Gale not to catch such a blatant unconscious reference, but she didn't appear to, and so it would remain the last word.

As if he had sensed the silence, the waiter arrived to pour out the rest of the bottle. "Showoff," Eve called Gary when instead he ordered a triple espresso. Eve's elbows rested on the table, her chin on the palms of her hands, her fingers tucked under her cheekbones. Now her question was to them both, and it came with her permission to tell her it was none of her goddamn business. Still, she'd wondered all this time — what if she and Paul had been the ones to divorce? — if they felt they'd done the right thing.

Paul sat forward too, but to protest that it *was* none of their business. "You can't ask that question," he said.

"It's *the* question," Eve said, "for our whole generation. Either you think about getting divorced, and don't, like us, or do, like them. *No one* hasn't thought about it." She'd turned to face Paul, and again she rested in the cup of her hands.

"The Christian Right hasn't thought about it," Gary evaded, "or so they pretend." His impulse was to protect Paul.

"Okay, fine," Eve said, "I apologize."

"It's awful timing," Paul said, "to talk about divorce on a wedding day."

"I said I'm sorry." This time she didn't turn to look at him.

"You considered it too?" asked Gale. She lowered her shoulders and raised her eyes to meet Eve's, for the first time in all these years seeing her as an equal.

"Of *course!*" By placing her forearms on the table, her hands palms-down, fingers still curled, Eve looked like a lion. Or a sphinx.

"When?" Though it was true about their generation, Gale had always thought Eve and Paul were exempted. This was shocking, but not altogether bad news.

Eve's expression was both fixed and ambiguous. "The first ten or fifteen years. Especially the first ten."

Gale asked, "Why?"

"Jealousy, the same as for you. Only ours was professional."

Under the table Gary squeezed Gale's thigh as a way to keep himself from announcing, "I knew it!" As a midlevel architect married to Chloe, a star, he knew from experience that it's pretty hard on the old ego. He knew the culture conspired to make it even harder, so that if he'd been Paul, he wouldn't have done very well being married to a doctor with a national reputation, being himself a perpetual associate professor.

It was Paul's bad luck to obtain tenure in a university whose new president would have fired him gladly but for union rules. Paul's insubordination was as notorious as the flagrant abuses of power committed by the president known around campus as the Naked Emperor. In the beginning Paul had been like that boy in the fable who dared speak the truth, but unlike that fable, this one didn't have a happy ending. Especially not for Paul, who became demoralized. And blamed Eve.

"I understand" was what Gary heard himself say. "I really do."

But Paul looked crushed.

Gale admitted out loud to the feeling she'd had all day, of wishing to have those years back to do over again.

Like a fact checker's, Paul's response was a bit too explicit. "Do it all over? No thank you, no fucking way. I'm just waiting for the son of a bitch to die, so I can get my own life back. What's left of it."

The value of talk being the foundation of Gale's profession, Paul's expression of anger meant he had her full attention, as she listened sympathetically to the blatant examples Paul conjured one after the other like linked scarves from a false-bottomed hat. It was even worse now than back in the seventies and eighties because, painfully slowly, dissenters had been marginalized. Protest was no longer quashed, as in the sixties; it was simply ignored. Democracy was an optical illusion.

"We who couldn't be bought out in those early days now question ourselves for holding on to absurdly high standards. Wouldn't it have been easier to have agreed to the early-retirement package and just have gotten the hell out of there?" As Paul asked this, he looked to Gale for an answer, but it was Eve who smiled comfortingly, and Gary who said again, "I understand about this. I really do."

Gale said, "I know what you mean, Paul. Thinking back, splitting up isn't the worst thing that happened to me."

"Oh really?" Gary asked. "What is?"

"Okay, that is," said Gale. "Sure. But at another level, the worst thing had already happened long before. All our splitting up did was confirm a belief I already had, that I didn't count." As if to exhibit the relationship of mind to body, Gale could feel herself concealing her exposed neck, retracting it with her shoulders.

The concept of entitlement was completely foreign to Eve, who'd dealt with overt discrimination while never doubting her ability to become a better doctor than those men who believed women were born to be nurses. "As if nursing isn't the most honorable profession there ever was. Talk about the disenfranchised!" In other words, of these four, Eve was the only one who seemed to have survived her childhood intact.

Paul was still with Gale, though, grateful for her identification with him. "I have to ask. If I were your patient, would you have told me that about yourself?"

"It would depend, but no, I don't have a rule against it. I never found it very helpful when the doctor feigns immunity." Implicit was that in training she'd been taught to do just that.

"I should have found another job, I guess," Paul said, "rather than having been fatally undermined."

"I feel the opposite," said Gale. "Maybe you shouldn't have stayed, maybe I ought to have. And if you feel you stayed too long, I feel I might not have stayed long enough."

"But you can't know one way or the other," argued Eve, too practical not to be content with doing your best and accepting the consequences. "We'll never know."

"Do you mean me?" Gary asked Gale. "You should have stayed with me longer?" There was nothing he would wish more, other than that he could have resisted Jeannie in the first place.

"Yes, I'd like to know what difference it might have made."

"But that's my point," Eve repeated. "You can't know that."

"I know," Gale said tolerantly. "All I mean is, I wish I could. I wish —"

"Dot-dot-dot," said Gary.

"Fill in the blanks," Paul said, as if these were the directions for a test.

Gary seized the opportunity to sign the check with his room

number, and eventually, like hosts at home, Gary and Gale walked Eve and Paul to the front entrance of the hotel, to tell them good night and see them off.

"So you got rid of your spouses. Now what?" asked Eve in a voice that was too matter-of-fact to require a response.

"Now what?" Eve asked again as they stood by the door, huddled like teammates. Shouldn't somebody be deciding what play was next?

"We won't know that until tomorrow," Paul said, laughing. He suddenly sounded as clumsy and extraneous as Eve. "So we might as well just go home." He was envious of Gary for not knowing his own future, not even the next half hour.

After Eve and Paul's cab made a dramatic U-turn and vanished, Gary checked his watch. "It's still early, believe it or not." Sandra had already been asleep for three hours, he verified, promising himself not to mention her again, not even, like this, to himself.

They walked in slow motion across the lobby to the elevators, where a set of doors stood open, closing immediately after they stepped inside.

"Those two look familiar, don't they?" she asked about their own blurry, sepia selves looking back like old photographs. This time, when they looked at their own reflection in the brassy fingerprinted doors, they looked shopworn.

This might have been why Gary asked Gale, so tritely, "My place or yours?"

∞

In its glass of water the bride's bouquet leaned against the wall behind the bureau like a skeptic at a cocktail party. But its fragrance was romantic.

"What are these called?" asked Gary about the slender trumpety flowers lined up like Shaker pegs on a smooth maple rack. When Gale told him "Freesia," he responded, "Apt, as images go?" but this time it was a question. He was wishing they could pick up from that moment at Dick's Last Resort, when for one false second it seemed they could be irresponsible enough to have unsafe sex.

Gale stepped out of her shoes and unfastened the clasp of the pearls Bob bought for her on their honeymoon at Coral Beach, in Bermuda. She dropped them into a little pearly heap on the bureau. "Freesia is a perfume flower," she knew to say, because on that trip to Bermuda they'd ridden rented mopeds to visit the perfume factory.

As he took off his tie, Gary asked, "I mean, we're free now, aren't we?" He draped his suit coat around the chair back. "That was a gallant gesture of Bob's. Very touching." He didn't mean the pearls, which he didn't know about, but Bob himself, when he presented Gale the bouquet.

"You mean the car gesture?" If the gift was so touching, how come it had bothered her so?

"I meant the bouquet." Gary unbuttoned most of his shirt but waited for a stronger signal than Gale's taking off her shoes and her pearls. "But that too."

"It's how Bob expresses himself, giving a big gift instead of putting the same impulse into words." She removed the sapphire ring Bob's mother had given her in the same spirit. Would they next have to do the same with Sandra, to evoke her, but only in order to dispel her? And would Gary as self-servingly exaggerate — distort — Sandra's good intentions in order to make them bad?

"Like, 'I love you'?"

"For example." She unzipped her dress, but she too was unsure how they should proceed.

"I love you, Gale." In the mirror behind Gale he saw across her back the bra strap that made the open zipper an upside-down A. This wasn't adultery, though. This was a family re-union.

Now Gale found, like Bob, she had trouble saying it. The once easy habit had leached into her soil, disappearing the way a foreign language does when it's not used.

"I loved you and I love you, both," he said. He felt an immediate impulse to sound less like a land claim, so with mock regret he added, "But by 'both' I don't mean both you and Bob. Sorry."

As she laughed her shoulders lurched forward enough to shrug her dress off as if off a hanger, and because the dress was expensively lined in a slippery fabric, it fell plumbly.

"There's one of the reasons why I love you. You're so" — she stepped out of her dress as if out of a puddle — "so efficient! All day I've been imagining you without that dress on, and look, in two seconds, presto." He was talking so fast he could have been selling her the idea.

"Now you," she said. She'd been anticipating that they would each shower separately and emerge in the hotel's cozy terrycloth robes. This was less coy, all right.

Without taking his eyes off her, Gary performed a step-by-step worthy of an instructional manual — the rest of his shirt buttons, suspenders, fly, boots, socks — and in his pinstriped white boxers, she in her white silk bra and half-slip, they could have been a pair of paper dolls to dress up in matching paper outfits.

They sat primly side by side on the end of the bed. Close up, the faint pink stripe was visible in Gary's oxford cloth shorts, and tiny, pale blue flowers bloomed ever so prettily in Gale's lap. Pink and blue, as if for these unsafe times, whereas in their own era, birth control consisted of planning ahead each morning by swallowing a pill, and unless you planned to get married that week, there was no talk about blood tests.

"I don't have a condom, do you?" Surely there would have been a vending machine at Dick's Last Resort.

"Of course not." It was the one sure advantage of a marriage like hers and Bob's. Gale doubted Bob had ever used one, even in the army during the Korean War; by then he would have been newly married to Priscilla. "Wait." If she were Margo, what should be her questions at this moment?

"I'm okay," he told her.

"Wait. This is new." She felt like a virgin. "What do I need to know?"

He and Sandra had met deep enough into the eighties to know to proceed with extreme caution. "You need to be assured that both Sandra and I are negative, and that neither of us has been —" But he couldn't say "unfaithful," since now he was.

"With someone else?" There was something stirring in having this checklist: theirs wasn't going to be a random act of passion after all, but a deliberate risk. Gale would be required to trust him, as once she had.

"No, neither one of us has been." Of this he could afford to be certain because, until now, neither one of them had sufficient inclination. "Now I'm supposed to ask you too, so —"

"No. In my twelve years with Bob I've never." Nor was there any reason at all to doubt Bob. Wasn't the security of his conservatism one of his attractions?

"And Bob?" But he wasn't serious. How could anyone married to Gale desire to have sex with somebody else? Only he himself could have made such a mistake.

She reached up under the little café curtain of her short slip in order to bring down her pantyhose and bikini underpants. "So that's it?" she asked. Her faithful-servant diaphragm was waiting discreetly in the next room. "So now we're down to birth control?"

"Done." Gary stood and dramatically stretched the elastic waist of his boxers. He'd noticed her inability to tell him she loved him, but he was sure she did, and sure she would. "May I show you my vasectomy scar, up close?"

∞

Though the top sheet and blanket had been neatly folded back on both sides, Gary and Gale twirled like a pair of helicopter rotors, their downdraft blowing the covers off the bed to make the mattress a landing pad. Having already delayed these twenty-four hours, he couldn't wait any longer. "Let me inside you," he asked, "please," as he pushed in and, apologizing not only for rushing but for everything, splashed her with himself.

She'd forgotten the smell when it wasn't confused by hygienically unscented jelly smeared on a rubber disk dusted with cornstarch after use to keep it from getting stressed out. This better smell was wet leather and damp wool, asparagus snapped off underground, geraniums. She could taste herself because, as if they were honey bees and the byproduct were propagation, she put his fingers into her mouth to spread him. The taste was dandelion milk.

"Sorry," Gary said, keeping his hands in motion to reassure her it wasn't over.

"Still, isn't it odd it only takes a minute, when the space between before and after is of such consequence?" She was keeping her legs open to him, straddling him.

The significance of the crossed boundary was for Gale not unlike her sexual initiation, which like this had been equally momentous and disappointing. She and that boy named Bruce could have been randomly selected for each other, given how little they seemed to have in common beyond the fact of their both being hired to wait tables at a summer resort. Directly afterward — this was before the concept of female orgasm had been imported to Ohio — she wondered what all the fuss was about. Whether a girl's first experience occurred on the official wedding night or, as for Gale, under the umbrella of a buckeye, the official state tree, the act itself was disproportionate to the preliminary effort of postponing it.

She rolled onto her back and lay, legs hinged open, like an old family dog wanting its stomach scratched. Gary obliged, but his hands on her belly was an even better feeling than she'd been capable of dreaming it the night before. His adventuring fingers probed and pressed, and sensation was transformed from the concrete to the abstract and, beyond, to the absolute. Gale saw colors streaming by like flags from every nation joined to become ribbons of joy, reds and yellows, rivers of blues too beautiful to have been seen ever before. Gary was good. Not only that, he was goodness.

Now, for once, he saw he could be the messenger of pure good news, the bearer of gladness itself, the provider, the source. All he'd ever wanted to give Gale, he gave her. And all at once she received him.

If Gale hadn't wakened herself the night before, bolting from this very dream, she still wouldn't have been able to imagine this amount of freedom, no matter that the unconscious mind cannot be restrained. Her own hands on Gary were like moths drawn to porch lights, madly flying in place.

"Don't stop," he told her, because by trying she could bring him right back. Sculpting a firm shape with friction, with her hands she made him come up like a vase on a potter's wheel, and this time he would hold his shape as long as she wanted him to. This time, in the meantime, she'd be the one whose glistening tissue softened like butter.

"Oh. My." Now she was the one who told him, "Don't stop." For her first occasion of extramarital sex, this was more like it.

∞

"Shortness of breath" described them both. For this problem the remedy was the mini-bar, stocked with water in mini-bottles that were supposedly shipped from the Arctic Circle. They felt as pampered as in a first-class stateroom on an ocean voyage. Nothing they might need could be very far away.

He never felt this comfortable. "Why don't I feel guilty? Am I a total shit?"

Since they'd have to speak of it eventually, and this was a way to postpone addressing her own guilt, she asked him, "Did you, back then?"

The iced water, or a real chill, or both, prompted him to pull up the sheet. Gale, still too warm, shrugged it off her side. "Yes and no," Gary said. "I felt, I guess, allowed to think of myself as a work-in-progress. Like a building always being renovated, always improved."

"Did you consider it your 'prerogative'?" Gale let her tone communicate what she felt about male entitlement.

"I guess I did. It seems such an ancient idea now. How could it even have existed in the modern era?" He saw this sounded like he was making an excuse.

"Why her?" Gale was not interested in his theories, only the facts.

"No good reason, except that every time I turned around she was there, noticing me. She was watching me cut the grass, hang the rope swing, pitch to Charlie, and, sure enough, I began to notice her too." Since the process was step by step, it was easy to describe it.

"And where was I? In general, I mean."

"Busy, very busy."

Gale barely remembered those months of their marriage. She did recall looking forward to that August, when both kids were signed up for a ten-day overnight camp no farther away than Concord. Neither Gale nor Gary had parents their kids might have gladly visited, so it was to have been their first chance to be all alone in their own house. Needless to say, with so fresh a trauma as their father's sudden disappearance, the kids never made it to camp, not that summer or any other. In an out-of-body sort of voice Gale asked him, "So what was it you noticed about Jeannie?"

"The backs of her knees, the insides of her elbows. Hinges. What fascinated me were her angles, all those moving parts."

"Like a toy."

"Yes," he admitted. "She showed me how to take the chain off a bike and put it back, what's inside a clock radio, how to develop my own film. You remember how she'd made a darkroom in the Golds' basement that fall?"

"So she invited you in and the chemicals made you swoon?" With some bitterness Gale remembered the so-called father-son photography project, in which Charlie lost interest instantly because it was only black-and-white film, and for that there was always Polaroid. "Don't you know the Paul Simon song about everything looking worse in black-and-white?"

The way it happened was that Charlie would split immediately and Gary and Jeannie would be able to hide in the darkroom with the full protection of the Keep Out sign on the door. None of the kids would dare barge in because, cleverly and dramatically, Jeannie had demonstrated for them the way light always spoils the film. At first Gary simply let Jeannie show him how to make pictures, but soon they were hiding in this tiny locked room, where the red safe light gave them new identities: a young woman on the make, making it with a man ten years older who ought to have known better.

"You haven't answered my question, you know." Gale examined Gary's pores while waiting to see if he could remember what she'd asked him. Under his eyes they were enlarged.

"Why her? I thought I did." He couldn't feel his arm beneath Gale's heavy head, but this was not the politic moment to retrieve it.

"No, not that question." She could wait.

"Wasn't *I* the one to ask 'Am I a total shit?' Or did you?"

"You're close." Now she pulled up the sheet after all, to cover herself while she presented a theory. "You asked why you don't feel guilty — now, with me — but your calling yourself a total shit means you are. As you should be. My question was whether or not you felt guilty with Jeannie."

"But I said yes and no, didn't I?" He could see this was evasive, but he didn't want to be interviewed like some research subject. "So I guess not?"

She helped him out. "I was so angry, I never gave you a chance to let me know you were sorry."

"I was!"

"Of course. You *had* to be. You lost everything on account of a misdemeanor, which was not even considered by the culture at the time a real crime."

"Not that I'm excusing myself, but it's true: the jury deliberated less than a minute." Sure, there were two or three sessions with some social worker, who had no sympathy for Gary's side of the story, but basically he had been found guilty, by her, without a trial. "Open and shut."

"I punished myself, too, for that."

"Then could I ask why you kept refusing to see me? It seemed so —" Punishing was what it felt like.

"So much like my mother?" Gale's eyes opened with the realization.

"Now that you mention it," he teased gently, since they both knew that nobody was her mother's equal. "All I know is, for about five years whenever I picked up the kids you'd leave a note — instructions — or there'd be a babysitter or somebody. I couldn't even get the kids to show me a picture of you."

"That's because I weighed more than you did." She saw his look of disbelief, so she kept on. "I was fat enough, long enough, to have to get rid of every article of clothing you'd ever seen me in. Only the approach of my fortieth birthday prompted an insight: if I stayed fat I'd hate myself forever, even more than I hated you. More than my mother hated me." This was an indulgence in itself, because her mother had too many problems of her own to have hated Gale, and Gale knew this. Still, at the time, her mother being one of those women who weighs herself every morning and eats accordingly, it had been an act of revenge — ultimately against herself, if not her mother — to get fat. It justified her mother's rejection of her.

Gary put his hand on Gale's hipbone, which once only an x-ray could have been able to detect, on a thigh muscle no longer embedded in the bubble wrap of excess weight, on an ankle whose circumference had increased exponentially but which now, as before, his hand could reach around, fingers touching. How could it be that the human skeleton can be responsible for two such different bodies?

"Then I met Bob, whose strongest qualification at the time was that he was incapable of rejecting me." She didn't mean to make it sound as if she'd placed a classified ad — "DWF Seeking No Surprises" — but that particular lesson was one she'd learned for life.

"So how'd you meet him?" Gary wondered whether this too could have been avoided.

"Once I lost about half the weight, I made myself go to Philadelphia, to the national meetings I'd skipped. I ran into a Barnard classmate who was a psychologist and Bob's next-door neighbor. Still is." When Gale first met Bob, he didn't know she was neither as thin nor as fat as she could be, only that she had the most luminous smile he'd ever seen in his life.

"And?"

"She introduced us. We played tennis."

"I play tennis," he said, interjecting himself like a poor sport. "But did you used to play? I guess I forgot that."

"No, I learned with the kids. Did you always?"

"Sort of," Gary said. "Are you any good?"

"Very." Gale could honestly say this, because the leaner she got, the meaner her serve was. "Bob and I were this year's mixed-doubles champions at the Philadelphia Cricket Club." As Bob and Priscilla once were, before her drinking got in the way of her game.

It was too threatening to consider Bob an athlete in addition to everything else, so Gary asked, certain he was faster at this, at least, how soon they'd gotten married. At this nobody could beat his and Gale's record.

"That took a while, naturally, and Bob understood my reluctance. Just as he wouldn't be capable of marrying another alcoholic, I'd only be able to remarry after such a fanatic deliberation that any raw impulse would surely have died in the process." It was an argument, as with her serve, she aced.

"I was a raw impulse? Which should I be, flattered or insulted?" The set of his mouth showed that he felt chastened.

"This isn't about *you*, Gary. What I'm trying to explain is what happened to me. Since you asked." Now she sat straight up against the headboard, tugging the sheet with her.

Automatically, but also genuinely, he said, "Sorry." Next he said, "Please." And then, "Go on."

She did, because she needed him to hear this. "Raw's the opposite of safety, so I knew if I could feel safe I'd be happy. Deliberately, I tested Bob, inspecting him with a checklist." She could see the creases on either side of Gary's mouth, nestled like spoons.

"Not unlike raw meat, perhaps?" And now he smiled.

"Like a car, I was going to say."

"A Saab Turbo, no doubt." Now he found her foot with his and pressed his arch against her instep. "I understand what you're saying. You refused ever to be impulsive again, correct?"

"That's right."

"Until tonight. You changed your mind, I guess."

"It was easy as long as you were on the opposite side of the world, but —"

"— it's impossible now that you aren't," he said. "Say it."

"It's true."

"I know. Say it."

"It's impossible to pretend I don't love you."

"Would that be the same thing as 'I love you' or just a double negative?"

"It would be the same thing. It's the same thing. Which is why it's impossible."

He said, "Let me ask you this, though. How far down this checklist were you when Chloe and I split up and I tried to get you to see me?"

"Too far, that's the problem. I'd already decided to marry Bob."

"You'd told him?"

It was hard for her to admit: "Not yet."

∞

It wasn't surprising when, that night in Philadelphia, she and Bob had argued about everything. Instead of having postponed her flight until Saturday morning — in order to see B.B. King at the Orpheum with Gary — her plane was delayed anyway, by thunderstorms. By the time she got to Philadelphia she was furious, at herself, for not being capable of risking seeing Gary. She could plainly see she was afraid of upsetting the life she'd reconstructed, and yet she knew, even at the time, such caution was dangerous. Bob attributed her panic to having been alarmed by the rough flight, and though it was too bad she couldn't enjoy the dinner party in her honor, it wasn't the end of the world, not even when Gale had so much to drink he couldn't avoid a nasty comparison with Priscilla.

Clearly, her own courage having failed her, she'd given Bob an opportunity to question his decision to marry her. Too much wine had made her so combative she challenged each person around the table. She was like a debate team assigned the opposite premise, hotly defending positions she herself didn't believe in. Then, when she felt ashamed for having embarrassed Bob, she made everything worse by apologizing so profusely she appeared to be mocking him. Bob's friends were too timid to voice concern, but it was in their eyes, so at the end of the evening Gale attacked Bob for having such dishonest friends.

The following morning she'd promised it wouldn't happen again, but he'd told her, "Darling, it's understandable. You had a terrifying flight down from Boston, and you drank too much wine too fast. Don't worry, we all understand." God knows, this explanation would have been preferable to the truth, that their relationship was dependent on a great denial.

Gary asked, "What is it? You look distressed."

"I'm imagining that I agreed to see you that time, imagining this night being that one instead, in our own bed." She knew it was unrealistic to assume there wouldn't have been complications, but at the moment it seemed entirely believable.

"We'd have had these ten years?"

"Twelve."

"That means you'd have agreed to have me back?"

"I don't know, but —"

"You can imagine it?"

"Yes. Which is more than I was capable of at the time."

Gary said, despairingly, "I shouldn't have been surprised by how quickly our marriage came apart, since I knew before going to architecture school that it takes less time to dismantle than to build."

She perched on her side, like a board that could tip either way. "What about after an earthquake? When a building's been declared structurally unsound, isn't it hardest of all to rebuild?"

"No, you go system by system." He turned to face Gale with his whole body, lining it up against hers, close enough to be varnish. "With a checklist."

But the irony failed to impress her, since it was too awful to think he could have been fundamentally changed in the five years since their divorce. "You probably wouldn't have passed my inspection."

Confidently, he disagreed. "But I'd been humiliated, don't forget. Chloe had left me, so I'd gone from being the villain to becoming the victim. The judge even awarded me a settlement."

"What? How come?" She hadn't been told this, no doubt because their kids believed the news would have depressed her, or made her angry.

"Because Chloe's career demands made it impossible to keep up my practice. It's not the argument my lawyer made in court, but the judge believed it should have been made on my behalf. He turned our divorce into a case of unequal protection under the law. I was the sacrificing wife, the judge declared." Since it was Gary's one courtroom triumph, he'd gladly detail it, if she was interested to hear. Was she?

"Wait a minute. Although you weren't asking her for money, the judge required you to?" Gale was aware that, under this draped sheet, she and he also looked like one body, indivisible, one nation, maybe even under God. But this was no pledge of allegiance, and, for fear of being misjudged, she wouldn't want them to be judged by anyone, in any court. "What did she say?"

"Chloe wasn't there, which doubtless influenced him." Gary rolled onto his back, as if the hotel room ceiling were the night sky brimming with stars. "The judge asked me how much it would cost to design my own dream house."

"Come on."

"Really. He gave me a few minutes to calculate it, then to my estimate he added another hundred thousand." Gary laughed, the sound overwhelmingly noisy. "That's for the land, he said."

Gale got caught on the edge in his laugh, and reacted. "So it was a conspiracy. It was the same old shit, in other words. Men disenfranchising women."

He protested, but she said he ought to have protested the judge's willingness to punish Chloe for being too successful.

Now Gale also lay on her back, crossing her arms, flattening her breasts.

"Don't, Gale. You weren't there, you don't know." He threw back the sheet and went into the bathroom, shutting the door as if expressly against her. He was so exhausted he barely recognized himself in the mirror, so he decided a shower might help. He'd been afraid they would waste their time together by one of them falling asleep, but it hadn't occurred to him that they would argue, wasting this short time together on problems — no matter how important — that were even bigger than their own.

On the rim of the tub was a small can of shaving cream and a razor, so Gary shaved, using the chrome of the nozzle for a mirror. Hot water rained on him and, feeling more hopeful, he let the rising steam obscure his regrets, carrying them over the top of the shower curtain. Surely this was normal, although unexpected, because the more comfortable they were with each other tonight, the more complicated it was going to be in the morning. But he saw that he didn't want it to be simple. From now on, Gary wanted it to be a mess.

As if Gale did too, she pulled back the shower curtain and stepped in over the side of the tub, under the water. Her voice didn't sound like her own, but the words could only be hers. With lathered body gel and shampoo covering her like a veil, but vanishing down the drain like the ghost of hurt feelings, she explained it.

"It's what we weren't saying. I need to admit I feel very guilty right now. I wondered if you do too."

"I do." But he asked her, "Now what?"

She answered by turning inside the circle of his arms to press her back against his front like two sides of a coin. "Now it's been said."

The palms of Gary's hands fit her breasts perfectly, but more surprising to him was the way they felt fleshy, softer than Sandra's much larger breasts were. That Sandra had had her breasts done was no secret from anyone, but that hers and Gale's could feel this different was an unpleasant surprise, at least to him. He was determined not to compare their bodies, because the age difference gave Sandra an obvious advantage, but it hadn't occurred to him that Sandra's breasts could compare unfavorably. The man in the street would tell him Sandra's are as good as it gets, but these he now held in his hands were more like nursing breasts emptied by a sated baby. These had fed his children. They made him weep with desire.

7

THE NIGHTS WERE LONG BY THE END OF OCTOBER, BUT not long enough. The drapes were drawn, so there was no daylight to turn the lovers instantly into two humble creatures with no special powers. There was the clock, though, whose big red square digits were irreversible. It was a firm 6:27, and though Gary rationalized that since Sandra was on Arizona time they still had two more hours no matter what, Gale could more easily imagine Sandra breaking down the door with the fire ax from the corridor (if such a weapon still existed in public spaces in these violent times). "Anyway," she said, "I simply can't anymore. I'm down to a single layer of skin all over."

The trouble was, his recently shaved face made her need to keep her hands there, as if she were deaf and reading his lips with her fingers. Nevertheless she threw out a new idea. "Let's get out of here, go take a walk, get some air. There's a lot I didn't get around to asking you." She pulled herself up onto hands and knees, into an arch, to ask, "Tell me, how's your mother?"

So their laughter rolled them to the edge of the mattress, and Gary answered, "The same."

He'd have preferred to carry Gale's scent around with him from now on, but needless to say, Sandra would recognize it as not her own. He took another, quicker shower and, as if to show

Gale what a good husband he'd become, made the big bed: stretching the sheets like a camper, tucking them in like a soldier, tossing the four pillows against the headboard as if going for extra points.

Admiring his vitality, Gale said, "They could just declare this hotel room a sperm bank. There's at least a lifetime supply."

"If this were sperm, we'd be in big trouble," he teased. In case she meant he was a sperm whale, he thought her wet hair, slicked back and dark, made her look like a seal.

"No way." She was much too tired to imagine a pregnancy.

"But did you discuss it, you and Bob?" Then he permitted his real feelings to show. "I've always hated the name Bob. It's so *Bob-like*."

However possible it was to laugh about Bob's name, she wouldn't be so disloyal as to say how eager he'd been to have another child. All Gale said was "Of course we did."

"I couldn't handle it," Gary admitted, but he meant her having a child by somebody else.

"Neither could I," she replied ambiguously. One night at dinner Bob's daughter confronted them, saying it was her right — and Robert's and Grant's — to know whether they intended to have children, as well as what provisions for them were contained in the prenuptial agreement. It was the only time Gale had seen Bob tell Jane this was none of her business, although in fact, against his own lawyer's advice, Bob had refused to have any contract with Gale beyond the wedding vows. As if Jane were still a child, when she wouldn't apologize Bob ordered her to leave the table, after which he apologized to Gale for his greedy children. Bob had missed his own kids' childhoods, but it was for another reason than his own second chance that he'd wanted Gale to have his child. It was so a child of his could have the experience of a better mother than Priscilla.

"But you could have, technically," Gary said, shrugging on his wrinkled pinstriped jacket, checking the pockets to make sure he still had his key, "or at least theoretically." The thought of Bob in the delivery room filled Gary with envy: he wanted exclusive rights to Gale in that moment of giving birth.

"Margo and Charlie needed me to mother them," Gale said because it was the truth.

"Thank you for that." They walked down the carpeted hall in silence.

In the elevator, he noticed that as her hair dried it turned its true color again. "Why does platinum mean gold when it should mean silver? Platinum hair is now my favorite color."

"I call it gray." The car landed with a self-correcting lurch.

As they crossed the empty lobby he said, "Sandra convinced me to color mine for my thirtieth reunion, in case you were wondering."

"I was, but it makes you look the same as before." Then she said, "This was Bob's forty-fifth college reunion, which means that when he graduated, you and I were finishing first grade."

He was doing the same calculation — in fifteen years he'd be sixty-six too, a senior citizen like Bob — but Gale shifted the frame of reference and asked how old Sandra's little boy was. "Not little," he said. "Jason was four when I first met him, and now he's ten." The air outside was considerably more damp than it had been the night before, and he realized he'd forgotten how unpleasant the coast can be when you're unused to the humidity. This time of day at home was cool too, but not like someone's basement.

"So, Charlie's age." He would understand that she intended to draw the parallel.

"It's these same next years I'm —"

As if knowing he was about to say "going to miss," she finished his sentence for him. "Going to love. You're going to love his young adolescence." Then Gale added, ominously, "Jason will never need you more."

They cut across the four lanes of Huntington Avenue and hurried past Dick's Last Resort, with its wrought-iron chairs and tables piled up out front, chained together. Such life-in-the-big-city precautions made their having given themselves over to each other in this place seem unrealistic, even unwise, and by daylight Gale felt cheap and untrustworthy. In this part of the city, where hotels and shops sustained each other's needs, Sunday morning was downtime. Neither Trinity Church nor the Christian Science Mother Church was open for business, not yet. Virtue was completely absent.

"What are you suggesting?" Then, before she could answer him, he changed the emphasis. "What exactly are you telling me?" They were riding an unusually steep escalator, which was also long enough for him to realize that if Gale were to tell him over and over when to come and when to go, in the process he'd die of old age. This wasn't what he had in mind.

"You're not assuming we ride off into the sunset together, I hope." She held the rubber rail firmly because she hoped he wouldn't seriously suggest this.

"What are you proposing instead?" He was fifty-one years old, and he wasn't going to waste all the rest of his life finding himself. "I'm not likely to conveniently disappear again, you know. I've done that once." He knew he had no right to make it sound simpler for him than for her when, as she'd pointed out, in his case there was a child involved. Nevertheless he asked roughly, "Do you propose a double suicide?"

The escalator dropped them at one end of a long corridor of closed stores whose display windows and doors were protected by iron grilles. They rushed past the stores like shoplifters making a getaway, and in an equally hard voice she asked him, "Did you say 'double' or 'murder'?"

"Oh, please, don't even suggest it." But his desperation felt equally frightening.

"For the record, I didn't." She spoke these words into his

open mouth, where they would be absorbed eventually, like all sound.

∞

If they were in Paris, they could have a bowl-sized cup of café au lait and a croissant, served by someone who'd think it was normal to have made love all night. Instead, the only place open was a Dunkin' Donuts, presided over by a guy whose only words were "Here or to go?"

"Here," said Gary, but by default. The sugary air was unpleasantly insubstantial, no matter that it was possible to buy albino onion bagels. If they were in Tucson, he'd get the coffee to go and they'd drive off into the stunning sunrise.

This coffee was so watery that the half-and-half made it look more like tea, but the heat helped. Grateful, she held the cardboard cup with both hands, noting in a barely audible voice that they looked like the only customers who weren't homeless.

"We have the opposite problem, don't we? We have too many homes at the moment." Then Gary corrected himself, lowering his voice to match hers. "But those aren't the most serious of our worries."

To prevent Gary from returning to matters of life and death, she retrieved his earlier mention of his college reunion. She hadn't known him then, so the past seemed safer ground than the present or the future.

The University of Virginia was such a throwback when Gary was there that it had slaves' quarters which were still called that. Mint juleps were labored over by eighteen-year-olds who cut their chemistry labs all semester. It was a hideout for the exceedingly late bloomer who'd have been eaten alive if he'd been accepted by the Ivy League. It was perfect for a Baltimore boy like Gary, who looked forward to years and years of college preparation in the form of multiple student deferments. "Greetings!" came the surprise letter from his draft board, but — "Jesus

Christ, you scared the hell out of me, you son of a bitch!" — it was just a prank by his demented roommate. The real letter came the next week.

Since he didn't have a conscience yet, he'd hoped for some major flaw and gotten himself examined so scrupulously no fine-toothed comb could have given him a better going over. "Sorry, son," he was told by the family doctor, "I sure hate doing this to you."

As it turned out, although Gary couldn't manufacture a defect, he was at least the only child of a widowed mother, until the fact that his father wasn't dead, just missing, came to the attention of the draft board. Could he explain? Sure, his father had been missing his entire life, and because his mother had no desire to remarry — Gary left out that the feeling was mutual on the part of every gentleman caller — she'd never bothered to obtain the required death certificate.

But wait. In the meantime he'd gone on to graduate school and, finding Gale, had gotten married himself. By the time of Nixon's "peace is at hand" escalation of the war, a daughter and a son had been born, giving Gary more dependents than was necessary. Five years out of college, he'd graduated for a second time. And been licensed.

Now he let go of so much air he could have fainted, watching his life flash before his eyes like someone about to make a crash landing. "But Charlie and Margo have already improved on me. They're both doing it right, aren't they? Differently, but both right."

"It's a relief," said Gale, "that somehow or other we succeeded in making it possible for Charlie to believe in the value of a commitment." She knocked on the Formica countertop, taking no chances. "But there's still Margo."

"She'll be fine," Gary reassured. "She'll be all set. She was the one who made me come to the wedding, did you know that?"

It was Charlie, Gale thought. "No."

"Yes, beginning in June, all summer she was after me to agree. Margo said you wanted me here." He looked so tired, the skin under his eyes was a purple. "No?" Despite his utter fatigue he could figure this out, and did. "Yes? I love it. See what I mean? Margo will be just fine."

"Manipulating people?"

"Deal-making." Gary slapped the Formica for a sharper sound, a conclusion.

"She never asked me, so I never said if I wanted or didn't want you here. Actually, I assumed you'd come, unless —" She'd thought it was poor form to be on your honeymoon for your son's college graduation.

He was about to say "Never again," but he caught himself. Given this night, he could imagine getting married a fourth time.

Gale was laughing as she told him, "Earlier tonight, Margo wasn't pleased with the way things are going, but now I understand. She was afraid she'd used an incorrect formula or said the magic word inside out."

"Created a monster?" His stomach roared like one, but it only served to make him wish for a real breakfast, rich in cholesterol and calories. "Let's get out of here. This Dunkin' Donuts could be anywhere, including Tucson or Philadelphia. Let's be in Boston." Not that calories need replenishing, but Gary had spent all his.

Being in Boston meant what, though? They could take the Green Line car to Coolidge Corner and hear Russian, or go the other way, to the Italian North End. The Orange Line would take them to Dorchester, for Haitian Creole, or to Chinatown. The Red Line went to Somerville for Vietnamese, or the opposite way, to South Boston's Irish neighborhood. The most relevant question right now was who has the best breakfasts?

There was a cab stand in front of the Lenox Hotel, directly across the street, and though they'd decided to ask to be taken to Southie, the driver of the cab first in line was a middle-aged black man. Since there was no assurance that race relations had improved sufficiently in the many years they'd been away, Gary said, "Good morning. We'd just like to take a ride around the city." It wasn't worth risking a man's dignity for genuine Irish soda bread.

"We're tourists," Gale added, instantly understanding Gary's decision. "What do you think we should see in Boston?"

He drove them along the Black Heritage Trail, where the Underground Railroad ran beneath the gold-domed State House. On Joy Street he pointed out the first African Meeting House and its museum, and then he zigzagged to the corner of West Cedar and Pinckney streets, where he paused so they could admire a flower shop's windows, lit to showcase the season's last purple Eventide asters next to dark peonies known as singledoubles and the hardy mums that lingered into fall here in Zone 6. Next door was a gray brick house, and there he stopped the cab to have them read the bronze plaque designating this building as an African American Historical Site for having once been a safe house.

Asked where they were from, they answered separately, together, but this was no problem for the driver, not even when they both changed their answers to "Brookline, actually." And where would they like to go now? According to Gary's watch, it was time to go to the hotel.

Because they'd disappeared from his rear-view mirror, the driver knew not to hurry. He stopped for every amber light and moved on at the green only so as not to look suspicious. Now he saw them, now he didn't.

Each familiar Boston landmark upset her more, and now, with the driver circling the hotel like a plane over Logan, it was the public library: all the hours she and the children had spent there, all the books she'd read them all those lonely bedtimes. She was weeping yet again, futilely. "But it's not up to me," she told Gary. "If it were, I'd take it all back, do it all over."

"Sshhh. I promise, it will work out. Sshhh." With his fingers he brushed her hair back from her face, then with both hands he rubbed her neck, trying to release some of the pressure she'd let collect there. "We still have time. It will work out."

Usually Gale would be the one offering such consolation. Everything was always so *clear* to her — it was her job to see through things, as if emotions were windows — she would be the one comforting. It was an awful, and liberating, experience to need help, and she badly needed help with all this tension in her neck, and everything else. The driver helped too, soothing her from the front seat, not invisible anymore. "It's all right," he reassured her. "Don't worry, dear."

Nothing could have meant more to Gale than not to have to worry about the cab driver's needs. She said, "Thank you," but it caused her to cry all the more that she felt such complete gratitude. This was what "coming apart at the seams" must mean. This was "losing it" for certain. "Oh," she wailed, "No!" Over the years she'd seen so many people whose lives were ruined by choices made in their ignorance, but her own explicit weaknesses were so familiar to her by now, she'd believed that naming faults was the same as overcoming them. And look by how much she'd been wrong.

This wasn't exactly bad news as far as Gary was concerned. He'd been worried — panicked — that, bloodlessly, she was prepared to see him off at the airport with merely a "good luck to you and yours." This behavior of hers was new to him, and he knew it was right because he felt identically.

His hands were hot on her tight neck but, like steamed towels, still refreshing. The cab driver had gone up to Massachusetts Avenue and circled back and was resting by the curb in front of the Colonnade. The sun was up. The Christian Scientists were on their way to church across the street.

The driver was too cool to say "Here we are, sir," but he

couldn't keep the meter running if he shut the car down, so over his shoulder he said, "Here we are, sir."

"Yes," Gary said, "okay." To Gale he said, "We're here." He gave the driver a 100 percent tip.

Gale got out of the taxi and thanked the driver for his kindness, even though in his cab she'd made a terrible realization. For her there was no point anymore in asking Now what? Her life wasn't a romance novel, so the answer couldn't be simple. It struck her now and hurt like a blow from a blunt instrument: the answer exists in the entire rest of their lives.

∞

The doorman's job is to avert his eyes and not expect his "Good morning!" to be returned by every hotel guest. The advantage of the card key, similarly, is not needing to ask for a room key from the desk clerk, who doesn't know whether to say good night or good morning to people who stagger through the front door. Phone messages being electronic, human interaction with so-called service personnel was no longer necessary. So far, so good.

When the elevator reached Gary's floor, Gale pressed the Door Open button's angled parentheses, but there was nothing more to say, and anyway, he'd be seeing her very soon. He just stepped across the threshold and turned back to watch the two sides of the door meet in the middle. She pressed one floor up and realized that the need for sleep was indeed equivalent to the other fundamental bodily urges she'd met all the rest of this night. The doors opened again, and like him she merely stepped across the metal threshold onto the hall carpeting and down to her room. If Housekeeping had come by in the interval of her absence, she could have been convinced by clean sheets and towels and a restocked mini-bar that the whole thing had been a fantasy. God knows, she'd fantasized it often enough.

Gale set the alarm clock for less than an hour from now and

was about to call the front desk for a backup wake-up call when she noticed the flashing red light on her telephone. Guessing it was a message from Margo with instructions to meet in the lobby at a certain time, she was startled to hear Bob's recorded voice.

"Good morning, darling. Everything's fine here, including Amanda. You must be down at breakfast. I'm at the hospital now, just leaving." Bob didn't say for where and, except maybe to play racquetball, it didn't occur to her to assume he would be heading anywhere but home.

Without taking off her clothes, Gale got under the covers and pretended numbly to have just arrived in Europe after an overnight flight. Under those circumstances a nap makes all the difference, or so she told herself as her heavy body fell toward sleep like a jumbo jet closing the distance to the runway. Remaining were tasks like wake up, dress, pack, check out, all of which could be performed by her surrogate self and after which point Margo could take over. With any luck, Margo also might have stayed out later than she meant to.

These weren't thoughts, however, but sensations: simultaneously in-body and out-of-body, so that she herself, as Gale Oakley, didn't exist. This version of her was hanging like a curtain between nothingness and the void. Not to worry. Maybe this was what death felt like. On the other side, possibly all would be quite normal again. The feeling was of completion. This was why she felt exhausted: it was very hard work, closing open circles.

Her breathing slowed enough to stall, so the only reliable activity was the digital clock's electronic transformation — zeros becoming ones, ones twos, threes fours — dots of light like soldiers imprinted with meaning. The only noise was the hum required by the passage of time.

Meanwhile, one flight below, Gary was just inside the door of his own room, having made no noise opening or closing it. He'd been smart enough to remove his boots out in the hall. Now he leaned against the entryway wall and waited for his eyes to adjust to the darkness he had created by lowering the shades and overlapping the heavy drapes. If he got thirty minutes' sleep he'd be lucky. He was trying to imagine himself into some sort of meditative state, whereby fifteen minutes supposedly does the trick all day, when he heard the terrible noise of a light switch.

From there he couldn't see the bed, but the light made a trapezoid and reached almost to where he stood. "Oh, hi," he said, more like a teenager caught in fibs than like a burglar. "I'm just coming in." He thought he might as well not start out lying.

"So I see." She sat up in bed. Her hair had been pressed so flat against her head, its curl was completely ironed out. She was the one scrutinizing him, however.

"You okay?" Of course Gary was referring to her having had too much to drink.

"I don't know yet."

Gary shed his clothes layer by layer and brushed his teeth noisily, conveying that in spite of the fact that the rest of the city was starting over, he was finishing up.

She followed him unsteadily into the bathroom, but to sit on the toilet, voiding her overstressed bladder. Though Gary had the protection of his boxers, she was naked. He said something she didn't hear over the noise of the toilet's flush, so Gary repeated it.

"You're asking me what time's the *brunch?* As in, will I wake you in time?" She was also brushing her teeth, but to get rid of a bad taste.

Trying not to cave in at the outset, he said, "I know, I was out way too late."

"Have fun?" she asked, as if she'd already caught him in her trap. The thick washcloth held a pool of water she splashed against her face. When would she have power, if not now? She took her time.

"I really ought to sleep," he explained with a yawn. He shuffled toward the bed.

"That's surely true, but I doubt it will be possible." She patted her face dry with the sleeve of the terrycloth robe hanging on the bathroom door. "I'm about to take my shower, then I'll get all dressed up in another brand-new outfit. *Then*, at the brunch, I'll go get patronized all over again, only this time it'll be worse, because I managed to miss everything. Bob will make me feel dumb again."

"Don't worry, Bob's gone." He was pretending to sleep, breathing more loudly than was normal for him.

"Oh?" She leaned against the doorjamb. "Since when?"

Gary could feel himself slipping out from under himself, like skates on ice.

"Gone for good, you mean? Or just temporarily?" She'd been awake long enough now to be alert. She aimed the bedside reading lamp on his face and said sharply, "You answer me!"

He was too tired to realize that his attempt to be helpful to her was at the same time unhelpful to him. "I'll tell you all about it in the morning. But really, hon, leave me alone for a minute, huh?" Because he saw his mistake, he said, "Yes, I know, it's already the morning."

He'd missed his mistake, which was in saying "leave me alone," as if she had no rights at all.

Harshly, she said, "You don't know shit, you know that?" Once it had been necessary to get a restraining order against Jason's father, so she knew this feeling.

He couldn't follow the sequence, but he didn't try to, either. "I promise," he said, only wishing she'd turn off the goddamn light. "You're blinding me," he protested.

"Sor-ry." She sounded like her son, obeying Gary even when he was being treated unfairly.

"Thanks. I'll just sleep while you're in the shower, okay?" So he escaped.

Another mistake he'd missed was that she'd noticed something, but couldn't decide which question, when or where or why — she knew *who* — mattered the most. While she was deciding which to ask, Sandra said, "I see you shaved."

∞

After he attempted to phone Gale, Bob had called Margo to ask about the brunch. Margo could hear a loudspeaker in the background, but then, in the hospital someone was always paging a doctor. She was telling this to Gale, who said, "Not anymore. Now they all wear individual pagers."

"Oh, right." But neither of them wondered if this meant Bob could have been calling from an airport.

Gale was driving down the ramp of the Colonnade's parking garage, shocked by the transition from that darkness into this harsh daylight. Fumbling in her purse for her sunglasses, she also wished to conceal herself from Margo's scrutiny. Already Margo had told Gale she looked like someone barely making it to the end of final exam week.

"So where were you?" asked Margo. "Out?" She was appropriately self-mocking, because this was what she herself had replied throughout her adolescence.

"Dunkin' Donuts."

"Now why didn't I think of that?" Margo laughed, pulling a twenty-dollar bill from her wallet and holding it out to her for the parking attendant.

"I think coming and going is free for hotel guests," Gale said as they were waved through.

"Speaking of being a hotel guest, there *is* room service in the better hotels, you know." Margo herself always took advantage of the continental breakfast as a way of not having to deal with anybody without having had her caffeine.

"Gary and I were out, walking." Gale made a right turn and crossed on Dartmouth to Copley Square, where she and Gary had sat only a few hours earlier on that wooden bench near the fountain, between the two treasures of Trinity Church and the public library. In a Romance-language country they would have been a conventional sight, but in Boston their kissing prompted drivers to beep their horns in encouragement.

Margo said, "Sorry about last night, by the way. I never in my life used the word 'elope' before, and I certainly shouldn't have accused you of abandoning me. Sorry."

"I'm sorry too, for making this complicated." Gale's reflexes were slow, and she needed prompting from the driver in the car behind, who honked when the light turned green. "There's the Dunkin' Donuts," she said.

"I believed you, Mom. God." But Margo could see that for Gale it was a treasured souvenir, not just a place. For so naively believing it would be nice for Charlie if she brought their parents together, Margo could only blame herself. If she were more conservative she'd have staged some sort of run-through, to get everything out of their systems ahead of time. Yes, that's what a proper conservative would think to do.

"I suppose it wasn't *un*complicated before, though, was it?" Gale asked.

Margo shifted in her seat, to better guess what her mother meant. Was she saying she'd never stopped loving Gary? Or something less impossible to comprehend? Whatever it was, Gale seemed to have shrunk under the weight of it. And now she pulled over to the curb, where a fire hydrant provided Gale a place to stay while she considered what to tell Margo.

But Margo spoke. "It was a good try, Mom, even if it looks like you might have oversimplified. Last night, once I thought about it after we talked, I saw how your marrying Bob was to try to do your best for us, regardless of whether or not it might have been best for you." Margo said this with such simplicity, it could seem like a compliment rather than the epiphany it was.

Gale was trained not to miss such a moment as this, but her

thanks seemed inadequate to the gift Margo was giving. "I'm so grateful to you for being able to see this." She reached over to caress Margo's cheek as she said, "If the child can be father to the man, she can also be mother to the woman. As you are." Gale would have been glad to apologize for not being as good a mother as she'd desired to be, but instead she preferred to say, "I'm so lucky you're my daughter. Thank you." She made it sound as if the choice had been Margo's to make and, out of all the mothers, she had picked Gale. This absurdity made Gale smile, and, perhaps to slyly reassert the original order, in her most motherly voice she asked, "But did you manage to have fun with David and the others?"

"You're welcome," Margo answered first, and then she seemed content to respond, "Well, it was a better place last night than the night before, but basically I'm getting so sick of that scene." One of the things she'd wanted to talk about with Gale was this feeling of being an outsider, not only to the club scene but to everything. "It takes so much effort to project yourself beyond those extremes that the whole ordeal feels pretty manufactured." This in itself wasn't something Margo ordinarily disdained — what was more manufactured than Orlando, where she had become a designated player? — but combining that with everyone coupling all around her had been too much. "So, no," Margo said, "I wouldn't say it was fun."

Gale pulled away from the curb and crossed the shopping street to turn left onto the leafy boulevard called Commonwealth Avenue. The sun was directly overhead, but lots of people were clearly just getting their day going, walking generic or name-brand dogs while holding cardboard cups of coffee, whose value was likewise indicated by trademarks. A street person pushed a shopping cart inside of which, a perfect fit, was a blue recycling bin being used for refundables collected from trash bags. The cart's proprietor rested from his labors on a typical green park bench, drawing smoke from a cigarette that was also likely

begged or borrowed. Children in strollers or on bikes with training wheels were being guided, but in the opposite direction,
toward the Public Garden, which was, in Michelin terminology,
worth a detour. "I love this city," Gale said, but with a strong,
audible regret.

They approached Kenmore Square, which had never bene-
fited from any kind of plan. Margo knew all about Fenway Park
because she'd re-created it, including the Green Monster of a
wall, in Orlando. She liked the way the ballpark was right in the
middle of things, and she remembered how as a child, during the
season, she'd be lying in bed and, depending on the wind, hear
the fans' roar. Farther along, the green transit trains came up
from underground and became trolleys. She liked that too.

Making a left onto Kent Street, at the domed synagogue that
looked like a planetarium, Gale took a short detour. Slowing to
turn right, she pulled to the curb again and stopped. Here in
Brookline, eternal in its everlasting brick, was her children's elementary school, unchanged by time: in the classroom windows
were orange construction-paper pumpkins with black triangle
eyes and grins with missing teeth. "I forgot about Halloween this
year," Gale said. Where she lived now, as Margo knew all too
well, the houses were too far apart for children to go trick-or-
treating on foot, so parents had to drive them from house to
house.

"It's tomorrow," Margo said. Her last real Halloween had
been right here in this cozy neighborhood, where every house
offered candy. During Chanukah and Christmas the decorations
would make clear which house was which, but Halloween was
everybody's holiday. In their Chestnut Hill, Pennsylvania, neighborhood, which was even fancier than the nearby Chestnut Hill
here in Massachusetts, every house was obliged to have Christmas lights. Behind floor-to-ceiling windows, gigantic trees proclaimed an excess worthy of Martha Stewart. All the men wore

red pants and green neckties embroidered with holly berries or candy canes. The eggnog was lethal, and someone always tripped on a rug or down a few stairs, but since every man who lived there practiced one of three professions — law, medicine, banking — there was usually a doctor in the house.

Priscilla had always given the Christmas Eve party, because her mother and grandmother had handed it down along with the angel for the top of the tree. What a shock it was when Gale told Bob the point of having a house in the Virgin Islands was so they could spend school vacations in a state of relaxation rather than with tension headaches caused by good cheer laced with false hopes. Gale had tried giving the party once, their first Christmas, but her expectations were confirmed when Bob's children failed to include her children on their Christmas shopping lists. The next year, and every year since, Gale and her kids and Bob spent Christmas on St. John, where, one by one, his children and his mother became all too glad to join them. At eighty-eight Grandmother Oakley was "strictly ideal" according to Charlie, but Gale admired her for holding out against easier conversions to tropical winter weather. Gale loved St. John for the holidays because the perennial bushy poinsettias were bigger than sacrificial evergreens.

Margo really wanted to ask whether her mother and Gary had had sex in addition to their doughnuts, but instead she asked about Charlie and Beth. "How soon do you think they'll have their kids? Because this is where they're going to go to school too, aren't they?" Margo didn't mean to sound critical, just envious.

"Soon. They could do worse, don't you think?" To prove her point, Gale said this public school system was better than most private schools.

"True." For once, Margo didn't need to contrast her own bad experience. She surprised herself and her mother too by saying,

"I'd give anything to have this simple a life." Of course her ability to say so meant she probably never would, or could.

∞

Sandra's strategy for getting through these next few hours was to count backward from the time of their flight. If they planned more than enough time at the airport to return the car and check the bags, and doubled the hour it had taken on Friday to cover no distance at all through the tunnel, they'd barely arrive at the brunch when it would be time to leave it. She'd made two other, related promises to herself: to hold off drinking until after take-off, and before then to attract zero attention to herself. She wished this had been her goal the day before, but as her mother put it when she married Gary, "Better late than never."

To her pointing out that he'd shaved, Gary had again used the available truth, that he'd gone out for breakfast. "Yesterday," she'd answered, "you didn't bother to shave. You went straight from the Cape to the hotel dining room." He'd said, "But today I did it differently," so she'd responded, "That much is pretty obvious."

But she had no overall plan. Especially after having had a bit too much to drink, she could use a moment's orientation in order to decide what, or what not, to think. Even though she'd tried to keep him from escaping into the camouflage of sleep, he was so far gone so quickly he didn't even snore in the usual way. If there was a use to be made of these fifteen or twenty minutes, she'd find it. In the meantime, meaning would accrue, like interest.

She packed both their suitcases, putting their combined dirty laundry in one and in the other some specially requested *Cheers* souvenirs: four decks of cards for her mother, and for Jason a glass mug he would use for pencils until she said he was old enough to drink beer. The jacket that matched her gold dress was with a note in Gary's handwriting, so at least he'd checked in on her at some point to make sure she hadn't choked on her own vomit. Which she hadn't. Things could be worse.

At the other extreme, where things could be better, was the abstract possibility that "nothing" had happened, but the chances of that were so slim her gambling mother would have advised her not to take the bet. Clearly, then, the reality lay somewhere between life and death, or, to be exact, somewhere just shy of those two: tolerable/intolerable. How did that sound?

After a long shower she spent a lot of time on her hair, getting it to spring back to life, and then she dressed in the last of her specially purchased outfits, a pinto-inspired black and white suit with a skirt short enough to display her well-exercised legs. Gale had legs too, but Sandra had the added advantage of breasts. Cantaloupe-sized, Gary called them the first time she let him see them.

Once she got him home, she'd make sure he remembered that she'd rescued him, and if he didn't seem to, she'd remind him. Plus, she'd given him not just permission but encouragement to build his dream house, something neither of his two other wives had done. With the settlement from Chloe he'd invested in commercial real estate, but the crash of '89 occurred before he got his money out. The reasons he moved to Tucson were two: he disbelieved he could ever make another comeback and, in making himself a list of the most consoling landscapes in the world he'd traveled, it turned out the desert won. Immediately he found Sandra, who convinced him that his devalued property made perfectly good collateral. That she also had a piece of land to sell him was only a bonus. The real beauty — even Gary said so — was the way she helped him realize there was enough of him left for her to see his genius. For example, she'd never appreciated the stars until he came along and pointed out constellations through windows he'd had cut for that purpose alone. Like him, she could be thrilled by millions of stars seen from more millions of miles away. She'd brought him back once, so she could do it again. And this time it would be easier, since the house was already built.

Sandra didn't rush for the phone, in order to let the noise begin to waken Gary. "Hi," she answered, then, "Hey!" and "Hi!" again, this time to show what a good idea it was for Jason to call precisely that moment. "*Sure*, Jason," she said, "he's right here." To Gary she said, "Your son wants to discuss something important with you. He won't say what."

Gary didn't open his eyes, but he held out a hand for the receiver and knew to hold it against his ear. "Hey," he also said, but without any energy, "what's happening." It was a mere greeting, not a question.

Jason's voice was uniquely deep for a ten-year-old. Completely prepubescent, he nevertheless sounded more like an old man whose whole life had been an adventure and who'd be only too glad to recount it from start to finish. "I made my costume," he began, "which I've been working hard on this entire time. Guess what it is?"

Nothing at all came to mind. Gary said, "I give up."

"A jack of hearts!"

This meant nothing to him. Working to ascribe meaning, again Gary failed. The phone slipped from his hand.

"Sit *up*," Sandra said. "Talk to Jason!"

He did. Or at least he listened.

"First Nana bought me three white T-shirts and red, blue, and yellow permanent paints and a black laundry marker. Then, as I was about to draw freehand, on the way home we passed this copy place and Nana bet me it's possible to blow up a playing card really big. Actually, three cards." Jason paused, because Gary was supposed to ask him, "And is it?" But he went ahead and provided his own answer. "It is!"

Gary listened to Jason's enthusiasm over Nana's carrying a deck of cards everywhere at all times, and to Jason's meticulously detailed description of the huge cards: the queen's head-dress, the king's belt buckle and the jeweled grip of his sword, the jack's mustache. "The ten's too plain for me," Jason explained, "so I decided to exaggerate a year or two. How old is a jack anyway? And that's how I also came up with the idea of the mustache. Cool, huh?"

Gary said, "Very."

"Mom's holding a flower — ever notice that before about the queen? — but it's okay, I made it a cactus bloom. I gave you an old-fashioned haircut that curls under, plus a beard. You ought to grow one."

"I wish I'd thought of that," Gary said. "No kidding. But let me get this straight: you drew —"

"*Traced.*"

"Traced three face cards onto three T-shirts?"

"Yes!" Jason waited for him to get it.

But Gary had to say, "I don't get it."

"We three will be the Hearts family on Halloween! It took me sixteen hours total." Then he asked, "Can I talk to Mom?"

Sandra compensated for Gary, because she not only instantly understood the medium, but the message too: "You're so smart, sweetie. What an original idea!" Then she said, "I know it, us too, we both can't wait to see you in a few hours. Love you."

Sandra hung up the phone. "I said 'Love you' and guess what Jason said? 'Heart you.' Pretty cute for a boy, don't you think?"

"Sure," he said, his tone implying, "if you say so."

"Hold it right there," she said, her hand raised like a crossing guard, "we're talking a ten-year-old here, okay? We're not comparing Jason with Madison Avenue."

"I agree it's a cute idea." He tossed the sheet back and went into the bathroom. At the sink he put shaving cream on his face and, white-bearded, he said, "Jason thinks I should wear a beard. You think so?"

"You know I hate beards." But she couldn't let him get away with making her apologetic. She had the advantage, and she wasn't going to lose it to him over nothing. "At least the Hearts is a friendlier name than the one you gave us, the Burrs." When she first heard his name she said, "Ouch!," implying prickers, but now Sandra shivered as if she'd caught a chill. "Brrrr."

Gary took a cold shower, but just to wake up. Back in his less dressy brown boots and a tan suit he almost hadn't brought — never assuming he'd wear each of the other two out, around the clock — Gary checked his reflection. What a good idea to wear the cactus flower tie Sandra made him buy. Look how it drew attention away from his face, which by now was a poor imitation of his own, as if he'd died and this was the best they could do with his remains.

"How do I look? I mean, to you," Sandra asked him. She didn't pose herself, and neither did she smile.

"Good, just like the day I met you." As long as Gary could stick with the truth, he would.

"Thanks, but as you might remember, we met at night." As she crossed the room to give him a chance to appreciate all she'd done for him, starting that night, he picked up their two bags to make his arms unfree. So she took the opportunity to remind him, "You weren't in very good shape when I found you, were you?" If she made Gary sound like a stray dog she'd found and fed and bathed and brushed, all the better. At the time, he said she'd saved him, taking him in.

"No" was all he said. It went without saying that he wasn't in very good shape right here either.

When Sandra leaned in to kiss him she dizzied him with her perfume. "Let's go get this over with and get out of here." She meant get out of Boston as well as this predicament.

Again Gary checked his image in the full-length mirror on the closet door. Everything was the same in this room as in Gale's, including his reluctance to leave. At least he looked more presentable than he felt.

In this extra minute she got an idea, and before she'd tell him what it was, she had Northwest on the line. "Yes, unexpectedly we have to get back home sooner than the plane we're booked on." She had the tickets in her purse, so it was easy to provide information. She told Gary she couldn't believe she hadn't had this idea yesterday or the day before, since she'd had the feeling as soon as they arrived at the restaurant and Cousin Ed took over.

Instead of saying something like, "Give me the phone," Gary had a better idea.

"Two," Sandra told the airline representative.

"One," said Gary.

∞

Bob took a cab whose driver looked to be about his own age and distinguished enough to have been a white-collar professional, although in the Soviet Union. He had a book of maps to read but almost no English to speak.

Eve's father's house was on the far side of Brookline, almost on the Chestnut Hill line, a coincidence Bob and Herb had established as Bob was leaving the hotel the night before. "I'll drop you off," Herb had volunteered, "the wedding's over anyway, isn't it?" Needless to say, it confused him that there could be two Chestnut Hills.

The real problem had been Bob's, however: the desperate feeling of going home alone to Priscilla's huge empty house. It was so uncharacteristic to act with spontaneity, he'd almost failed to recognize that what he'd done was act an urge. No matter that while they were gone mail had been delivered for Gale, proving her existence; Bob's impulse was a need to give his own wishes — for once — priority. Gale was absent, in spite of the fact that the pillows on her side of the bed bore the scent of her moisturizer. It frightened him that all his adult life he'd met the needs of his patients so conscientiously, he never understood this was at the expense of his own needs.

After Priscilla's death, Bob had wished for someone just like Gale to come into his life, and once she did, he told her all of his wishes had come true. There was one more wish he ought to have made: that she'd be there always. This didn't explicitly mean he feared she would leave him, but they hadn't their entire marriage gotten along as poorly as these last two days, and the cause of the tension was clearly, outrageously, Gary. His wife Sandra wasn't un-outrageous herself, but except for the drinking, it wasn't her fault. Bob didn't like to think in terms of people being driven to drink, because he'd always believed Priscilla's refusal to get help indicated that she was her own driver. In the case of Sandra, it seemed justified to blame Gary. In those foolish cowboy boots he surely saw himself as irresistible, though if you asked Bob, Gary looked like a delayed adolescent. This was what made him dangerous.

Since the cab driver could make no sense of the dispatcher anyway, instead of shrill radio static they listened to Mozart. After two tries, Bob managed to decipher the word "engineer" — "Bridge!" the driver shouted in exasperation — but that was the extent of their conversation about employment opportunities in what was now Russia. As they came for the third time into Cleveland Circle, Bob also raised his voice — "Stop!" — so he could call from a pay phone. As it turned out they were, and had been for some time, only a few hundred yards from Herb's house. They were supposed to have continued straight, toward the reservoir, then turned left and gone uphill to the big stucco house with the best view.

"There's my car," Bob said, although strictly speaking it was Gale's car. On their tenth anniversary he'd given her this tin-colored Mercedes, presenting her the keys in a little envelope that said, as if written in a southern accent, "Happy Tinth!" Unlike yesterday, she hadn't complained then that it was too generous of him; rather, just like Charlie, she'd said she planned to drive it until their twenty-fifth, if not longer. He had every intention of reaching that anniversary too, although in the year 2007 he'd be seventy-nine.

"Beautiful house," Bob told Herb, who answered the door himself because this was something he never grew tired of hearing. The front hall was marble from the quarry Michelangelo used, as if Herb were a Medici, or at least the governor of the commonwealth.

"Too big since my wife died, but for her I keep it." Herb exaggerated: his wife had been the one who'd thought it was too big, from the very day he bought it.

Bob said, "I know exactly what you mean. Me too." For this shared experience alone, he was glad he'd come back.

"I knew I was right about you. You're Charlie's grandfather, I said, but Evie said no." Herb added, "Half the time I'm wrong because I forget, so do me a favor, will you? Tell Evie I was right." With a comforting hand on Bob's arm, Herb asked, "How long ago did your wife pass away?"

For simplicity's sake Bob decided to answer, "Sixteen years." He'd been married to Gale for twelve, and it had taken two to get her and a short relationship with someone else first, in between, in order to relearn the basics.

"Mine's a year last month, so the gravestone's only a couple weeks old. It's why Beth postponed the wedding." Bob's expression conveyed a confusion, and Herb said, "You might not have heard about it." By "it" he meant the postponement he himself had told Beth wasn't necessary at all.

"No, I didn't hear she'd died. I'm sorry." Bob was too polite to ask why Herb waited an entire year to get the stone carved, but this was because he was assuming it was on account of Herb's grief or, as Gale would suggest, his denial. Bob knew little about religious customs other than his own.

Herb received Bob's sympathy with a nod, and in a rush of words he said, "But I didn't mean to trap you at the door to listen to my troubles, did I? Come in, come in! Nice wedding, wasn't it? Beautiful car you gave the kids." Herb put a fraternal arm around Bob, who responded by having a feeling of gratitude he was about to express when Herb asked him, "What's your name again?"

Just then Gale came in from the terraced yard, through the door on the other side of the house. She answered Herb's question for him, but as an exclamation: "Bob!" Since she was coming to see if Gary had arrived yet, she felt caught in the act. "Oh!"

"Hello, darling," Bob said and closed the distance between them with eager strides. "This is my new wife," he said to Herb without wishing to further bewilder him.

It took Gale these two seconds to remember it would be appropriate for her and Bob to kiss each other hello.

"Wait a minute," Herb intervened. "And here I felt sorry for you!" Revealing that he wasn't as dumb as he feigned, he bestowed upon Bob a conspiratorial wink as he told him, "You're on your own from here on in, pal." As Herb crossed the marble floor he was careful to land each step toe-heel, toe-heel, for the best resounding effect.

Because she couldn't look into Bob's face immediately, with deliberate precision Gale noted his gray-and-white-checked button-down shirt and silk paisley tie, navy light woolen blazer, medium-weight gray slacks, shined cordovan penny loafers.

In response to her thorough inventory, Bob asked, neither seriously nor self-consciously, "How do I look?" It was a small joke between them, because he always looked the same, and wanted to.

Only once had Gale tried to get him to switch from Brooks Brothers to something a little more daring, but he'd politely refused her: "I guess I'm not confused about who I am." He noted the shadows under her eyes, and her nervous hand over her mouth, as if she were trying to stop herself from saying something she didn't want to say.

Apparently he didn't want to hear whatever it was. "You were right. I shouldn't have gone back home. I was being overly cautious. Obsessive, as you might say." He took that hand of hers in his and said, "At the hospital everybody did fine without me, but I didn't, without you. I didn't do fine at all."

In addition to his words, Gale also heard, from the cobblestone courtyard outside the front door, the sound of two car doors being shut. Like someone about to be in an accident, she braced herself.

"As you said about Jane yesterday," he went on, "it's easy to fly here from Philadelphia for a few hours. I didn't want to miss the opportunity today to tell you everything I might not have put into words sufficiently, or often enough. I need you to hear me before you —"

Gale shut her eyes so tightly she saw little bubbles of colored light, like balls being thrown at her from a distance. She couldn't bear to hear him say "leave me," but the word he chose instead was "respond." This was even harder to imagine.

"Promise me this, will you?"

She nodded her head, which meant yes.

But it was only David Haynes arriving with the woman he'd met at the wedding reception, who'd believed him at first when he claimed to be related to the famous jazz Hayneses, but who nevertheless agreed to show him where to hear good music in Boston once he confessed his was the other, untalented Haynes family. "I had to drop back by the hotel for the directions," he explained, "but I figure it's no longer my job to keep track of everybody. Hey, I thought you left town, man." David offered his hand to Bob and kissed Gale, then presented Sondra. "We're not the last ones, though."

For Gale, the feeling extended beyond relief, into reprieve.

"Gary and the other Sondra — *San*dra — were still checking out. They said to say they're coming." He only meant it would have been a good thing for them to say. "Actually, they didn't," David corrected himself, "but I assume they are."

Sondra glanced around admiringly and told Gale and Bob, "Your house is beautiful. David told me all about the times he visited."

David said, "No, theirs is in Philadelphia, this one is somebody else's. Whose it is I have no idea, do you?"

Like someone afraid of missing something, Herb reappeared and was instantly rewarded, claiming credit not only for owning the house but for remembering that David was the best man. "This guy here keeps confusing me," he said, gesturing to Bob, then patting him on the shoulder. "But luckily I'm the kind that likes surprises."

It went unsaid that Bob and Gale were the kind that didn't. David took the opportunity to mention the Saab again, as an example of the best surprise he'd ever witnessed.

"Here she comes," said Herb as Margo came in from the terrace. He announced that he was about to give Margo a tour of the house, and anyone else who wanted to come along was welcome. "She's an architect," he added, implying she wasn't the first architect who'd wanted to see his house.

Just as her mother had, when Margo saw Bob she said, "Oh!" But at least she had the presence to add, "Hi, Bob." If there was any reason at all for anybody to laugh, she'd have risked something ironic like, "The plot thins."

8

GALE TOOK BOB DOWN THE STONE STEPS INTO THE LOWER garden, where she remembered there once had been a swing set, replaced, when the grandchildren grew older, by a vegetable garden divided into quadrants. Now it was only daylilies, and Eve had already pointed out to Gale the variety that had been named for Herb.

Because Herb was no philosopher, he couldn't put into words that the reason he chose to grow daylilies was that, if you have enough of them, you don't notice that they only live for a day. As with a hedge of bright, trumpety hibiscus, the eye is daily drawn to the full bloom, away from a confrontation with the passage of time. You don't remember that yesterday morning's blossoms have become shriveled cylinders of spent flower, translucent petals removed from basic life support. There's no such thing as extraordinary measures in this system, so you're a fool if you don't go into the garden every day, all summer long. The lily named for him had a plum-colored eye.

In Gale's garden — that is, Priscilla's — the perennial border had been so ingeniously designed it served as a perpetual calendar. Every kind of flower called to mind another — peonies that looked like poppies, dahlias like camellias, mums like anemones, roses hybridized to resemble peonies as well as dahlias and chrysanthemums — and the show kept rolling too, from earliest spring until the second frost. Priscilla's own favorite had been the rainbow-inspired iris the Greeks named the "eye of heaven." According to the gardener she'd hired to keep the garden, eternally, the iris marked the start of Priscilla's own small yearly growth spurt. Her good time of year — her only — began when the iris leaves spiked their way out of the chilly soil, bearded arrowheads blooming on stiff slender shafts aimed for the sky.

Gale and Bob gazed beyond Herb's daylilies toward the reservoir and Boston's skyline, the three distinct dimensions of near-middle-far providing ample perspective. Actually, though, they were merely waiting for each other to speak.

Gale's apologetic tone of voice contrasted with the disembodied content of her observation, but at least she'd found a way to begin. "My profession was founded on the belief that unresolved experience will continue to seek resolution until it's found."

This went without saying, and besides, in medical school Bob had thought about becoming a psychiatrist, so he knew there was more to say. He waited.

"It was stupid of me to think, to whatever extent I did, that Gary and I wouldn't have had unfinished business," she said.

Unwilling to allow Gale to excuse herself, in case this was her intention, Bob assured her, "You and I have unfinished business too."

"I know."

"I feel mine takes priority." Bob blinked, then fixed her with his eyes, whose irises pristinely resembled a pair of blue planet Earths as seen from space. "You are my wife. I'm your husband. You married me."

Margo's tour of the house had been postponed by the arrival of Gary and Sandra, so Margo used the commotion of Herb's welcome as her chance to escape to the garden. But there were her mother and Bob facing each other, and Bob had both of

Gale's hands in his. To Margo it looked like they were getting married again. Before she could altogether disappear, Gale said, "Hi, dear."

Margo walked across the grass to them and said, "Charlie sure pulled a fast one, didn't he? He got me to act like the magician's assistant, the one who gets sawed in half when the trick fails." In other words, they should know not to blame her. She was a victim too, because Bob's presence here meant, at the very least, that she'd lost her planned time with her mother.

"It's nobody's fault," said Gale.

"Easier said than done," Margo said, ignoring Bob. She felt that terminology like "in the long run" and "deferred gratification" lacked heart. Only a coward would call these word-packages a sentiment.

Bob said, "I'm sorry to ruin your plans, Margo, but your mother and I will be driving back to Philadelphia from here. We hope you'll come along."

"No thanks." Margo wasn't proud of the feeling she had, so she wasn't going to let him, of all people, see it. It was the same feeling she'd had when Gale said she'd be marrying Bob.

"We'll still have tomorrow," Gale offered.

But it wasn't Margo's job — the way it *was* her mother's — to put herself in someone else's place. She was allowed to feel exactly what she felt, which was that, once again, she and her feelings meant nothing at all to her mother. Clearly, it didn't matter to Gale that she'd been counting on their time alone together. How could her mother think it could be the same with Bob there?

"Wait," Bob said. Margo had turned her back on them.

"I've *been* waiting!" It didn't matter that she was twenty-seven years old. She recognized herself as the girl whose needs were last on the list.

Gale knew Margo wanted to discuss Orlando and whether or

not, or how, her projected move might be a mistake. Gary had told Margo that Disney was a good way to get credentialed in the field, but only Gale knew how insecure a big move like this would make Margo feel.

Anticipating their move to Philadelphia, Margo had argued, "Why can't Bob move to Brookline instead? His own kids are at boarding school."

"He can't move his practice," Gale had answered, as if she and Bob had ever seriously discussed it.

"And *you* can?"

"Well, mine's still being established, so it makes more sense to move mine." Gale had been naive as well as very wrong about this. In fact her practice had stalled when she made the move, for the simple reason that in Philadelphia she got no referrals because nobody had heard of her work.

"Let him commute," Margo'd challenged, "or let him wait until we get out of high school."

"Honey, we've been over and over this, believe me, and I feel that what's best for us all is for me to move the three of us there. He has such a big house," she'd offered as if it were hers to give. Actually, Gale hadn't understood at this point that according to the terms of Priscilla's will, Bob was more or less required to continue to live there.

"For your information, you're making a dreadful mistake." All Margo had meant at the time was in regard to her own life.

Bob's daughter Jane had liked Agnes Irwin during the few years she'd gone there before being sent off to boarding school, so, despite the long daily commute, it seemed a logical place to send Margo, even though Margo was coming from a happy and successful freshman year at Brookline High. In this new, all-girl school, where the other students had all known one another since nursery school, Gale vainly tried to console Margo by saying, "Girls can be mean without always meaning to be."

Because those girls had successfully made Margo feel inferior to them, she had firmly believed she was inferior.

Gale recognized what a disastrous choice the school was, but it took a while for her to figure out an alternative, by which time Margo was going to be a junior and, or so the college placement adviser said, she ought to focus her concentration there if she ever expected to amount to anything.

From this vantage point of Herb's daylily garden, it seemed miraculous to Margo that she hadn't destroyed herself with an eating disorder or a pregnancy or by getting kicked out of school for plagiarism and then lying when confronted with the hard evidence. God knows she'd tried, in all three ways, but apparently — like Gale, like Charlie, even like Gary — she too had become a survivor. Each of them had made it out of family situations that could have been better but also could have been much worse. And by this means Margo saw that she was able to put her needs aside for the moment, because she'd learned how to.

"Margo, listen, please," Bob implored. His blue eyes were intent on Margo now, and she met him more than halfway. "All of a sudden," he said, "it hit me for the first time — the very first time, I think, in my life — that I could have done things all differently. Especially with you."

The three of them made an equilateral triangle now as Bob continued, "Charlie was always so much easier to please than you, and I don't mean this at all critically, only as a fact. As a result, I missed being as good a father to you as I'd wanted to be. Charlie needed so badly to please everybody all the time, he never questioned me. But you did. I had a chance, in other words, to hear your needs, but didn't." He wasn't as uncomfortable speaking these words as he might have imagined he'd be. Not that he'd imagined it. "Do you remember asking me why I didn't move to Brookline if I wanted to marry your mother, since there was only one of me and there were three of you?"

Margo nodded. This had been on their first visit to see Bob's house. She hadn't been at all impressed by it and had asked Bob where all the neighbors lived.

"I said it was impossible. Now I can see that it was not only *not* impossible, it was a better idea. For those three years I could so easily have been a visiting physician here, so much more easily than it was for your mother to move, before she was fully established in the field, to an unreceptive city like Philadelphia. Then you could have finished high school the way you'd planned." Margo opened her mouth, but Bob wasn't finished. "I couldn't see until it was all over that your high school experience wasn't at all the thing you'd had in mind. It just didn't occur to me. I'm sorry, dear."

Mostly, when he called her dear, she felt patronized. "It turned out okay," she said, sounding like Charlie.

"I could have put the goddamn house into a trust," Bob said with a bitterness that was as new to him as to Gale. "I wish I had." Even right this minute he made a discovery. "I know how much I wanted my children to have a good mother, as if yours could make up for theirs. But my own kids had been so long gone from there, it seems there was no bringing them back. How could there be? And why should it be you who has to sacrifice?"

Margo said, laying her head against his shoulder, "Oh Bob, it's okay. I never appreciated enough what you did for my mom, the way you treated — *honored* — her. And made her feel safe." Margo could tell without looking that Gale's eyes were closed and her mouth was trembling. "And as for me, well, you were there, weren't you? You tried." She didn't mean to criticize her own father, who had also tried, though not there. "Thank you, Bob."

"I'm sorry." Bob wished to give Margo the equivalent of a car; that is, of offering himself as her father. "I'm so sorry," he said again, now that he'd finally understood this was the thing Margo wanted.

"Thank you," Margo said, and meant it. "However, that's all I want to hear at the moment. You two finish on up now, or whatever, and I'll meet you back in Philadelphia tonight or tomorrow morning. We'll still get our day, Mom." As if Bob and Gale were sitting in their places at Priscilla's dining room table and Margo still had homework, she asked, "So now may I please be excused?"

∞

There was too much food, and the bagels were so fresh and Sandra was so hungry, she ate two of them. She'd never seen them before with cranberries, so once again Herb told her she was his favorite. He wasn't the kind of host who intimidates guests into drinking more than they might have if left to their own devices, but he was the kind who coaxes guests into eating more than they would choose. Herb presided over every meal as if it were a survey.

"Rate this," he charged Sandra, who never liked cream cheese in the first place.

"I've got your number, Herb. You're an old-fashioned flirt." Still, she took his littlest finger into her mouth. "That's it. Enough."

"Like it?"

"No. What the hell is it?" The orange juice was spiked with champagne. She gulped it down to chase the taste, and he poured more from a pitcher.

"Guess."

"That's what my kid says a hundred times a day." She took another sip and pretended to be aggravated. "Pickles."

Herb was thrilled. "Close. Capers."

She always confused anchovies and capers. "I hate capers. How could you do that to me?" She always confused "masochist" and "sadist" too. "You're a masochist, Herbie."

He beamed.

Now that they were on a nickname basis — he should call her Sandie — she said, "You've got to explain this to me: why would anybody, given the choice, not get married here? I mean, forgive me, Herbie, but there's no comparison between this place and yesterday's ordinary house. This one's so —"

"Majestic?" Herb was a capitalist, trading up on her zest.

"That's exactly the word! Plus, romantic. It's right out of a fairy tale, so what better place could there be to get married?"

"And that's what I said when I offered it to them, but kids these days, you know, they're so — what's the word here? — frugal. They're so frugal in what they will allow themselves to want." Herb had no idea that Beth's argument was with the very concept of the fairy-tale wedding.

"But yesterday's *was* Beth's house growing up, I guess, so maybe that's a good reason."

Herb countered with, "My wife would have loved nothing more than having her first granddaughter's wedding in the garden." Of course he was speaking entirely for himself.

"I can understand, and I was very sorry to hear about your wife. But, and I hope I'm not offending you, there's always you. So here's to you, Herbie, and to second chances." Sandra drained her glass and had a fabulous idea. "Maybe I could introduce you to my mother, huh? She's single. I could plan your wedding for you, right here in your garden. How about it?"

Herb asked, "Is she Jewish?"

"Not yet," Sandra exaggerated.

He patted her on the head as if she were a star pupil. "I like your entrepreneurial spirit. So, will I like your mother as much as you?"

"Better, because she's available and I'm not. I'm already happily married." At the moment this too was a bit of an exaggeration.

David Haynes brought Sondra into the dining room to ask Sandra where Gary was. He said he had to get back to New

York, so he wanted to say goodbye, but his eagerness to leave conveyed that he intended to get to know Sondra better before the last shuttle to La Guardia. The feeling looked to be mutual.

Sandra had kept one eye on Gary the whole time, but this conversation with Herb was distracting, because she could so easily imagine her mother and Herb having a fine time together. Of all the men in her mother's life, not one of them had been rich. What a nice change. "On the terrace," she answered. When David shook his head, Sandra said, "Not on the terrace? Then whose tan suit is that?"

David looked through the screened window and said, "Paul? I already found Paul."

"*Paul!* Then where the hell's Gary?" It was true: Paul's tan suit was just like Gary's, except that Paul's academic version of it didn't fit him. Almost altogether sober, Sandra had reflexes so sharp she hooked her arm through David's and said, "We'll go find him." To Herb she said, "Be right back, Herbie. Hold on to that thought."

David reluctantly let go of Sondra's hand and got dragged off by the older, paler, less exotically named woman, who seemed so determined — as if now she had two reasons, her own and her mother's — not to let Gary ruin everything.

"That's okay, Sandra, just tell him for me —"

"No, I know he would hate to miss you. You're Charlie's best man, after all." Could he argue with that?

As they went from the dining room into the front hall, Margo was emerging from the small bathroom under the staircase. She asked, "Have you seen these faucets? Curlicue dolphins that look Pompeiian."

"Come with us," Sandra said. "We're on a search. We'll check all the upstairs faucets." She grabbed Margo's hand and pulled her along.

Because the house tour had been postponed by Bob's arrival, Margo hadn't been upstairs yet. So she wasn't opposed to the idea, especially when at the top of the stairs she saw two wall sconces that alone justified the excursion.

The first bedroom they came upon had what Margo identified as a trademark Schumacher print, but everywhere. Sandra told Margo she personally thought it was an overkill effect, since you could barely see the bedposts holding up the canopy. "Too darling!" she pronounced it. The print-on-print made the room spin.

In the hall a faux-marble table held a real Tiffany lamp, whose shade kaleidoscoped the jeweled light. Margo too closely inspected it, so Sandra tried to rush her, saying David had a plane to catch. "Hurry!" she coaxed.

David's worry showed in his face, and it didn't look like it was only about his own schedule. Margo missed seeing it, though, because the wallpaper had been so skillfully applied, not a single seam was visible. She was thinking how much she'd hate to be in a museum with Sandra if she was always this impatient. Of course Sandra had no taste to start with, but Margo knew that already.

"Empty!" Sandra said at the door to another guest room, this one more formal, done in a green she'd never been fond of. "Where could they be?"

"Who?" asked Margo.

"Gary," David said. "I was looking for him to say goodbye." The absurd thing was that back at the hotel, while they were checking out, they'd kind of already said goodbye. That is, he'd said, "See you," which was good enough for David.

"And who?" Like a dog on a leash, Margo resisted being led. "Gary and who?"

Sandra didn't feel it necessary to clarify, so she didn't. She shifted her weight from one foot to the other and back. She could outstare anybody.

"No way," Margo told her. "Not me." Bob and Gale had come up from the lower garden soon after her, but Bob had just proved anything was possible. Margo already knew too much. She turned back toward the stairs and said, "Come on, David. Not you either."

"Wait!" It wasn't as if Sandra wanted to burst in on Gary and Gale all by herself. She hurried after Margo, who silently escaped down the carpeted staircase like a princess in magic slippers. David was right behind her.

From the top of the banister Sandra called to Margo, "No fair."

"Think about it," challenged Margo from the safety of the marble foyer stairway, which reverberated. With a peculiar expression on her face, a mix of pretend horror and real amusement, Margo asked, "How could you ever think I'd want to discover my parents together? I could be scarred for life."

∞

On the terrace, Margo found Bob. He and Eve were trading opinions on a colleague of Eve's whose work was written up in *Newsweek* before *The New England Journal of Medicine.* "Bad form," Bob said, without assuming it had been intentional on the part of the researcher. "Too bad," he added sympathetically.

"Where's Mom?" Margo asked this so casually Bob wouldn't think to worry. And Bob answered that he supposed she and Gary were saying goodbye. Bob appeared so unthreatened, Margo relaxed too. In Herb's yard there was no maple as gaudy as the tree next to the Gold house, but even if less theatrically, the leaves had turned here too, where summer and fall nicely coexisted.

But Sandra was less confident. She'd cut through the kitchen and gone out the side door and onto the wide lawn, which narrowed like a funnel at the stone steps into the upper garden. There was a rose trellis at the far end, with bright red cottage roses that still managed to be in bloom. Gary and Gale stood facing each other and, because Sandra saw this must be the place Herb had had in mind for the wedding ceremony, her own panic intensified irrationally. From the top of the garden stairs, it looked as if Gary and Gale could be getting married. Sandra screamed at them, "What are you doing? Stop that!"

She rushed down the uneven stone steps and ran across the grass. When she reached them, to keep from falling forward she lurched back and her high heels sunk in. She was fixed to the spot.

Gale tried to speak, but Sandra interrupted to tell Gary, "Just look at yourself. You even *look* guilty!"

Maybe, but he felt more like a guy who'd just lost everything to a twister that had roared through.

Gale wanted to suggest that Sandra might be overreacting. It wasn't like Gale to ask people to tone down their feelings, but she simply couldn't confront Sandra like this. Sandra was behaving like a crazy person. What if she was?

"Don't you *dare* criticize my reaction!" Sandra crossed her arms in front of her to keep from slapping Gary and pushing Gale to the ground.

"Wait," Gale managed to say, "I know just how you feel."

This stopped Sandra long enough for her to see that it could be true. She stepped from her shoes and sat down on the grass, folding her legs as if this were a yoga class and she could learn how to be at peace in the next hour and a half. If this took that long, however, there went their plane. "Okay, sit. Talk to me. I'll give you three minutes."

When Gale sat, Sandra made a helpful discovery: all Gale's height must be in her legs because, seated, they were exactly the same size. She could look directly into Gale's eyes, and did. And said, "Take off your sunglasses."

Luckily, Gale looked terrible. The skin around her eyes was puffy and discolored, and the distinctive olive green had become a generic gray. Her straight silver hair had turned to pewter, framing her bony face, and the skin on her neck was loose enough to crease. This was helpful too.

"Right now you have the advantage, don't you?" Sandra said. "No, don't put them back on. Look at me. Do I deserve what you've done?" She raised her hands to either side of her own face, her pink manicured fingers like eight arrows telling Gale where she must focus. "Look! Gary and I have a life. This person is his wife!"

And what if Gale herself had been able to shove her face into Jeannie's, to ask if she deserved this? What if she'd stood up for herself instead of disintegrating? She felt the same nausea at this moment as on that Saturday morning when Eve sat at Gale's round kitchen table to tell Gale what she'd learned about Gary and the babysitter. Witnessing consequences, whether caused *to* or *by* her, made her equally sick to her stomach.

Sandra charged Gary next. "And you, who were you when we met? You were Chloe Fortunado's castoff. A reject. Broke. Out of work. A ruin, you yourself said."

"Yes," Gary admitted.

"Who believed in you anyway? Who loved you?"

"You."

"And I've spent my best years on you because I saw you were good. Talented, sure, but a good person. Worth the trouble. Of course your mother raised you to think you were better than everybody else — everybody but her, that is — but I trusted you. I never believed you'd take advantage of me, because you owed me too much. Because it was me who saved you." Sandra smoothed the black-and-white-print pleats of her short skirt and popped her shoes free, brushing dirt from her heels. "And just for your information, we're not missing this plane. Not me, not you either."

Then she thought of another thing she wanted to tell Gale.

"You see, I'm not like you. I don't think it's inexcusable to fuck up. And I'd certainly never kick him out for fucking you." The rest of Sandra's sentence was, "The way you did."

Gary reminded her, "Since you weren't there, you don't know what happened."

"Oh?" Now Sandra looked to Gale. "Correct me if you have another version, but mine goes like this. You ask him if he loves her — the girl, that is — and he says no. You say get out. He goes. End of story." She shrugged, and her breasts rose into the V of her neckline. "Well?"

Gale said, "I never asked him." Until last night.

Gary said, "I never loved her," but as an assertion. As crucial evidence.

"That's what I've never understood, frankly. I'm not complaining, because otherwise, of course, I'd never have met my husband. But, especially for someone smart enough to become a psychologist, it seems real dumb." Now Sandra addressed Gale. "You must have been really freaked out to make such an enormous mistake."

"I was."

"So if you don't mind my asking: how come?" Sandra leaned forward over her lap, bypassing Gary, toward Gale. "I've always wondered." To protect herself she said, "Not that it's any of my business."

Gale said, "It's *the* question." Her elbows were locked, her arms set like props keeping the barn door closed after all the horses have escaped. "But I can't answer it in a few words."

"So it's none of my business, you're saying?" Fuck her. "I'm not so ignorant, you know, that you have to use simple sentences whenever I'm around. And it's not like only people who have college degrees are allowed to see a shrink, when every second person in the country's in a twelve-step. Who do you think you are, condescending to me?" Sandra pressed her shoulders down and took in a reservoir of air. "You can fuck my husband maybe. You can't fuck me."

Gary attempted a rescue. "This is impossible. We're all too tired and too worked up." The rescue failed.

"Speak for yourself — your*selves* — because Bob and I, the idiots, got plenty of sleep." Sandra checked her watch, as if to say the time for sympathy had run out.

But Gary had things to say too, so he tried again. "You just be quiet for a minute, will you? Jesus." Gary's famously warm hands were clammy. "I'm not proud of myself, not for anything I've done. I cheated on my wife and bailed out on my kids for eight years while I — I guess you'd have to say — chased my shadow." The circles under Gary's eyes were concentric. "When I woke up, lo and behold I had become a hired hand. My wife became my employer, and I barely noticed, until she let me go, what I'd become." Without any self-pity he said, "Those were my dues. Fair enough."

Now, though, he looked to Gale for some pity. "I'd hoped you would let me see you. I tried to get you to see me, just to *see* me."

"But I couldn't be seen by you."

"I never understood."

"I couldn't let you see how unhappy, how bad —" Her mother's words to her had been "how disgustingly fat" she was. "I didn't want you to see that I'd been devastated by you. What if I still loved you? Would I let you reject me twice? And since the first time you had no reason to betray me, why wouldn't you — how could you not? — again, if you had a decent reason? I thought you couldn't possibly love me."

"But what if I already always did?" Gary could let Sandra hear this because it was the truth. It was Gale he wanted to believe it.

"No, you couldn't have, then," Gale replied, "but only because I believed you couldn't. I was incapable of thinking you could." She'd already told Gary why.

Sandra said, "I just don't get it. What's the *reason?*"

"My mother died," Gale said. "She killed herself. My mother killed herself." The precise and entire answer to the question was "But not soon enough."

∞

The party was over. The New Jerseyites were herding up their kids, so the kids were scattering. Eve called two of them down from an apple tree with almost horizontal branches and offered to check the gardens. From the top of the steps she performed her piercing Manhattan cab-hailer whistle. Sandra jumped up. Such a he-man whistle had been her girlhood ambition too, but it was still unfulfilled.

"Visiting hours are almost up," Sandra said. Without a look back, she climbed the stone steps unsteadily, as if she were boarding a small boat in a swell.

Bob was coming across the lawn, having volunteered to check the lower garden for kids. Intercepting Sandra, he asked, "What's up?" Since this was her kind of question, she laughed and said, "Visiting hours."

In the lower garden Sandra and Bob circled the daylilies, and Bob called back to Eve, "Nope," to which Eve yelled down, "Thanks anyway."

"That's about it, huh? Thanks anyway," Sandra told Bob and smiled. "But nice meeting you."

"You too." He really meant it, too. "I admire you."

"You do?" She tipped her head, and now her smile wasn't ironic. "I got a different impression. Funny."

"The impression you got is that you reminded me of someone I had a problem dealing with. It was only a first impression, though, and an incorrect one. You were uncomfortable. You had every right to be. You drank too much."

"Scared to death," she admitted.

"Yes."

"You too?"

"No, but I should have been. I should have seen how anxious Gale was. Instead, I thought it had to do with Charlie or returning to Brookline after so much time."

"You wanted to. Think that."

"I suppose," Bob said. No, he would have to admit it hadn't occurred to him to worry. "No, in fact I take too much for granted." For one thing, he hadn't seen how exotic daylilies were when you looked them right in the eye.

Sandra told him, "She's lucky to have you, if you ask me." Bob had already aged better than Gary ever could. "You could have been a movie star if you hadn't gotten into medical school." Now she laughed out loud, to let him know she knew how dumb this sounded.

"Well, thanks." He was taking nothing more for granted, beginning now. "He's very lucky to have you." Bob didn't want to say his name, though.

"No joke. The shit."

"Exactly." A breeze moved across the reservoir, its path a fan of ripples. Above, honest-to-God Canada geese took advantage of that current of air, their own more purposeful V directing them toward South Carolina.

"Look at that. So how do you think those birds decide who gets to lead?"

Bob knew for sure. "It's so hard, they have to trade off. The lead goose has to break the air."

"Goose? Oh yeah, I see the neck now. Huh. We don't have geese in Tucson. Only what you'd call birds of prey, I guess." She laughed. "You know, like vultures eating human carcasses in old cowboy movies."

"Sounds like, 'A nice place to visit, but I —'"

"God, that's *all* I'd need." The thought of Gale living across town made her literally shiver. "Don't even think of moving there."

But neither was he immune to feeling threatened by their common although quite uncertain futures. "What do you suppose they're saying to each other?"

"Goodbye." For good measure Sandra added, "Or else."

So they were both able to admit to wishing they hadn't scared each other off. They could have used, and been, allies: he could have advised her not to have so much to drink, and she could have told him he was a complete fool to fly home. She did anyway, now. "I couldn't believe you did that. I, at least, had no choice! But you voluntarily got on an airplane? That's criminally foolish."

"I know. I had a second thought at the airport, but I talked myself out of it. It was when I walked through my own front door that I knew what a mistake —"

"I wish you'd called me right away. See, that's what I mean. We should have teamed up."

It was a funny thought, so they were both smiling as they went into the upper garden. Gale and Gary were sitting on a stone bench, straddling it like a seesaw, gripping the edges with both hands, clinging, and before Sandra could tell him time's up, Gary said, "I know. Be right there."

Bob and Sandra were confident enough to keep going, up the next set of steps, across the lawn and the terrace, into the house. Herb greeted them just inside the door, but it was to Sandra that he said, "There you are! I was afraid you left without telling me your mother's name."

Sandra smiled. Things were getting better every minute. "Maggie."

"Maggie! How could that be Jewish?"

"She's changing it. What should she change it to?" Sandra patted Herb's arm. "Seriously, though, didn't you say you sometimes come to Arizona? Will you promise to visit us?"

"Right now I'm thinking of a cruise." Herb had to ask his daughter, "Where's it go again, Evie?"

Eve answered blandly, "Tahiti." She thought it was the worst idea he'd ever had.

Herb said, "Right. Where what's-his-name lived."

Sandra said, "Marlon Brando."

"Ha! You're a funny kid." He patted Sandra's golden curls. "Gauguin. Paul Gauguin, the painter. Know him?"

"He's why Marlon Brando was inspired to move there, I heard."

Herb must have thought that was a perfect answer, because like a good audience he clapped his hands.

Margo came from the library, where she and Paul Gold were resting up after the chaos of helping to get New Jersey on the road. Paul had asked her what her plans were, and she'd told him they were up in the air. "But without parachutes."

"Good, you're here," Sandra told Margo. "Bob and I were just talking about you. We agreed we'd be a team next time. Right, Bob?"

Margo was so skilled at reading between the lines, she knew what Sandra had in mind, and said, "Don't count on it. I'm eloping."

"Next time?" It took Bob a second to realize she'd meant Margo would also get married one day. "We'll be ready," he said like a good sport, but discreetly he knocked on the banister, for better luck next time.

∞

As if the stone bench were a real seesaw, it seemed they had to get up together or both would fall. His hands had absorbed the stone's temperature, and when he placed them against her cheeks she said, "It was you putting your warm hand on my back, all this. Finally your hands have cooled off."

Gary closed the short distance between them, sliding toward

her. If she picked up her legs and put them around his waist, they could become a double helix. Nobody could separate them. "No," he said, "they haven't cooled."

But she didn't do her part, instead reminding, "You can't miss that plane." To start the process, she pushed herself back, not unlike an airplane backing away from the gate.

"You're still much more practical than I am." His arms landed in his own lap. "I could see missing it. I could see never going back. You and I would take a different plane somewhere new. Start over."

"Like fugitives." She unfolded the wings of her sunglasses, her only disguise.

"I've started over lots of times already. It's not hard. I've gotten good at it." He refastened the top button of his shirt and slid the knot of his necktie back up the inch he'd loosened it. "I'd be an itinerant contractor in some new part of the world that needs buildings."

Gale stared at him. "That's a serious invitation, isn't it?"

In ten seconds he had the whole thing planned out. "We'll be very happy."

"There's the difference between you and me. I've never started over like that. I'm not impulsive enough to, but I've also never had the opportunity to. I've always made the best of what I had, because —"

He interrupted to correct her. "That's not true. You were impulsive enough the night we met. And last night."

"— because I had children, I was about to say. So last night I must have felt they'd become adults. Sending Charlie off to his own future must have seemed to me like a permission to be that free."

"Charlie was oblivious." Gary didn't mean this as a criticism, only a fact.

"Yes, but Margo's still here." Gale watched the toes of her

shoes point her in the direction of the stone steps. There was too much to say in that short a distance.

"Margo's more successful than both of us put together," Gary said with a simplicity equal to his pride.

"Margo *isn't* oblivious. Margo has so much on her mind these days. She's the opposite of Charlie." Gale had to wonder how she'd managed to pretend this wasn't the case. "You saw. Margo wants it both ways, like a child does."

"Wants what both ways?"

"Fantasy and real life."

He was hoping she would say what Margo wanted was the same thing he did. "You're so clinical, Gale."

"It's what I do all day. It's my work. It's what I've caused to happen in my life." She said, "It wasn't easy."

Since this was an opportunity for him to apologize, he did.

Gale said, "I understood there wouldn't be patients lining up to greet me in Philadelphia, but I had no idea how demoralizing it could get. In Philadelphia I had to start over."

"So you *can* do it, see?"

"I hated it." She allowed herself to laugh nevertheless. "There's no such thing as an itinerant psychotherapist, for your information." She heard herself echo Sandra's "for your information," but she left it alone. Saying this goodbye was complicated enough.

"We'll move back to Boston, then."

"Stop!" Angrily, she said, "Don't oversimplify, don't trivialize." Gale could so easily have told Gary that her entire life had been his fault.

"Sorry." One thing he'd perfected over the years was how to express his regret.

She shook her head. "No. It's too hard." And here too she meant everything.

He chose this moment to risk asking the question with the yes or no answer. "This isn't the end again, right? Just tell me that much, yes or no."

"No," answered Gale without any hesitation.

They were at the bottom of the several stone steps that were too narrow for them both. "Wait, you have to say more. Will you call me? Can I call you? Will you meet me somewhere? What are we going to do next?"

She evaded his gaze.

"I know you can't *know,* but give me some idea," Gary said. "We're not a scientific experiment, we're a couple of middle-aged —"

"Contentedly married —"

"— lovers."

"Contentedly married."

"Not anymore." The more she complicated it, the easier it looked. "It's over for me," Gary said, already imagining what he'd tell Jason. This time — as opposed to telling Charlie and Margo that he and their mother weren't able to keep their marriage together — it would be the simple truth.

But Gale's point was, with *Bob* it wasn't over. The sorrow he'd expressed to Margo in the daylily garden was about missed opportunities he intended to make up for, to correct. This was a capacity their marriage also had, Bob was wanting Gale to see. If she were to walk away from him, it would be giving up on *two* dozen years: the dozen they'd already had, and the dozen to come.

Gary couldn't see Gale's eyes behind her sunglasses, but he saw the creases in her forehead, her mouth set in a worrisome way. Her determination had been such an asset in their marriage, with the one exception of that day she told him to pack his things. Now, reminded of the way she looked that morning, he could see her teeth were pressed together, the unrelenting muscles of her jaw confirming his egregious behavior. He wanted to say "Stop!" but he took what there was: she'd answered no to his question; no, it wasn't over, again. But she'd already turned away from him, to climb the stairs.

"You said it was my hand on your back, all this," Gary improvised, putting it there again, stopping her from continuing up. "So just remember it, because it will still be there when you go to sleep tonight and when you wake up. Every night, and every morning."

∞

Gary shut the heavy wooden screen door behind them without letting it make a sound, so once more their mere appearance was for Bob a surprise, and a relief. Sandra, timing them, was giving them one more minute before being forced to go out after them, so she could afford to be glad for her own sake when they showed up. She was in the midst of a show-and-tell with her pictures of their house — "Gary's dream house," she said — so she pretended not to have heard them come in. "This is our room," she was telling Eve about the bed he had designed. The blades of the ceiling fan blurred like a pinwheel.

Passing the next picture to Herb, she said, "Here's our son's room, see? Each cubby has a different color door. Jason's very artistic, very good color sense. And here's the pool."

"Very nice," Herb complimented Sandra, and to Gary he said, "You could be famous, for all I know. Very good, very unusual. Were you somebody's disciple that I would have heard of?"

"Pop —"

"What, that's a rude question?"

Eve said, "You always ask people if you should have heard of them. It looks like, if they're not famous, you're not interested."

"Don't be ridiculous, Evie," Herb said. "If I've got a Fortune 500 across the table, or some superstar, I want to know it. At my age I can't know everything ahead of time anymore."

Because he looked hurt — whether feigned or not — Sandra

told him, "Herbie, on your way to Tahiti, stop by. We're right on the way, right, Gary?" She put the pictures back into her purse. "And anyway, for all we know, you could be a famous patron of the arts."

"See? That's my point," Herb told his daughter.

"So you'll come?" Sandra extended a hand to Herb, and he kissed it.

He said, "Tell her to change her name to Johanna, or Hannah. Whichever one she prefers." To Gary he said, "Good luck professionally." He didn't seem to sense that Gary could use luck personally.

A bell sounded, two rings, and Herb surprised everybody by bringing a slim phone from the pocket of his jacket. Herb shouted, "Hello?" and was richly rewarded.

"It's the kids!" he announced. No matter how much money he had, Herb still used the expression "It's your nickel," as if the younger generation weren't capable of valuing conversation. It always startled Herb when his children and grandchildren didn't call him collect.

Charlie and Beth were really just calling to thank everybody for everything, which in itself was another way of demonstrating that they'd arrived intact. Since their *casita* had two phone extensions and Beth and Charlie were both talking at the same time, on the first full day of their marriage they'd instituted the awful habit of making ordinary conversation impossible.

Worse, Herb switched from his portable to the phone on the hall table, so that the newlyweds could be on speaker phone. "We're all right here saying goodbye," Herb narrated.

Margo refused to be part of a group conversation, so she retreated to the library. She couldn't understand how Charlie could *not* have been bothered, as he claimed not to, by Sandra or Bob always being on the other end of the line. It was the principle she detested, the loss of privacy. True, she could have been less passive-aggressive by not calling her parents at their work numbers, where they weren't as free to talk, but Margo believed Chloe had had the right attitude. Chloe had asked Gary, in Margo's hearing, why, when his children already had two parents, would they need a third?

"What's it like at Rancho Alto," Beth's father asked. "High?" He was accustomed to diluted connections.

"Mucho ideal," answered Charlie.

"Rockies," Beth elaborated, describing the panoramic view of fields of wildflowers and, not far off, freshly snow-capped mountains.

"What kinds of wildflowers?" asked Herb, but Sandra said, "Shame on you, Herbie. You don't expect they've gone hiking already, do you? This is their *honey*moon!"

Eve Gold couldn't decide which seemed the more improbable: Sandra and her own father so chummy, or the fact that Sandra had just become Beth's stepmother-in-law.

Gary told them, "Thanks for calling," as a way of demonstrating he was overloaded, unable to think of what else to say. So when Charlie answered, "Tell Jason we said Happy Halloween," Gary felt guilty, once more, for everything.

Sandra could have taken a minute to tell them about the jack-queen-king of hearts, but to economize — on time — she said, "I'll take pictures of our costumes for you. I've used up the rest of the wedding film I brought, on Herb and this great house. But with film there's always more where that came from, right?"

"Right," said Charlie. "Oh, and Mom?"

Gale indicated she was present.

"When you get home, please tell Bob again we're so thrilled with the car. We talked about it the whole plane ride."

"I'm here, dear," Bob said, "and I'm glad."

The short silence represented the confusion Beth and Charlie experienced, but they must have immediately thought Bob simply, purely, changed his mind about leaving. After all, they'd been dropped off first. "Ideal," Charlie replied again, which to him was all that mattered.

∞

In the center of this formal marble foyer, Eve and Margo stood between the two pairs of travelers, enabling them to avoid having to use the actual word "goodbye." Only Bob and Sandra exchanged a salute-like wave, after which Margo offered to walk Sandra and her father out to the car. Paul helped Gary remember how to get to the airport tunnel from there, and Eve said "You're welcome" to Sandra's thanks for everything. Still, when Sandra assured Eve, "We'll see each other very soon," Eve didn't know in which new, surreal capacity.

Gary and Sandra crossed the cobblestone courtyard to where their rented car was parked at the end of the line. Since only one car had "Keystone State" plates, Gary ran his hand along just that one. Not in his wildest dreams could he afford a top-of-the-line Mercedes — nor a bottom, used — but luckily money isn't everything. In Arizona the sunroof option would give you sunstroke, and the genuine leather seats a third-degree burn.

Gary told Margo, "Break a leg," because Disney work was always a performance, but then more parentally he said, "And good luck," to which Margo replied, parentally, "You too." She watched Gary maneuver an illegal U-turn, and let the car nearly disappear before she stopped watching.

Back in the house, Gale and Eve sat on the Persian-carpeted stairs like two little girls gossiping. With Gary gone, Gale could feel the muscles in her neck letting go to some extent. Even Bob relaxed enough to let Herb coax him into having a piece of the cheesecake.

This was when Gale asked Eve, "What would you have done in my place?" Eve would know this wasn't a question requiring a literal answer. What Gale wanted to know was whether, as Gale, she'd done the right thing, for herself.

"The same thing," Eve said simply. "Last night it looked like you had no other available option. Not for lack of trying to provide one."

"Oh? You mean *you* trying to provide one? The champagne?"

"Was just to let you sit a minute." No-nonsense Eve.

"That must have been why my life flashed before my eyes in that minute." Gale hunched over her knees, like on the illustrated card in the pocket of the seat on airplanes, and they both laughed.

"Paul's surprised it hadn't happened before, but that's only because he knew Gary better than you." Eve added, after a moment of reflection, "Which, however, is neither here nor there, is it?"

"Were you serious when you said our divorce spared you yours? That it could just as easily have been the other way around?"

Eve quoted herself from their conversation the night before: "Either you divorced and ask yourselves what if you hadn't, or you didn't divorce and ask yourselves what if you had."

Gale persisted. "Any advice?"

"Okay, yes: take your time." This was more useful than take two aspirin and call me in the morning.

"It *will* take a long time." With her finger Gale was tracing the pattern in the stair carpet, a border of decorative X's and O's in overlapping blues and greens. There was also a row of what looked like oval-shaped hearts, as if children not only made these rugs but designed them. Down the middle of the stairs were indigo peacock feathers with saffron centers.

"Yes, good," Eve coached. "Keep in mind how long it took to decide to marry Bob." She could have told Gale to then double that amount if she ever thought about leaving him. This was what Eve had advised Beth about Charlie when Beth asked for old-fashioned motherly advice.

"Two years to decide about Bob," said Gale, "and ten minutes to decide, after eleven years, to divorce Gary. I see." A failure of logic, in addition to the failure of the marriage.

Over cheesecake, Bob was being given Herb's and Paul's tag-team directions, which he said he didn't need, since Gale knew the way. Once more he invited Margo to ride with them to Philadelphia. She refused.

Convincingly she made it seem she had any number of plans, none of which included the back seat of her mother's car for the next six hours. It went without saying that on this ride Gale and Bob weren't likely to run out of conversation.

Bob felt a kind of confidence, but he also resisted knowing the details. Left to his imagination, he was freer to pretend there was a difference between what Gale had done to him and what he'd done to Priscilla.

Because Margo misinterpreted the expression on Bob's face, she feared she'd disappointed him, so she promised to come home almost right away. Margo said she'd catch up with David Haynes later on, in New York. She could always crash at his place overnight — it was their open invitation to each other — and she'd take her time getting there. With a window seat on the left side of the train, she'd be able to absorb the impact of these thirty-six hours, watching the shoreline disappear and reappear as relentlessly as the tide.

9

GARY REMEMBERED TO AVOID THE EXPRESSWAY ON THIS sunny fall Sunday afternoon. Like opposites converging by a reverse magnetism, the weekend leaf-peepers were returning from their peak experiences in the flame-colored northwest mountains and were met head-on by boaters coming from the southeastern Cape waters and those last few sails before first frost. The golfers only made it worse.

It was possible to drive through the middle of the city, and — as if an old shortcut were like a foreign language that is revived by immersion — Gary remembered that too. Cutting through a shut-down downtown, past Old City Hall and Post Office Square, he thought this earlier Boston looked the same and better. The new buildings were either good or bad, either something he wished he'd done or was glad he hadn't.

They passed the Apple Pie, which in daylight looked too ordinary to have turned his life inside out. Instead of "Private Party" the sign on the glass door now said "Closed." In the window sat a huge bowl filled with Granny Smiths, Macs, and Golden Delicious apples. The temptation was great.

"There's the Apple Pie," said Gary. The urge merely to point it out was irresistible.

Sandra said, "Don't remind me."

It began there — his asking "To be continued?" — but it

ended with Gale answering his question in the affirmative, sort of. "No," she'd said, meaning it wasn't over again. Because this was a double negative, he'd have preferred a yes, but it meant the same, didn't it? Even if she wouldn't say specifically where they'd go from here, Gale's telling him no meant that they had some sort of destination. Sure, he'd have preferred a clear yes, but no wasn't nothing. Anyway, the question had been his own. He could have put a more positive spin on their future than to ask if it was over again.

"Cousin Ed. Now there's a loser." That's all Sandra could think to say, but then she came up with, "Where was he today, by the way?"

Gary hadn't missed him. "Who knows? Maybe he assumed today was only for the out-of-towners. He lives here in Boston."

"That explains why his jokes are so old. God. You can't get me out of this place fast enough. All these historical markers. Who cares?" She refused to notice another one, no matter how significant.

Gary decided not to let her devalue everything. "History matters to a lot of people, Sandra. Me, for instance. As an architect, I'm inspired by the Custom House Tower up ahead. It's Boston's first and best skyscraper."

"Yes, you made that clear." She hated it when, like a teacher, he called her by her real name. Uncrossing and recrossing her legs, she added, "But primarily your own history, it seems."

They were under the expressway now and heading for the tunnel. Maybe the roadway would cave in. Maybe in the tunnel the water would break through and he wouldn't have to have this conversation.

"Your personal history, that is." Automatically, she removed her sunglasses.

"Look, it's not as if you didn't know I had a personal history, as you call it. I told you everything. You knew the whole story."

"Right. So blame it on me. Make it my problem that I'm

signed up for Modern History but the course is Ancient History."

He made the mistake of saying, "Not that you've taken either one."

"Correct, Mr. Advanced Degree." She glared at him. The nerve, when her cumulative average from the University of Arizona was way better than his undergraduate record. "But the difference is obvious enough even for a dope like me to recognize." Sandra might not have been capable right now of cooling down by making herself count to ten, but that didn't mean she couldn't count.

"You don't understand," he said, knowing as he spoke that it was the wrong thing to say. Meanwhile, the tunnel entrance noted the early death of a Lieutenant Callahan, its namesake, and inside the tunnel the grimy tile walls were curved, so you couldn't forget you were in a tube buried under the filthy harbor.

"Oh, but I do. Easily." She sealed her window to shut out the exhaust. "You see, because it would be no different if — at Jason's next birthday party, say — his dad and I slip away into the bedroom. 'Don't mind us, we're just going to fuck our brains out here in the next room.'"

"It's not the same thing at all." Gary's window was open so he'd die right away, but this meant she had to scream at him to be heard.

"'Don't mind us,'" she yelled, "'if we fuck right here in your face. Hurry, blow out your candles, Jason, we can't wait!'" She strained against her seat belt to lean closer as she screeched in his ear, "'Don't mind us, but we're so *turned on!*'"

The buzzing tires sounded to him like a swarm of killer bees, and it was as if everyone was driving too fast, trying to escape them. Gary doubted he could.

"And, while Jason's still opening his presents, you can hear us fucking, you can hear the headboard banging against the wall, and of course you hear every word — 'Baby! Baby! Don't stop!'

— and even our *breathing* is audible. 'We're so turned on we just *can't stop!* So don't mind us!' "

Behind their mid-size Ford was a tailgating Toyota 4-Runner, whose headlights were positioned so much higher than normal that its beams passed through Gary and Sandra like lasers. In the rear-view mirror the bullish insignia made it seem they were about to be trampled by a real bull, but the wall-like flat back of the airport limo-van ahead meant there was no means of escape. These outlaw cars belonged out west, where the off-road capability could be put to use, off-road. This was deadly: Sandra was going to get them both killed, especially if he told her to shut up. For once he decided to be careful. Maybe she'd make a mistake too, and he'd get out alive.

"'We're so *hot* we can't get enough, even if we're pumping AIDS into each other!'" Sandra recoiled from her own words.

Bingo.

In this decade of Jason's entire life, the child's father had failed every kind of rehab, including fatherhood. At the time of his brief relationship with Sandra, his drug of choice merely had made him impotent — so it was even more of a surprise to Sandra when she turned up pregnant — but since then he'd gone the whole distance. His at-risk behavior was a death wish waiting to be granted.

The right-hand lane was moving a little faster, so the 4-Runner cut from behind to pass them on Sandra's side. As his own odds improved, it became easier for Gary to hold his silence like a long breath underwater. He believed he saw a glimmer of light at the distant end of the tunnel.

As far as Jason was concerned, his father was a guy you might let buy you a present, but you'd never think of letting him come to your birthday party. He'd go into bureau drawers, into your mother's wallet, he'd steal the ten-dollar birthday check from your other grandmother in Florida, forging your endorsement.

There was no way you'd call him Dad. "Darryl" was as close as you'd get.

The limo-van braked and splashed them both with red light. Gary took it as a warning, no matter that he was the projected winner, of his capacity to lose the advantage. Reminding himself that she'd been the one to invite him to conjure up the unsavory image of Darryl, he held the words in his mouth a moment longer, smoothing the edges with his tongue. In the meantime, the white circle of outdoor light ahead was making this exhausted air less murky.

Sandra stared into the taillights of the limo-van, less than a car length ahead. She didn't have to be looking at Gary to see he was about to take the swing that would drive that pitch of hers into the stands.

Resurfacing in daylight, he blinked and then said calmly, "That's what I meant when I told you it's not the same. Nobody would have sex with him. Not even you."

∞

Bob and Gale were sent off as if they were the bride and groom, everybody's wishes showered on them like confetti. Bob drove, which was fine with Gale because her headache felt like the equivalent of driving under the influence. Their first few exchanges were about which turns to make, but once they got on the turnpike there were no interruptions until Sturbridge. Bob had the first few words of so many sentences in his head that he decided, rather than choosing the wrong one, to let her pick.

Her problem was slightly different, in that she couldn't decide whether to apologize for herself first or to thank Bob for his own responses. If she'd been capable of such maturity herself — but when she was young, seventeen years ago — her first marriage would have had the benefit of a doubt. If she could have given

Gary the time to understand the meaning of his infidelity, she too could have understood it. She still didn't. This was the least of her immediate worries.

What about her own infidelity? What was its meaning? How could a single act feel both liberating and like being taken prisoner? It had felt involuntary and at the same time quite chosen, given that she'd had twenty-four hours to say no.

"Was it my fault," asked Bob, "or inevitable?" He couldn't wait any longer. They were already past Newton.

"It wasn't your fault, and I don't know about inevitable, but I promise I'll tell you everything I can. Two things for sure right now are that I am deeply sorry and, equally, grateful. Thank you for coming back. I'm sorry you had to." If that sounded like a speech, so what? She should have said it right away instead of practicing it.

The trees grew bigger and better in these western suburbs, but the late season made the giant oaks acorn-colored, their pointy leaves cylindrically curled like capes around thin brown stems. No tree was the equal of the sugar maple back in Brookline. Red and yellow didn't make pink here, but regular old orange. This was nature undomesticated, unowned.

Possibly because Bob was required to keep his eyes on the road, he decided this would be the right time to tell Gale he wasn't altogether unfamiliar with adultery. "I was unfaithful to Priscilla, which is what made me nervous last night."

The expression on Gale's face was cartoonish, the surprise so great.

"In Korea, an army nurse who couldn't believe I'd only had sex with one girl, and only then, the first time, our wedding night. She made me feel it was somehow her duty to educate me, and my duty to want to be educated."

To her further surprise, Gale was almost charmed by the clichéd image of Bob as a medic infatuated with an army nurse in Korea, two thirds of his life ago. "What was her name? Something sweet?" Gale was more curious to know whether Bob remembered the name than what it was.

"Audrey Miller, from Buffalo. We didn't stay in contact, if that's what you mean." Bob's grip on the steering wheel was so tight he could feel the tension in his whole arms. But there was a task to perform, so he guided the car toward one of the automated tollbooths, in a lane designated for cars with nothing in tow. Pulling away from the machine, Bob slipped the turnpike ticket into the special half-pocket on the visor. He settled into the travel lane and set the cruise control precisely to the speed limit.

"How long had you been married at that point?"

"A year, I guess. I was called up as I finished medical school, so I was an army doctor without a specialty in a war that was just ending. Priscilla had insisted on moving back to Philadelphia, so —"

"Let me guess," Gale offered nonjudgmentally. "You saw yourself as trapped, your career defined, in effect, by her refusal to remain in Boston. You were already thinking you'd made a mistake."

"So it seems I'm not uncommon?" It wasn't Bob's impression that Gale had many patients his age, given that his generation's bias went against getting help, no matter how trapped you might feel.

"Yes, I think you are, in staying married all those —"

"Twenty-eight."

"— years. Had Robert been born yet?"

"No." The silence signified both his having thought about ending the marriage and his not following through. "Nobody divorced in our world, so it would have been a scandal even without children involved."

"I can imagine it. But wouldn't your mother have done okay? She seems fairly independent, worldly, smart." Gale concluded she would have done fine.

"Not Priscilla's. Not Priscilla."

"So you spared her back then in order for her to drink herself to death twenty-five years later. You sacrificed yourself?" She was asking if that's what it felt like.

"Yes and no. She always said she sacrificed her life to me." With a sigh he said, "And she had a point. She could have been much happier. With someone who kept banker's hours. Someone more fun."

Gale wanted to ask a question, but wasn't sure whether Bob would ever have entertained the thought that Priscilla might have been unfaithful to him. Maybe that "wasn't done" either. But more importantly, perhaps it would be a needlessly wounding thing to ask in these present circumstances.

And as if to demonstrate he and she were on the same wavelength, Bob said, "I used to wish she would be unfaithful to me."

"Was she?"

"I doubt it. I don't know." There went Framingham, now Worcester, and all the small towns in between that didn't exist as turnpike exits. His life had been like this: only a few opportunities to get out.

Gale was wondering how he couldn't have known whether or not Priscilla had been having an affair, until she remembered she hadn't known about Gary. That is, she'd been aware of not having enough time for him, but not what he was doing with his own time. If she hadn't been so stunned — this was the whole point — she'd have reacted differently. Or at least this was the thing she'd come to believe. Feeling joined with Bob in this disclosure of his own, Gale said, "Thank you for telling me about Audrey Miller." But there was no comparison between his betrayal of Priscilla and her own of him.

Bluntly, clumsily, Bob introduced the other time. "The other time was different. That was a romance. By then Priscilla was a wreck."

Gale heard only the one word. "Romance? Do I know about this?"

The sun was in his eyes, round and orange. They were driving directly west toward it, as if right into it. Bob lowered the visor, giving himself a task, adjusting it. "Maybe I made it seem she was the woman after Priscilla died, before you. Caroline, her name was. I might have been afraid, if I'd been more specific, of frightening you away."

"Ah," said Gale, but implied was "Eureka!" because this was one of those discoveries that was going to change the way people live.

"You needed to believe about me that, no matter what, I'd never be unfaithful to you. Maybe I thought you'd trust me less if you knew about this. I wanted you to believe I would — I will — never be again."

"Caroline." Gale was scanning directories in her head. Was there a Caroline in the Garden Club? At Gulph Mills? Among the mothers of boys or girls at the Academy or Agnes Irwin? Or would she be another nurse? Or a doctor? And what was this feeling: hurt? anger? jealousy? It was overpowering her.

"She's gone. Her husband was transferred to Chicago. She could be dead for all I know." He didn't mean to make it sound like he wished Caroline were dead, only to show how long ago it was by now.

"You don't have to rationalize not telling me. I'd prefer you didn't, in fact."

∞

Logan Airport had such a great view, it was a pity to leave. Sandra couldn't believe she'd heard herself say this, but it did happen to be true about the view. Just across the runway was the harbor, and the blue water supported a white triangle of sail that restrained a portion of the wind. At the top of the sail was the Greek letter omega.

"The end," she said.

"No," Gary replied. "It's only the class of boat."

"I was being poetic. Omega is a way to say the party's over." Any minute now, the ground crew would call their flight.

He was pretending to read the Sunday *Globe,* but it was depressing to be reminded that some cities, unlike Tucson, have cultural lives. The arts section seemed to be telling him, There's so much to do here! As opposed to Tucson, where there isn't enough.

"I used to know practically the whole alphabet, didn't you? Delta Kappa Epsilon: that's your fraternity, right?" Learning this about him shortly after they met had given her hope that Gary could come back to life, since DKE at Arizona was as notorious a party house as it was at UVa.

"I barely remember those years." At the time he believed he'd never forget them.

"Well, mine were more recent."

Gary watched the boat come about and sail away on a diagonal. Another regret of his was not having sailed in all these years. It was one of the few skills he had, growing up in Baltimore, but like so much else he used to feel good about, the opportunity was gone. The plane at the next gate was heading to Los Angeles, yet when he lived in that city with Chloe, with a whole ocean out his window, he'd never sailed. He must have withheld the pleasure from himself as a punishment. He must have thought it was necessary to give up everything he cared about.

First-class passengers and those with small children were allowed to board, so Sandra's patience was soon to be rewarded. In another ten minutes they'd be strapped into their seats and ready for takeoff. There wasn't a cloud in the sky.

A powerboat skipped like a stone, creating a wake the sailboat crossed, bobbing like a rocking horse. "I'm getting a boat," he said urgently, as if that very day.

"Fine."

Of course: he'd gone to Arizona because it's the desert. It was his own conspiracy against himself. If he'd *tried* to deprive himself, he couldn't have done it better. "I'm a total sucker," he said.

And Sandra said, "I thought I was. You just said you're getting a boat, and I said fine, even though we both know that they don't make boats in Arizona. Let's go, they're about to call us." She stood up as rows fifteen and above were summoned for boarding.

"I used to love to sail."

"I know. Friday night you talked about teaching Margo to sail at the Cape. That's why I mentioned the sailboat out there." Which she wished she hadn't. "That's us, let's go."

"I've suffered enough," he said matter-of-factly.

"Me too, so let's go, we're boarding." Their bags had been checked through, and though her mother had requested a Massachusetts lobster, Sandra didn't trust the dry-ice packing. They had no carry-ons beyond her purse and the *People* she'd bought.

Almost frantically Gary riffled through the newspaper looking for classifieds. "I know there used to be a boat section. I used to read it."

The last thing she wanted in her lap was a Sunday paper she'd seen enough of, but she said, "Then bring the damn thing, but quit stalling." She'd get him to teach Jason to sail too. East on Route 10 there was Wilcox Playa and, north, another Arizona lake, big enough to have been named after Teddy Roosevelt. Like everything else in her life, she'd make this work.

Looking like an absent-minded professor trying to reconcile the mysteries of the universe with getting to class on time, Gary was guided to the gate and led down the incline and across the threshold, all the while actively realizing what he had done to himself. His arms overflowed with the preexisting alternative to the life he had ended up with.

In his window seat he read the supermarket coupons and real estate listings like a man in need of basic food and shelter. Then he found the recreation section and read boat specifications as if they were assembly instructions. He'd deluded himself into believing he'd hit bottom and bounced partway back, but now he could see how he'd been in a free fall, and still was. His capacity for self-inflicted hardship was bottomless. Not anymore.

The glossy inserts from rival department stores offered merchandise to meet every single need Gary could have, so he pretended he had won the lottery and could choose anything he wanted.

"Now what?" asked Sandra impatiently. "Is this your midlife crisis?"

His eyes burned with a horrible realization. "I wasn't even going to allow myself one!" That's what he meant: he was a coconspirator in his own downfall. He hadn't ever said no. His eyes were wild.

"If you act suspiciously, they're going to think you're a terrorist." Coincidentally the flight attendant closed the overhead bin above their seats, snapping it shut, and asked Gary to fasten his seat belt. "See? They're keeping an eye on you." Maybe if she spoke to him like a child, he'd obey her like one. "Just go to sleep, okay? You're way overtired."

Like a child, however, Gary was discovering the power he had to say no. What if he'd said no that Saturday morning when Gale told him to leave? He could have said, "No, I won't." He should have said, "I'm sorry, I'll get counseling and I'll never do it again," but first he should have told Gale, "No!" And if she'd asked, "Why not?" he'd have said, "Because we love each other."

While the flight attendant instructed them about what to do in case of an emergency landing, Gary thought about saying no. He was able to imagine his having said no that morning as a way of practicing *really* saying no this afternoon. As they taxied away from the terminal, he decided to keep his discoveries private for the moment. It was like having a secret: he had power. This was a first.

The power he had was to be alive twice: the first time when he was married to Gale, and again with her this weekend. All the rest of the time in between and since — today, for instance — his vital signs made him out to be alive, but he'd been brain dead.

He'd "seemed" happy and would admit to even having "felt" happy, but his heart hadn't been beating the way it could. The surprising thing was that while Gale was certainly a handsome woman, she lacked the confidence to project her beauty. She still tried to disappear by ducking her head and raising her shoulders, same as always, only now it made him love her more than ever. She needed him. He pledged not to disappoint her ever again.

Gary could see that Sandra's absolute sense of herself had made her very appealing to him. Her pretty mother, Maggie, had given Sandra her looks, but more, her steady verve. And Sandra had passed it on to Jason like a family heirloom. All three of them were about to start hating him, but none of them would be destroyed. The way Gale was. The way he'd been.

What this proved was that, like Gale, you could appear to have everything going for you — two parents with 2.0 kids in a Cincinnati suburb with a golf course as its town green — but not manage to have self-worth. Or you could be like him — nothing going for you, thanks to less than one embittered parent — and have achieved the exact same result. By this formula, he and Gale seemed intended for each other, as — well now, here's an idea — did Bob and Sandra, who — as opposed to the losers he and Gale were — were both clearly winners. So this was a temporary role reversal for both Bob and Sandra, but Gary was confident they'd bounce back. Taking into consideration their former partners — Priscilla and Jason's father, Darryl, to name just two — you could certainly say things hadn't always been perfect for them. And they'd done fine. He didn't need to feel guilty. This in itself was a nice change.

From the flight deck came a greeting and the news that they were next in line for takeoff. There were meaningless details about altitude and, displaying hierarchy, the captain said, "Flight attendants, please be seated," as if they, who were responsible for these hundreds of people, couldn't have known to seat themselves at the right time.

The plane pivoted and took off.

∽

Bob broke apart the heavy but artificial silence by asking, "May I please say one more thing?" Though Gale didn't answer, Bob continued. "When I told you my own infidelity had made me nervous, I meant last night. I need to tell you about that, okay?" Again he glanced at her, but she was like a statue in profile, aloof, a stone figure with her eye on the horizon.

"I left my car in the driveway by the front door, and when I went into our house, at first all I saw were the things that belonged to you, all the perhaps minor but still distinct choices you'd made to make it our home. The blue watery wallpaper, the sanded cherry floors no longer stained walnut, the sconces reaching out to greet me with their light. For an actual moment, as I stood there by the front door, I felt very secure. I felt you there. Then I went into the kitchen."

Because Gale cared about cooking, the kitchen was entirely hers, wholly remade into a comfortable welcoming space, the new heart of the house. "What frightened me was the difference between the kitchen now and what it was before, and what my life would have been without you in it."

Bob was determined to tell her. "It's hard to describe, because in fact at first I sat there at the kitchen table and listened to the telephone messages. I checked in at Jane's and talked to Amanda briefly — she's fine, did I tell you? — and I called the hospital to check up on my patients. Everyone was doing fine, as I think I said. Things seemed normal."

Now they were passing yet another motorist pulled over by a state trooper in an unmarked car, this time the effective camouflage of a green Dodge minivan. To Gale the impaled speeders looked like roadkill.

Bob persisted. "But something was clearly happening to me, because when I went upstairs next, into our bedroom, again I noticed your things all around, and once again I felt pleasantly reassured." He checked to see if Gale seemed to be paying attention, but still it was her unnerving immobility he noticed.

"This was different. Instead of seeing before and after, the way I could in the kitchen — the indoor-outdoor carpeting replaced by the Mexican tile, the Formica by butcher block, the housekeeper sitting alone at the table instead of kids eating the warm cookies they'd made by themselves — everything I looked at in the bedroom vanished. I looked at my bureau, and your face disappeared from the picture frame, all your clothes from the closet, your earrings from the box Charlie made you at camp, your novels no longer on the bedside table. It was as if I had a terrible power to obliterate the things I care most about. Nervous doesn't begin to describe the feeling." Because this had been a lesson — a "life lesson" wouldn't exaggerate the experience — Bob had no choice but to say it out loud, even if she interrupted.

But she didn't.

"Last night I imagined you felt about me the way I'd felt about Priscilla during my affair with Caroline. The same horrible disregard. The same horrible, arrogant disregard. Nobody — neither Priscilla, nor I, nor anyone — deserves to be treated like that. I finally understood what it feels like." Bob wanted to tell Gale he finally understood what a suicide must feel like, but he really didn't want to claim this awful authority. Nor did he want to alarm her by seeming to identify with her mother.

She knew the feeling, naturally, but she wouldn't say so just yet. Let him finish.

"I disappeared too," Bob told her, the amazed horror in his

voice sounding like a special effect in a movie. "I vanished too!" By now he'd slowed the car way below the speed limit, enough to make them a hazard on the road. He didn't care. "Who I was no longer mattered. I meant nothing to you, so I meant nothing at all anymore. Instantly, I ceased to exist."

The fright he'd experienced had all the symptoms of a heart attack. If he weren't a doctor, he'd have called himself an ambulance.

Now Gale said, "I know the feeling."

"It was unbearable!"

"I know."

"Being about to die."

"I know, I know."

"Do you?" Bob was anxious to hear how quickly she could answer him, but he also needed to see her face.

"Feel that way about you? That you don't matter? No." Gale showed him her wide-open eyes.

Bob had to ask, "But did you last night, with Gary?"

She was thankful she could honestly answer "No."

He believed her. Bob realized he believed her because he felt himself breathing. He had a pulse.

Trees and more trees. Leaves being shed, landing on the ground dull side up, shiny side down. Leaves the same color as the sun. The same mix of despair and hope made Bob want to weep for the second time in two days, for the same reason.

Remaining, however, was that he'd lied. Gale tried to conceive of his misrepresentation of Caroline as anything other than the lie it was: it was a lie. He hadn't risked admitting the truth, even though perhaps it could have been helpful for him to have told Gale how he'd come to know so strenuously he would never, ever be unfaithful to her. Gale could see how the truth might have worked to Bob's advantage: *for* him rather than, as now, against him.

Gale watched him drive, both hands on the wheel of the car

he'd given her on their tenth anniversary. His beautiful hands could be those of a concert pianist or — and now she sounded like Sandra — a pair of magazine models like Kay's daughters. But these hands of his were capable of intricacy, like a jeweler's. Bob could repair a human heart like a clockwork whose timing mechanism was off by a fraction of a second. He was skilled, and she'd trusted him. He was still skilled.

But trustworthy? He'd lied to her. Like a bullet in bone, this discovery was lodged in her body.

∞

Usually Gary felt confined. His legs were too long for coach class, and his seat always seemed to be over the wing. The passenger in the seat ahead would recline, and from behind the tray table would be lowered, and raised, and latched, repeatedly. Usually, flying was being in a cage, the way pets travel.

Airborne, Gary reclined his own seat back and lowered his tray table, taking this initiative as a further sign of his power. He'd supposed himself obliged to be taken advantage of forevermore, if necessary. But no. He'd resigned himself to being told no forever by Gale. But no! It hadn't proved necessary. There was a statute of limitations, and it had just expired. Now he was free.

"Now I can relax," Sandra said, ordering twin Johnnie Walkers for herself.

"Me too," he said, and told the flight attendant he'd have a Sam Adams.

Sandra reclined her seat back to be even with his, and her nerves were soothed either by the first sip of scotch or by Gary's own satisfaction, evident in the way the corners of his mouth turned up instead of down.

On the morning of their own wedding, Sandra had told Gary she would only do this once in her life. He'd amazed her by responding, "Well then, I guess that makes me the lucky man, permanently." Since her purpose had been to give him one final chance to back out, she had taken this statement as definitive.

Jason was why. Having given him the ultimate deadbeat dad, she wasn't about to make his life even worse: she owed Jason. But Gary wouldn't let him down. Gary had her convinced of this by the way he talked to her about his own childhood. And about his own children, whose adolescence he'd so regretted missing.

It was easy to believe how important his kids were to him. They'd both gladly come to the wedding, even though they'd had to leave right away for Charlie's Wesleyan graduation the next afternoon. They'd acted fine. Maybe it was just that, an act.

Now Sandra corrected herself. Doubting his kids was clearly just a distraction: wasn't he the one she wasn't able to trust? Sandra held a sip in her mouth long enough to let the scotch saturate her head.

And she recognized, as evidence, the way Charlie always treated Gary more like an old friend than a father, and how Gary — what a pathetic toast he gave, not even planned out — all weekend avoided seeming like the father of the groom. It was like he wanted to be the groom himself again, like a competition.

God knows, she knew he could be irresponsible, but not like this. It was dumb of him to buy a building in L.A. a month before the economy crashed and two months before one of the minor quakes preceding the big one, but at least you could consider those acts of God. This weekend he'd been on his own.

The trouble was, her own behavior wasn't exactly model. She'd lost some of her advantage by passing out like, well, a peer of the bride and groom. Not even. They were so straight, they'd probably never had one too many in their entire lives. Still, though, she was the newcomer. She was the guest.

Suddenly she felt afraid on Jason's behalf. Jason had been around — as a toddler he'd seen dozens of guys rotating through playground duty — but when Gary turned up, right away Jason asked Sandra if Gary could stay for a sleepover. To his credit, Gary remained on the top bunk that entire night, so that in case Jason woke up, he'd know he could trust Gary's word. In the morning when she went into Jason's room, she'd found her wide-awake son up on the top bunk with Gary, watching him sleep.

The scotch was sharp but also smooth. Stalling, Sandra initiated a perfectly safe conversation by asking, "What's your week ahead look like?" The opposite number to her usual, "How was your day, dear?"

"Fine," he answered.

"Halloween's tomorrow, remember." No! What about Jason's pumpkin? They forgot to get him one. Gary promised! Oh, poor Jason.

"Fine," Gary said again, as if the holiday had just been declared by Sandra.

"So everything's fine, it looks like." She hated drinking good scotch from a plastic cup, one, and two, her nail polish was beginning to chip. Three, "Not that you asked, but things have been better. For me, at least."

His response was to tip the brown bottle on an easy angle, giving himself, in profile, a very long sip.

His irritating silence prompted her to say, "You promised. You know that, don't you?"

Three times he'd promised, as three times now he'd betrayed.

"I gave you a lot of chances to get out, including one at the last minute."

There was precedent: Saint Peter.

"Listen to me!"

"I am," he said. "You gave me an opportunity to get out."

"And you didn't." Sandra extended the fingers of her left hand. There was his ring. Two, including the engagement. And he wore hers. "That counts as proof."

But they both knew there was no proof. By definition, the future is as uncertain as it is unknown.

∞

Gale took a break, intending to doze away the distance between Hartford and points west. The sun's position in the sky was no help, too low for someone with a headache already. In her driver's seat, Bob was the right height to protect his own eyes from the glare. And beginning soon, the rest of the trip was due south. He'd get them there.

So it was her chance to recall as precisely as possible what was actually said, what was merely implied. Where and when the conversation had taken place was clear: at her own dining room table, in Brookline, the same place she'd confronted Gary with the news Eve Gold had just given her. Bob wasn't seated at Gary's old place, because Gale took that place for herself.

"Will you consider it?"

"I can't, Bob. I can't even consider marrying you." It would have been true for her to say, "Don't take it personally," but to the best of her recollection (as they say on the witness stand) she hadn't gone that far. But she'd said, "I'm sorry."

He'd acknowledged his embarrassment at having determined her ring size without it occurring to him she could refuse the ring. This was Friday, so she had the whole weekend to change her mind and/or take pity on him, whichever one came first. She remembered smiling encouragingly, but as with a patient who still has a long way to go.

"I'll be waiting, however long it might take." She remembered this line very well, because it was such a cliché and yet delivered as if for the first time in history. She recalled feeling like a character in an English novel, refusing the hand of such a nice man. Counterpointed, though, was his quite modern question, "What did I miss?"

The candles burned all the way down. It was like an intake

interview, an inventory of the wounds she'd suffered. Her mother was recently dead, so her perceived inadequacies as a daughter were reinforced by her failings as a wife. She couldn't take any chances. Bob understood: he'd failed his wife.

Gale vividly recalled the sorrow in his face, but the force of Bob's admission was overwhelmed in that moment by her wishing Gary could have felt this guilty, when instead he'd caught Chloe Fortunado's rising star and been rewarded for taking advantage of wife after wife. Gale's anger had flared up in her, so instead of admitting to his affair with Caroline — presuming this had been his intention — Bob seemed to be accepting blame for not having solved Priscilla's drinking problem. Reasonably, he didn't want Gale to be this angry at him, especially when he was already feeling humiliated. In other words, she was to blame for making it so hard for Bob to tell the whole truth that he'd settled for half the truth.

Next example: having a drink after a French detective film at the Nickelodeon, and she'd asked Bob if anyone had ever left him. "Yes, a woman named Caroline," he'd said. "I was in love with her, but she was married and moved to Chicago." His way of saying "she was married" made it sound like she *got* married to someone else, then she and her new husband moved to Chicago. "Sad," Gale said, and Bob chose not to elaborate.

Should she have asked outright, "Say, Bob, how's your record on adultery?" He could have supplied the data, supported by statistical averages to show he was simply a product of the culture. "Nothing personal," he could have said. In that context she'd be obliged to understand.

However, just at that point in her own life Gary was sending requests through the kids, who'd told him about their grandmother's suicide. Wouldn't she please see him? Here Gale gave herself the benefit of the doubt: she wouldn't have wanted to be told about another woman Bob had once loved because right then she was relying on him to guard her against Gary. What if it turned out that, refused by Caroline, Priscilla had been Bob's rebound? Gale wouldn't want to fear making such a mistake in her own life, settling for Bob mostly as a way to resolve her feelings for Gary.

Bob could quickly clarify the chronology for her, but she didn't want the burden of an actual conversation, not yet. Anyway, did it seriously matter when the affair had taken place? Bob himself had said Caroline could be long dead for all he knew. Would Gale continue to use this ancient example from Bob's life to escape blame for her own infidelity? Would he let her? Would she allow him to let her?

The purpose of his admission was to say he wasn't perfect either. Period. Her reason for thinking back to their first serious conversation was as a reminder of how long she and Bob had been married. A year longer than she'd been married to Gary.

Bob was listening to the BBC World Service, the volume barely audible so it wouldn't intrude. How like him to let her work through the news of his own infidelity without his interpretation dominating. How like Bob to trust her. How like him, now, to have forgiven her. And why? For the single simple reason that he loved her that much. A feeling this unfamiliar wasn't easy to recognize.

She didn't believe there was such a thing as petty adultery — petty theft, yes — but to take Bob's side of the argument, it was hard to be lastingly troubled by a William Holden–like wartime fling forty years ago, nor was it impossible to sympathize with a Jimmy Stewart–like man trapped in a bad situation. Even if his romance with Caroline took place as recently as the last year of his marriage to Priscilla, that would still be seventeen years ago. It was over for good whenever it was Caroline moved from Philadelphia, however much time that was before Priscilla's final collapse. Sometime in the next two years there was someone else, but then she and Bob met and he waited two more years before she finally took that ring he'd offered prematurely. Gale counted five women in Bob's sixty-five years, not exactly a world record. With a fifteen-year disadvantage, Gary had had almost that many wives.

This was how she removed that bullet of Bob's disclosure, simply by letting it become a flesh wound. Were she to put herself in Bob's place even for a minute in these past twenty-four hours, there would be no contest. She'd already demonstrated with Gary's Jeannie that she wasn't big enough — smaller than both Bob and Sandra — to accommodate betrayal. Sure, she could absorb old news, but if Bob were to have had a current relationship? Forget it. Double standard? Absolutely. Some people were secure enough to allow their lovers to be free, but she wasn't one of those. She was familiar enough with her insecurity to know she would possibly always remain damaged goods.

This was why she'd rather be herself than Sandra: she could trust Bob. About Gary, ironically, her experience of him as untrustworthy had been reconfirmed. He was all too ready to reinvent himself this very day, as if it were his indisputable right to leave behind little piles of clothing as he stepped from one identity to the next. Yes, he'd deserved a second chance with her, but yes, there were reasons why she hadn't been able to give it to him. As there were reasons why he wouldn't get it now.

She yawned deeply, the exhalation sounding like a sigh. They still had hours to go.

So Bob entered the conversation. "I wish you could promise me you're mine until I die." He sounded more like a show-tune lyric than like himself.

"But I already promised that," she replied, their marriage ceremony having contained the traditional vows.

"That's what I mean. Nobody does, really. I mean, I don't expect you to feel you're under contract." But no, this wasn't what he meant. Against the advice of his children and his lawyer, he'd refused to have a prenuptial contract, because in marrying Gale there was another principle involved, called free choice.

"Marrying Priscilla, we used the old Episcopal Book of Common Prayer, where the vow is 'cleave unto one another.' The new language puts it in terms of life and death, too, but it sounds more metaphorical, less dangerous than being cleaved to. Don't you think?"

He squinted against the sun, and the lines at the corner of his eye also looked like radiating smile lines. But his voice sounded serious. As if he'd meant to introduce a discussion about etymology, she responded, "When I think 'cleave,' I think cloven hoof or cleft palate. You're saying it means two opposite things at once: to split as well as —"

"To adhere." Bob grasped the steering wheel. Yes, this was serious. "Along with Charlie, I love fidelity. And I prefer undivided — what would be Charlie's word? — allegiance. Still, the older and wiser in me requires me to call up a Middle English word that can be both at once. That is, divided and undivided."

Gale's categories were more modern, harder-edged. Her training had taught her how to look into herself for reservoirs of unspent anger, choked love; not words with two wholly different meanings. The question she was obliged to take back to her own couch was: was it to get back at Gary or, fundamentally, to punish herself? Which one did she want to hurt more?

"I don't think what happened has much to do with me, or not with me *as* me, not me personally." Bob appeared to have discovered this on his own. "It's between you and him. Maybe it's your revenge."

Gale had turned in her seat to see more of Bob's dispassionate face. "Revenge?" Against Gary, this was possibly the appropriate word, but against herself? She'd already done that with the weight gain, and never would again. Far more sensible was that she'd let herself be appealed to by Gary because she wanted him to desire her. And why? For revenge.

"Yes. So it's between you and him, the way if I ran into

Priscilla, God forbid, she'd probably — *we'd* surely — want to kill each other." At last he smiled.

"With a cleaver?" she asked at the same time as his, "With a cleaver." And they both laughed.

Then, because for once in his life the timing was on Bob's side, he pulled into the rest area that had been there right along in the signs telling them they were getting a little closer with each mile he drove.

He sped up the ramp and swerved right and, like a truck driver planning to call it quits for an hour, stopped the car. "Did you know this about me? I'm impulsive too," he announced, claiming his rights, asserting his own strong will. "And, I'm married." He pressed the emergency brake pedal and shut off the car engine. Releasing his seat belt, he asked, "Are you?"

Bob opened the car door and got out on his side. So did Gale, and they each came halfway around the front of the car to the middle, by the chrome star ornament, into one another's arms. The metallic gray hood was very hot from the two hours they'd traveled, and the visible heat shimmered in the air above the flat steel surface. The unusually orange late October sun angled off it and directly into their faces. So, in order to better see each other, they shut their eyes.